BETRAYED

penny DIXON

Matador
9 Priory Business Park,
Wistow Road, Kibworth Beauchamp,
Leicestershire. LE8 0RX
Tel: (+44) 116 279 2299
Fax: (+44) 116 279 2277
Email: books@troubador.co.uk
Web: www.troubador.co.uk/matador

ISBN 978 1780883 205

British Library Cataloguing in Publication Data.
A catalogue record for this book is available from the British Library.

Typeset in 11pt Palatino by Troubador Publishing Ltd, Leicester, UK
Printed and bound in the UK by TJ International, Padstow, Cornwall

Matador is an imprint of Troubador Publishing Ltd

To Sarah and Norman

Acknowledgements

I want to thank my parents, and especially my mother for encouraging me to write this story. I am extremely grateful to my brother David who filled in many gaps in my memory and furnished me with information it would have been impossible for me to research. Thanks also to Andrew Dixon, Ash Gabbidon, David Goddard, Janice Price and Sandra Walton who volunteered to read my first draft, and were loving enough to give me their honest opinions. I hope you will see the difference your feedback made.

I thank God for inspiration and the many angels who sat with me into the early hours of the morning, willing me to keep going.

Chapter 1

Issy looked deeply into his eyes and wondered if she could believe him. She wanted to trust him, wanted to lose herself in his pleading eyes, but he had lied to her before. He always had a way of making it right though, of winning her round. She found it hard to resist his raised eyebrows, his wide-eyed innocence and the small gap in his front teeth when he smiled at her.

He wasn't touching her yet, but she knew he would. She knew he would move to her, slide his arms down her back, pull her in close, and hold her hard against his beating chest. He would say, 'Issy, you know I wouldn't lie to you. You know I love you too much,' and she would allow herself to believe him, because the alternative was too frightening.

She would push her nagging doubts to the back of her mind and allow him to kiss the top of her head. At six feet two inches, he was nine inches taller than her, and liked to kiss her on the head. 'Pint Size Beauty' was his nickname for her, and although she didn't consider herself pint sized or beautiful, she loved it. She could tell what mood he was in by the way he called her. If he was joking about her size, like if she had to ask him to reach for something from the top shelf, she was 'Pint.' 'Alright then, Pint' he would say as he reached up, or 'this one Pint?' If they were going to church and she was tottering on a pair of high stiletto she was Pint Size. 'Come on Pint Size, we going to be late,' he'd joke as he pulled her along.

The full term he saved for their more intimate moments. 'Come here, my Pint Sized Beauty' were for the times when he pulled her up to straddle him, as he stood with his back to the wall, and said 'Come on, open up for me, my Pint Size Beauty' when she wasn't in the mood and he was trying to persuade her. She always gave in, didn't know how to say no to him. He was her gift from God.

She looked at him and remembered the first time she saw him. She'd just bent down to sort out a crate of beer behind the bar at the rum shop and when she stood up, she was looking through the opened buttons of a pale blue shirt into a chest of finely curled hairs, dark against taut, wavy muscles. Her eyes had travelled up, past the long neck and slightly squashed chin, past the upward sweep of cheeks and slightly flared nostrils, to the surprisingly oval, almost slanting eyes. They were not the usual deep brown she was used to, more the colour of the inside of a neaseberry, light brown with little specks. They rested symmetrically on his face. She'd never seen anyone with eyes like that and didn't notice anything else about him for the few seconds he looked directly into her.

'What do you want?' she asked, feeling that she had to say something. She was, after all, there to serve the customers.

'Gimme a Red Stripe,' he answered without moving or taking his gaze from her. She watched the words slide from his half-opened lips, and land on the counter in front of her. She looked down to where they'd settled, before looking up again.

'You want me open it?' she asked, reaching into the ice box for the beer with one hand, and for the bottle opener with the other.

'Yes, dat would be good, seeing as how I didn't bring a bottle opener with me,' he chuckled.

She held the bottle tight, hooked the opener over the stopper, and yanked it upwards. It slid off the stopper. She looked at the bottle, and up at him perplexed, as if to say 'this doesn't usually happen, I'm an experienced barmaid.' He chuckled again.

'Try again. Maybe dat one just stubborn.'

This time the stopper yielded to her subtle pressure, and the beer hissed a small sigh.

'How much?' he asked, as she handed him the bottle and his warm fingers touched hers. Not trusting her voice, she pointed at the board above the bar.

'My name's Lukan,' he said quietly, putting the money into her outstretched hand so his palm covered hers.

Wordlessly, she took the money and dropped it into the till.

'What's yours?' he asked taking a sip of the beer.

'Isabell,' she answered with as little expression as she could to disguise the discomfort she was feeling.

'Well, it's a pleasure to meet you Isabell.' His words slithered from the top of her head, down her body, following his gaze. 'You work here every day?'

'Nearly.'

'Well, maybe I'll see you again... Isabell.'

Issy recognised the signs and wanted to suppress the feelings welling up inside her. She had a weakness for a pretty face, and Lord, his face was pretty. So was the rest of him. She allowed herself to watch him as he walked away; leaned her elbows on the counter and propped her face in her hands as his long legs carried him away from her, the Red Stripe raised to his lips. His square shoulders and broad back were well defined through his shirt, damp with perspiration. His legs were out of proportion to his torso, but they were strong legs, sure legs, workers legs, she could almost feel the bulging muscles inside his loose-fitting khaki trousers.

She watched him till he turned the corner out of sight and sighed. She didn't need a Lukan in her life. She'd asked God for a nice, responsible man who would marry her and take care of her children. At twenty five she was ready for a man to settle down with, to have some more children with. A man who wouldn't think he was so nice half the women in the district should run after him. She'd had enough of the kind of pretty face that didn't want to settle down.

She couldn't find one in any of the places she'd been looking; not in the bar where she worked part time, or the dance hall, or the clubs in Kingston. So when they had the last Christian Crusade at her church she found herself praying to God to make a choice for her, because she had to admit, she hadn't done too good a job up till now.

When the visiting preacher, a large dark man with a high shiny forehead and big hands, asked, 'Who in this room is weary? Who is carrying a heavy load?' Issy felt he was speaking directly to her. Felt he had seen into her heart and felt the weight of each step as she'd walked in earlier. 'Whatever your load is,' he continued, 'Jesus will take it from you, will carry it for you. All you have to do is ask! Brothers and Sisters, if it's money you want, ask Jesus! If it's peace you want, ask Jesus! If it's love you want, ask Jesus! Some of you running here, some of you running there, trying to find love. You know what you *waaannt*, Jesus knows what you *neeeed*. Hallelujah!'

'Jesus don't just look at the face, he's not concerned with the shape, or the height or the size. Jesus is concerned with the heart. He knows whose heart will go with whose. He knows the right heart for you! He sees inside all souls. He is the greatest match maker in the world. If you're *tired* of running around, making one bad choice after another, let Jesus choose for you. Jesus said, 'Come all who are heavy laden; and I will give you rest.'

Issy felt his words in her solar plexus as a spinning tornado, spiralling up through her chest, filling her heart, her throat, making her gasp for air as it gathered speed, pricking the back

4

of her eyes to release rivulets of tears, before exploding in her head, making her dizzy, light-headed, unbalanced. There were others around her crying, reaching out to her with their pain. Pain met pain, anger, frustration, disappointment, loneliness, apathy, blame, regret, resentment; creating a vortex of fear into which Issy felt drawn.

She felt the misery of the argument she'd had with Easton, relived the despair he'd left in his wake as he walked away, felt the anguish rupture in her head. She fell to the floor convulsed, shaking and twitching as invisible electric currents passed through her body. She was crying openly, thrashing her head from side to side, not caring for her hair or her clothes, not caring who held her dress in place to preserve her modesty, or propped something under her head to stop her bashing her brains out on the wooden floor. She wanted to stop, to tell herself how ridiculous she looked, but something inside kept her going, searching for release.

'Come on sister, tell the Lord about it,' someone was saying close to her right ear, 'Jesus can fix anything. Tell the Lord. Tell the Lord. Tell the Lord.' Like a broken record her words revolved in Issy's head, till she found herself telling the Lord how weak she was, how vain, how fickle, how picky, how she didn't know what was good for her, how she was ready for the Lord to choose for her, to find her a loving man, not another pretty face, who would disappoint her and leave her. At that moment, she was willing to trade light-skinned, pretty haired children for stability and love. She prayed to God to send her a husband.

When the singing, and the praying, and the preaching, and the crying was over, she lay spent and limp, like a rag doll, soaked in her own sweat. Two strong, sturdy Sisters from the church hooked a hand each under her armpits and lifted her to a standing position. Her legs wobbled as they helped her to a bench, where she sat, head bowed, ashamed. The preacher wanted all those who had given their hearts to God to come forward and declare themselves 'saved.' Despite the eyes on her, Issy didn't move. She knew others were going up to the Alter to receive the blessings of the preacher, but she didn't feel saved, didn't feel like making a public declaration of the utter helplessness she felt. God hadn't saved her, just pointed out her inadequacies, and she didn't want to stand up and show this to the congregation. So she sat, head bowed, until the end of the service. Until her brother Norman, who, concerned for her emotional and spiritual welfare, came to claim her. It was he who had persuaded her to come to the meeting.

That was six months ago. God is obviously a slow and careful God, Issy thought, as the weeks and then months went by and no righteous, loving and mature man showed up to claim her as his wife. Life continued pretty much as it had done since Easton Blackwell left. She was done with that kind of man. So Mr Lukan, or whatever his name was, had better get it out of his head that she would want to see him outside of work. Of course he would see her again, if he came to the bar and she was working, he would see her again. That didn't mean anything. She should've asked him where he was from, because his accent wasn't from round here, she knew all the pretty boys round here.

Chapter 2

'Maas Vincent's looking for carpenters for a couple houses,' his Uncle Dudley said as he joined Lukan under the mango tree in the back yard of his mother's house.

'When?' Lukan enquired, looking up, then lowered his eyes as his uncle sat beside him on the wooden bench Lukan had made. He shuffled up to make space for him.

'Right away,' he said bending over to pick up a handful of tamarinds from the pile that Lukan had been eating. 'The man him had let him down, take another job, him need someone now.'

'You tell him 'bout me?' Lukan enquired eagerly, leaning back to look into his uncle's face.

'I tell him I know somebody, but I don't tell him who yet. I wanted to check it out with you first. Don't know if you want to go that far. Me know seh you is a home bowy.'

'Where?' Lukan was hesitant.

'Clarendon.' Dudley said flatly.

His uncle called him 'Home Bwoy,' because he'd hardly ever left Savanna-la-Mar. He didn't like it but it was a lot better than what a lot of other people called him.

'How much?' Lukan asked, again hesitant. He didn't want to leave Sav, but things were getting tight.

'Him paying the full rate for a good journeyman; and because of the short notice, him will pay lodgings for one month. If him like you, him will negotiate after the first month.'

Dudley shot Lukan a sideways glance to see how he was taking it, while thinking; the bwoy really need to get out from under the frock tail of those two women, his mother and that gal him take up with. And now she breed two more. They only babies now, but before you look round three times, they going to be big. He need to get out and start acting like a man. He probably don't know I see him washing her panties the other day. That's no job for a man.

He looked at Lukan again who seemed to be turning the information over in his head. He absent mindedly shelled a tamarind and chewed it, spitting out the black shiny seeds to join the others like a pile of obsidian glistening in the streaky light of the sun filtering through the leaves.

'Him might even pay for one or two trips back to Sav because him know seh is short notice,' Dudley added, hoping to shift the doubt from Lukan's eyes.

'When him want me to start?' Lukan's voice almost trembled.

'Tomorrow,' Dudley said quietly.

'Tomorrow!' Lukan shouted, shattering the calm of the late afternoon. A goat, lying a hundred yards away, jumped up startled, annoyed that his slumber had been so violently disturbed.

'No need to tell the whole world bwoy,' his uncle said in hushed tones.

'I can't just go tomorrow!' protested Lukan.

'Why? What you doing so important that you can't go tomorrow? Is not like you have any work doing here. How you think you going to feed them two pickney if you don't get some money soon. And as far as I can see, nobody building nutting round here.'

Lukan's heart was beating fast. His uncle was right, his money from the last job was nearly done. Jez seem to spend it like water, he could never work out how it took so much to feed two little children, but she liked them to look nice and he didn't have the heart to say no to her. His uncle was always encouraging him to save, but he never seemed to be able to hold on to his money.

But to go to Clarendon tomorrow? Without any warning, without time to get used to it, to get Jez used to it.

'Him need an answer quick,' Dudley said, sensing his nephew's fear. 'Two other people interested but they're not journeymen like you, but he will take them if he can't get anyone else.'

'Let me think bout it Uncle,' he said slowly, as though he was already lost in thought. 'Let me talk to Jezmine.'

'What you want to talk to her about? You mek that gal turn you fool. Luke, you're the man, *you* mek the decisions. She depending on you. You don't have to talk to her about what you do. You just have to tell her you going to earn money to put food on her table and fancy frocks pon her back.' He was standing up, looking down on Lukan. Now it was Lukan's turn to say, 'Not so loud, Uncle, she might hear you.'

'I don't care if she hear me. If you want I'll go in there and tell her, if you too frightened to do it.'

Dudley was frustrated. He'd promised to look after his nephew when his brother died in his arms. He couldn't take all of them but he agreed to take care of Luke because he was the timid one, the one with the skin that confused the doctors. Some people said it was obeah somebody work on the bowy's mother when she was pregnant, but no cream or pill could cure him. He figured that's why Luke was so frightened to go out in the world, but that clear up now. He couldn't understand the bwoy.

'You don't have to do that. I'll tell her.'

'So you going then?'

'I'll try it.' He couldn't still the tremor in his voice.

'Good.' Dudley's voice softened as he put a reassuring arm around Lukan's shoulder. 'Let's go and tell him now.'

'You want me to come?' His uncle normally worked out the deals. Lukan just showed up and did the work. He was no good at negotiating.

'Yes, the man want to meet you. If you going to be with his team he want to make sure you going to fit.'

'I thought you say him just want a journeyman?'

'Yes, but some of the team going to be lodging together and him want to know who will get on with who.'

Mr Vincent was a short, round man. Everything about him was round; his head, his face, his eyes, the holes in his nostrils, his mouth when he said words like come, and some. He had a small round belly, and his backside looked like a gourd. He was recruiting purely on recommendations, not having time to see any of the men's work. He had three houses to build for a man who had contacts in England, and had to double-up on his usual crew because of the tight deadlines his customer set. He needed joiners, electricians and plumbers, and when Lukan arrived, he completed the set.

They were to leave at eleven o'clock the following morning. He would pay for lodgings the first month and for two trips back to Savanna-la-Mar in that time. Because of the rush on the jobs they'd have to work every other weekend but would have Sunday afternoons off on the weekend they worked. He seemed in a hurry, and over the months, as Lukan got to know him, he realised that it was his permanent disposition.

Leaving his mother, Jezmine and the girls was hard. He'd never been away from them for more than a night. His mother cried like he was leaving the island, but the way Jez responded to him made him realise that it was his own fear that he'd been battling with. She understood that this would mean regular money for a few months and good money too. The only thing she seemed worried about was him running off with some other woman and not taking care of the girls. He vowed to her he would never do that. He owed her too much.

She was his first and only woman. He was a shy boy, frightened of the girls who used to tease him because of the white blotches on his skin, especially up his neck and the right side of his face. He was so self-conscious that whenever anyone was talking to him, he'd try and stand sideways so they'd only see his left side. It earned him the nickname 'sidewinder' as he'd twist and turn to maintain the side stance.

The doctor said it was birthmarks; there was nothing he could do about it. Sometimes those kind of marks disappeared, sometimes they don't; only time would tell. None of the girls were interested in him. In fact, they were very cruel. Like his nickname he became nocturnal, staying inside as much as he could in the daytime and coming out mostly at night.

By the time he was sixteen, he was six feet. His mother learnt how to make a special cream that she gave him to use and the blotches began to even out and blend with the rest of his skin. Another two years passed, he'd grown another two inches and with the continued use of the cream, had almost normal skin. Facial and body hair covered any residual imperfections. It didn't improve his confidence though, and he was grateful to Jezmine for showing an interest in him and for taking his virginity from him.

As they lay in the bed that night, the bed he had made, with the only woman he had known, his head raced with the decision he'd just taken. Jez had packed his clothes in a small brown grip his mother kept under her bed for an emergency. It had never been used, there had never been the need for any of them to stay anywhere overnight. Now he'd be gone for two weeks. How would he get on with people who didn't know him? Would he be able to sleep in somebody else's bed? He looked around the room in the glow of the lamp on the dresser he had made. The shadow from the sloping mirror set in the thick wooden frame slanted, like the tip of an arrow pointed directly at him. He was never happy with the pale blue, Jez

11

had begged him to paint it, he'd wanted to wax it, to allow the natural grain of the wood to show its age over time, but Jez had won him over, as usual.

He was thinking of not seeing his daughters every day, of not seeing this room every night, of not being with Jez every night.

'You going to miss me?' She said in his ear. It sounded more like a statement than a question, like she knew exactly what he was thinking, and was confirming out loud what was in his head.

'Um hum' he grunted.

She pulled up close, put her hand on his knee and ran it slowly up his thigh till she reached the bundle of flesh. Without pyjamas he was exposed and available to her hot hand.

Gently kneading him like dumpling dough, she murmured, 'Going to miss this?'

'Um hum,' he grunted again as he began to respond to her touch. It started with the tightening in his scrotum, like a puppeteer bringing a limp marionette to a standing position. She kneaded his swelling orbs, before sliding her hand up his baton, now standing fully erect. She held him with one hand and ran her fingers over the tip of his pole. His buttocks clenched involuntarily. He turned his head to kiss her and saw a tear rolling down the side of her face, just as the wick from the lamp burned dry and the light went out.

'What you crying for Jez?' he asked propping himself up on his elbow, trying to make out her face in the dark. 'You don't want me to go?'

'Is not that,' she said between soft sobs.

'Then what?'

'I'm just so used to you here all the time. I'm frightened you might meet somebody else.'

'Jez, you know me like nobody else know me. I couldn't meet anybody else like you.'

'You might meet somebody better.'

'Better? What you mean better?'

'Prettier.'

'What make you think somebody prettier would want me?'

'Because you don't know who you are.'

'Come here. Come and finish what you started. Let me show you I don't want anybody else.'

He rolled onto both his elbows, pushed her legs open with his knee and, pulling himself up onto both knees, lowered himself on top of her. He wanted to make her feel better, wanted to make himself feel better, wanted to dull the fear he was feeling at leaving her, and this behind.

She never refused him, even when she was pregnant, and he had to pull out and relieve himself by hand, in case he damaged the baby. She wasn't pretty, but she was willing. He'd heard of men with pretty women who had to go somewhere else for their pleasure because their women thought themselves too good. Not Jez. She didn't mind if her hair got messed up. In fact she had it in plaits most of the time, three thick ones down one side of her head and three down the other. She said with two children to look after she didn't have time for fancy hairstyles.

He was sweating, washing her in his salt bath. She held him in his frenzy, moved with him when she felt him getting close to his peak, opened herself right up to receive his seed and his fear. He held her, a raft in his ocean of mounting panic. He was leaving all he loved behind.

Chapter 3

Dudley watched as his nephew hugged Jezmine and his two baby daughters before getting into the jeep. He was glad Lukan was going. He'd been trying to get him away from that natty head gal for the last three years. He deserved better than her, he just didn't know it. Yes, it was true that she was the only one that would look at him when he had that horrible skin disease but that cleared up long time now, his skin was smooth a clear like anybody else, he had good hair and a fine, muscular, working man's body.

The bwoy could have anyone one of the girls in the district, but he didn't seem to notice. Whatever Jezmine was giving him couldn't be so good that he couldn't see the way women looked at him now. A bwoy that look like him, with a good trade, could get a pretty and respectable woman, but he insisted on staying hooked up with this ignorant one who only seem to know how to spend his money and breed pickney.

They have some fine women in Clarendon; he was bound to hook one of them. Without Jezmine in the way and without his daughters under his nose every night he would meet somebody else. He would make sure Maas Vincent keep him down there as long as possible.

Lukan didn't embrace Dudley. He stood in front of him, looked him in the eye and said, 'Thank you Sir.' Dudley nodded his head once, but kept his hands in the pocket of his khaki trousers.

'Don't let me down,' was all he said, and Lukan felt the weight of his expectations, and those of his mother looking through the window of her little house, too emotional to come out and say goodbye to her son.

Anyone would think he was going to the other side of the world, instead of 60 miles along the west coast. Years later when this scene was played out again, he *would* be going to the other side of the world.

As the jeep pulled off, Dudley turned and walked away. No one waved, it wasn't a particularly happy occasion. Jez gathered up the girls, rested one on each hip and went back to the house she'd shared with Luke for the last two years. The house he built on the side of his mother's little plot of land so she could have a roof over her head when Darcie, their first daughter, was born.

Her father-in-law told her to get out when he discovered she was pregnant. He was a church man, said he was a God fearing man, and didn't want any ungodliness under his roof. Her mother, a weak-willed woman who was dominated by her husband, said she had to think about Jez's siblings. It was a bad example to set her sisters.

It was the opposite reaction from Luke and Miss Inez, Luke's mother. She'd told him in the cane field after they made love, and he'd pulled up the loose trousers with elastic waist he always wore when they were going to do it, so that if anyone caught them, he wouldn't have a zip to pull up and a belt to buckle.

She'd waited till he was lying on his back chewing on a blade of grass.

'Luke?' she'd begun hesitantly.

'Hmmm' he'd replied still in his post-coitus glow.

'I think I'm pregnant.'

'What!' he bolted upright.

'I think I'm pregnant' she repeated looking down, between her bent knees.

'What d'you mean you think? You're not sure?'

'I'm sure. I'm pregnant.'

'How you sure?'

'I don't have any bleeding for two months now.'

'Mek you never tell me before?'

'It might have just been a false alarm; I didn't want to worry you.'

'And you want to worry me now?' He knew he wasn't making sense but it was the shock.

'I have to tell somebody.'

He too looked through his bent knees at the ground.

'What you going to do?'

'I don't know.' She really didn't know. She knew she could get rid of it, but she didn't know who to contact, what it would cost or anything. That sort of thing wasn't discussed in her house. The expectation was that you wouldn't get pregnant out of wedlock, and any pregnancy in wedlock would be a wanted and welcomed one.

After a long silence he put his arm round her shoulder.

'We going to work it out.'

Her shoulders heaved and rocked under his arm as she cried out her relief.

'What you crying for now? I said we'll work it out.'

'I know.' She couldn't explain the release she felt from the worry she'd carried for the last forty-eight days while she waited to miss another period. Of course, she wasn't worry free now, she was still pregnant, but she wasn't the only one that knew.

'What you going to tell your parents?'

'I'm not going to tell them anything.'

'But they'll find out as soon as you start to show.'

'Yes. And when they ask me, I will tell them. You don't know what Mass Benji's like.'

Lukan did know what Mass Benji, Jez's step father, was

like. He was one of those Bible-beating men who preached Christianity but didn't know compassion, who could rile against Satan, but only understood the good Samaritan as a parable.

Jez wasn't his child, and he'd never let her forget it. It didn't help that she didn't look like her siblings, the ones who came from her mother's marriage to him. They were all dark with smooth skin that shone when oiled, and hair that was easy to comb. Jez had the misfortune of having pale almost translucent skin, the kind with freckles that blended together to form large liver spots when she stayed in the sun too long. Her hair was thick and wiry and hard to comb, so for most of her life she lived in plaits, not dainty cane rows like her sisters, but thick yam-head plaits. She was tall and bony, so it wouldn't be long before her pregnancy would be showing.

It wasn't surprising that Jez and Lukan got together. They were the outcasts of the district, the ones who looked different, who were both ridiculed. They first turned to each other for emotional support, then started to comfort each other physically.

'I'm going to have to tell Mama.' Lukan said reflectively. He never kept anything from her. She knew that he was bedding Jez. The first time he and Jez had done it, his mother had looked at him and said, 'You have to be careful. Talk to your uncle about what to use.'

'I love her, Mama!' he'd blurted out. He needed to tell someone about his mind-blowing experience, the fire he felt in his groin that spread throughout his body, the way he'd lost control of all time and space as semen shot from him like a fully loaded cannon. He'd made it to twenty without a full sexual encounter. His uncle was beginning to think he was a batty man, but he was too self-conscious to approach any of the local girls, and besides, they'd all made fun of him.

It was a Friday night, there was a local dance, his mother

made sure he was looking good in a dark blue pair of pants and blue and white stripe short sleeve shirt. She felt it for her only boy, every time someone called him 'sidewinder', wanted to turn him round as he tried to hide his face from people.

He'd had a couple bottles of beer and was drinking a rum, and still couldn't find the courage to ask any of the women to dance, but he was enjoying the music. After a couple more rums, he went outside for some air and to rest his feet. Jez was out there too, sitting on a wall, a small flask of Appleton by her side. He sat beside her on the wall. There was no risk that anybody was going to come and tell him to move, to get away from their woman. Him and Jez was in the same boat. Nobody wanted them.

'You want to go for a walk?' he asked after a while.

'Alright then.' There was nothing here for either of them, and they could hear the music for miles.

They walked in silence for a while before Jez asked about his mother. She had a sore on her leg that was giving her a lot of trouble. The last time Jez saw her, she was limping.

'It's still giving her trouble.' Lukan answered.

'She just get one thing after another. I feel so sorry for her. And she's such a nice woman.'

'She think somebody set something on her.'

'What you mean?'

'You know what I mean.'

'Fe true?' she asked incredulously.

'She think they set something on me too.'

'What them set on you?'

'My skin. She think is one of my father's jealous girlfriends. She think she set it on her and on me so that nobody would want us. And for true Mama's been by herself since Dada leave. And nobody want me.'

'That's not true Luke. That's not true.'

'How you know it's not true. Who you know who want me?'

'I want you!' she said boldly.

'I know. You're my friend, but I wasn't talking about want in that way.'

'I wasn't either.'

He stopped. She stopped.

'You mean you want us to do it?'

It wasn't the most romantic of seduction, but it was what she meant.

'Yes, Luke.' She said slowly, even a little slurred, 'I want us to do it.'

It had been as easy and as uncomplicated as that, had happened in a bush under the moon. They kissed. He took off his belt and pushed his pants and underpants down to his knees, she lay on her back and took off her panties. He was rigid, he didn't know she wasn't wet. When he tried to push it into her she screamed, he pulled back.

'What's wrong?'

'It hot. You doing it too hard.'

'How me fi do it?' He didn't want to hurt her, but he was this close and wanted to feel what everybody else talked about at work, wanted to be able to join in the conversations.

'Come here.' She took his rod with both hands and lay back down slowly. 'Come to me,' she encouraged when he didn't move. He knelt down astride her while she guided him into her. He felt her soft skin against his throbbing, pulsating flesh, and as if from nowhere he felt a rush of energy that travelled from his chest, down through his stomach and out of the end of his penis. His body shuddered as jets of hot, thick liquid squirted out of him and splashed over the mouth of her waiting hole.

'Oh God! Oh God! Oh God!' he said over and over. The release was so powerful, so all consuming, that for a moment he forgot she was there.

Her laugher returned him to his situation.

'What's so funny?' He looked down at her.

'You said Oh God about fifty times. My name is Jez, you're supposed to call *my* name.'

He pulled himself off her. 'I'm sorry Jez,' he mumbled, shame washing over him. He didn't expect that to happen. Now even *she* was laughing at him. 'I don't suppose you want me anymore now.'

'We can try again another time.' She leaned over to kiss him before looking for her panties. As her bare arm touched his, he felt himself hardening again. He was surprised to be aroused again so quickly. Normally after he masturbated, it would take him hours before he felt like it again.

He put his hand down to where she was trying to wipe away his spunk with her panties. Moving her hand out of the way he felt for her clitoris. He'd heard the guys at work say it was a good way to get a woman ready, so it wouldn't hurt, especially if she was a virgin. He never thought to ask Jez.

'Are you a virgin?' he asked.

'Why you asking me now?'

'Because if you are, I have to rub your pussy tongue to make you wet, so it won't hurt.'

'Alright then.' She opened her legs a little wider to give him more access. He couldn't tell if she was wet from her own juices or from his spunk but the more he rubbed her the stiffer he got.

'Alright, mek me try it again,' he said, feeling a little more in control.

She guided him to her entrance and he gently lowered himself into her, and thought he was doing OK when she screamed and pushed him off her.

'What now?' He was worried, she sounded in real pain.

'I just feel like something inside me burst,' she said pulling her knees up to her chest as she rolled onto her side. 'Maybe you too big for me.'

She was too afraid to try again that night. They both went home disappointed, entrenched in their beliefs that they were failures.

When he got home, his mother looked up from her sewing, stared at him over the rim of her glasses and said 'you better be careful.'

'Careful about what?' he asked sheepishly.

'You know what I'm talking about,' she said and turned back to her sewing as he slumped in the chair opposite her.

As she'd already guessed, he used the opportunity to ask her why a girl would scream. She said it showed she was a virgin, and smiled. Inez didn't know who, but her son had made it with a virgin.

'It don't mean it will be that painful every time, just the first time.'

She didn't ask who, she was pleased his curse had been broken. She may not have thought so if she knew it was Jez, the district's other outcast.

They avoided each other for a few days, but as the only friend the other had, they had to find a way back. He saw her coming out of the grocery shop on Great George St: offering to help carry her shopping he asked how she was.

'There was blood on the back of my dress; it's a good thing I went through the back door when I got home. I didn't want Mama and Mass Benji to smell my breath so I sneak in and went straight to my room.'

'I ask somebody about what happen and…' he began.

'Is who you tell about me?' she rounded on him.

'I didn't tell anybody. When I get home that night Mama just knew that I'd been with somebody. I didn't tell her who, but I ask if it's supposed to hurt. She said, just the first time.'

He was walking fast to keep up with her, for she seemed mad as hell that he told his mother. 'She say it show the woman is a virgin.'

'So you didn't believe me? You had to go and check with your Mama. Is true what they say about you.'

'What! What they say about me?'

'That you're a Mama's BWOY!' she shouted at him.

He was stung. He could take anything from anybody, he'd learned over the years to deal with the taunts and the jibes, but he couldn't take it from the one person, apart from his mother, that he trusted. He was about to hand her the bag and walk away, when he noticed the tears streaming down her face.

'Jez! Stop! Slow down!'

They were well away from the shops. He reached out and held her shoulder to slow her down. 'Stop, Jez.' He said quietly.

She looked up at him, the tears unable to veil the look of bewilderment, of betrayal in her dark brown eyes. He kissed her. Without knowing why, or quite how, something in her made him know that the next time would be right, and he wanted that next time to be now. Every fibre of his body was on red alert. He tasted the salt of her tears as they mingled with their saliva and was relieved that she didn't pull away, she yielded slowly to him, and he pulled her close.

Chapter 4

'What time you call this Issy? You was supposed to be here an hour ago, and tonight of all nights too.'

'Sorry Mass Joe. Ivan still sick and Daisy didn't come till four, even though I tell her to come by three o'clock. Sometimes I could kill that girl! Then by the time I tell her what she have to do with Ivan, I miss the bus. I'll make up the time Mass Joe, I promise.' Daisy, her younger sister helped her out with the children when she had to work, but she wasn't the most reliable person God put on this Earth. But with Ivan sick, she couldn't risk leaving him even for a few minutes by himself, not after what happened to Isaac.

'Maybe it's time I get somebody more reliable.'

'I'm sorry, sorry, sorry, Sir. I'll make up the time.' she pleaded.

'You say that every time you late.'

'But I always make up the time. You not paying me for time I don't work.'

'Anyway, it's busy so put down your things and get out there.'

'Yes Sir.'

Issy hated the rushing around. The two and three jobs to make ends meet. As well as working in Mass Joe's bar she was also an auxiliary nurse at the hospital. She would like to do the full training which would pay better than the shop and bar work put together and improve her status in the district, but

23

she didn't have the time to get the qualifications to do the training. It was a tricky situation, the constant juggling. Since she turned twenty five she wanted a more stable life. Chapelton wasn't as exciting as Kingston, but she'd had enough of excitement, and Isaac's death had sobered her up, made her look at her life differently. She wondered if God was punishing her for not seeking him earlier.

After her youngest son's funeral she'd started going to church more regularly, not every week because she had to work some Sundays, but whenever she could. It was after Isaac's death that Easton started to fall apart. He took to drink, started spending more and more time in Mass Joe's bar, and giving her less and less money. In the end, he got so bad he couldn't work, and went back to his folks in Franklin. She couldn't cope with the other two children by herself. Easton's mother offered to look after them. Issy allowed her to take Ivan, but couldn't bear to part with Irene as well. She needed someone to love and to love her back.

That was two years ago, since then she'd been on her own, struggling to make ends meet, struggling to come to terms with her son's death, and struggling to come to terms with the loss of her relationship.

Issy met Easton in a restaurant in Kingston six months after moving from her father's house in Brandon Hill. She was only sixteen and even though she'd saved up the money for the fare and paying for her part of the rent her father was still reluctant to let her go and live with her older sister, Mavis. He said she was the most hot-headed of his six children and that Kingston would only make her worse. She'd begged and pleaded with him almost every day, pointed out how she'd used the little starter money he'd given her to make and sell grater cakes, drops, gizadas, and potato pudding, and how she sold them to school children and later to higlers and even a couple of shops.

'You don't have to worry about me Papa,' she tried to persuade him, 'I know how to make money, I can even sew a few dresses for people if I don't get a job straight away.'

Papa Elmers had finally given in. Beaten down by her persistence. Many a day he'd wondered why his wife had died and left him with five girls. He missed her still, even after all these years of marriage to Frederika, the wife he took six months after her death to help him raise his girls. She hadn't added to his family, for which he was partly relieved, but which served as a source of bitterness for her, and which she tried to take out on the girls. Many a time he had to come out from cutting a suit, or sewing a jacket, to sort out a dispute between his wife and one or other of the girls.

Two of them had left already. His first, Beatrice, moved into her Granny Elmer's house when she died a few years ago, and Mavis, his second daughter moved to Kingston to work in a haberdashery store, a job with prospects. His only son Norman, and Isabell's younger sisters Daisy and Sarah still lived in the house they were all born in. He was lucky, they were all loving children, but it was Issy who was the unruly one, hard-headed, and the one who clashed with his wife the most. When she finish school at fifteen, he tried to teach her his trade because she showed an talent for tailoring, but she was too impatient, wanted to be out earning her own money, only interested in running up clothes for herself and her sisters to look pretty in church on Sundays.

'All right,' he laid down his one proviso. 'But you have to wait till you're sixteen.'

With her out of the way there might be a bit more peace in the house, and he might be able to concentrate more on his younger daughters Daisy and Sarah, instead of constantly fighting fire between Issy and Fredericka. So, at sixteen Issy packed her grip and went to join Mavis.

'Two things you have to get straight,' Mavis warned as

they walked down North Street to the room that they were to share, 'you have to pay your side of the rent, because I can't support the two of us. And you don't go out at night without me. The men here are not like the ones in Brandon Hill. You don't know their family, some of them will tell you all kind of lies about where they come from, how they are from rich families, how they have money, just to find out how much you have and try to take it from you. Some of them just want to breed you up and walk away. You listening to me Issy?' Mavis checked as Issy gazed around her open mouthed at the large stores, the busy streets and the big houses.

'Yes Mavis I hear you.'

'What me say?' Mavis asked, not convinced.

'That I have to pay my rent and be careful.' Issy précised Mavis' speech.

'I mean it, Issy. If you give me any trouble I'm sending straight back to Papa.'

Later, as Issy unpacked, in the small, sparsely furnished room on the side of the owner's house, she was ready to burst with excitement. She was ready for a big adventure, Brandon Hill was so small, everybody knew her, knew her father and took everything she did back to him. It was like being watched by a thousand eyes. Here, she could feel freedom in the air. Not in this room, not with her sister, and the owners of the house who knew her father so close by. But out there, where they walked down the road and no-one knew them. Out there was freedom and adventure.

'I'm going to start looking for a job tomorrow.' Issy declared, shaking out a printed dress and threading it through a hanger before sliding it onto the rail of the small wardrobe in the room.

'Better to wait till Monday.' Mavis advised. 'Most places shut on a Sunday.'

'I'm going to find anywhere that's open and ask them.'

Waiting a day seemed so wasteful; she was convinced she could find a job the next day.

'Tomorrow I'm going to show you round the place, so you won't get lost without me. Monday you will know where to look.' Her sister was emphatic.

Mavis cooked salt-fish and steamed cabbage with fried dumplings for their dinner on the small stove, in the tiny room at the back of their bedroom, and Issy updated her on all the happenings at home.

'Are we going out tonight?' Issy asked eagerly as they washed up the plates.

'Don't bother think about spending your little money going out. Wait till you get a job and know that you have some regular money before you start thinking about wasting it.'

Issy didn't reply, she didn't see spending her money going out to have fun as a waste. Maybe Mavis didn't see it as important anymore because she'd lived here so long, but she knew she had to abide by her sister's rules or be sent home.

As they lay side by side on the double bed which took up most of the space in the room, exhausted by the travel and the excitement of the move, Issy asked a sleepy Mavis.

'Is it true that a lot of women meet nice men in Kingston?'

'There's one or two good ones, but you're too young to know the bad from the good. The best thing you can do is concentrate on your work and forget about men. If that's what you come here for you might as well go home tomorrow.'

If I'd listened to Mavis I might not be in this situation now, Issy thought as she wiped down the counter and turned to the next customer at the bar.

'Red Stripe, please. Isabell.'

He was wearing a pale green shirt and a dazzling smile. Leaning on the bar the muscles in his arms bulged out to support him, and light bounced off his pomaded hair.

'You have a good memory,' she gave him her barmaid smile.

She knew one of the reasons Mass Joe put up with her lateness was because she was good at her job. She had an easy way with the customers, made the men feel special by flirting with them. She'd learnt it in Kingston.

In her first job in the small grocery store, she dealt mainly with women, old women who didn't like the busyness of the bigger stores and wanted a personal service, wanted to have their salt beef sliced instead of having to pick it out of the barrel themselves. After a few months she was bored though, seeing women all day and going home to Mavis at night, who seemed hell bent on keeping her away from night life. She'd been to one dance and Mavis had stuck to her side like burr to cotton.

It was in the shop that she heard about the job in the restaurant.

'My brother had to let another one of his bar girls go for dipping her hand in the till. You can't trust them. It's not like he don't pay them good money, but they never satisfied. Him having to run the bar himself and do everything else.'

'Poor man,' Issy said as she weighed the sweet potato, 'where's his bar?' she added.

'It's the one on the corner of Oxford Road and Halfway Tree Road. It's a good spot and him get very busy, but he can't keep it going without some workers he can trust. Miss Vera lucky to have you' she added, as she paid for her purchases.

She couldn't wait to get away from work, and went straight to the bar in the quiet time between the end of lunch and evening customers. Jack Williams looked her up and down when she said she heard he had a job.

'How old are you?'

'Seventeen,' she lied.

He looked her up and down again.

'You do bar work before?'

'No Sir, but I learn quick.'

'I don't have time to train anybody. I need somebody who can do the work right away.'

'Sir, give me a chance, I learn really quick.'

'I tell you, I don't have time to train anybody. I'm too busy.'

'But if I had experience you would take me?'

'Come back when you have experience, people come and go all the time,' He turned back to wiping down the optics.

She looked around the bar, it was bright and the open door let in cool air, or maybe it was the big fan in the ceiling which was going round at half speed. To the right of the bar were about ten tables covered in bright, multicoloured plastic tablecloths. It looked like the kind of place decent people came to. A pity, she thought as she turned to the door.

'Wait!' Jack Williams called.

She turned.

'Where you work now?'

He looked surprised when she told him.

'You ever serve food in a restaurant.'

'Yes,' she lied. How hard could it be to bring out a plate of food from the kitchen?

'All right then. I could use some help at night in the restaurant. You interested?'

'Yes Sir, I'm interested.'

'Can you start tomorrow?'

'What time Sir?'

'I'll give you one week trial, six till eleven.'

'How much Sir?'

The figure was more than she was getting for longer hours in the shop.

'All right Sir. I'll come tomorrow.'

That was the start of working two jobs. No need to give up the shop one. Mavis wasn't happy about her working nights but she knew the place had a good reputation. As Issy saw it, it would get her out of the house at night, and she'd get paid for it.

That was then. She didn't want to be out of her house at night anymore. Didn't want to be chatting to men at the bar, didn't want the attention of this face smiling at her.

'My memory good for things I want to remember,' he said quietly taking the bottle from her. She had no difficulty with the bottle opener tonight. She was too worried about what was happening to her sick son at home to pay this pretty face much mind. He paid. She moved to the next customer. He sat a while longer before going outside where they were setting up a sound system for a big open air dance to celebrate Jamaica's independence from England. It was going to be a long night.

During her first half hour break, she went outside to see what was happening. Although it was only half past nine, a good size crowd had gathered, people were beginning to dance round the edges of the space that was left as the dance floor. It would be another hour and a half before the dancing would get going, till the drink and the beat made it impossible for them to stand or sit still.

It was a hot night, no breeze, and the air was thick with anticipation and pride. Not many of the people there really understood what independence from England meant, but Norman Manley had made it sound like a good thing. Jamaicans would be able to do what they wanted without always having to ask England for permission. Jamaica was no longer a child and didn't need permission from a parent to run her life. Jamaicans would have control of their own industries, their sugar and bauxite, they would keep all the money they made and not have pocket money from England. Jamaica would be free, after years in bondage. People didn't know then, the price they would have to pay for that freedom.

Tonight they just wanted to have a good time, to rock to the rhythms of Calypso and bop to the beats of Ska, to hold and be held by somebody on the dance floor, to drink a few beers or rums, and if they were lucky, to spend the night with somebody.

As Issy watched, a part of her still wanted that life, even though it hadn't got her what she wanted, she still wanted the energy of it. The church, or more accurately God, promised her something more permanent than the pleasure of a good dance. People were coming from all over the parish. They would usually hold this kind of dance in May Pen but all Issy knew was that something went wrong and it move to Chapelton. She wondered if Easton would come. That's partly who she was looking for. He wouldn't come into the bar because he owed too much money to Mass Joe. No, if he came he would bring his own bottle of rum, he wouldn't bother with ice or coke or any of the things that made the drink a pleasure, he'd long stopped drinking for pleasure. Since their son's death he only drank for comfort and to forget.

She was about to turn and go back to work when she saw him on a bench under a tree on the very edge of the crowd, just visible in the lighting that had been rigged up by the sound men. His pale grey pants could have been white once, as could his grey open neck shirt. That's how she always picked him out in a crowd, always dressed in white when he went out, that and his height. He was usually head and shoulders above most men in a room.

He was wearing white the first time she had met him in the restaurant in Kingston. She was serving his table of four, two men and two women. She didn't see them come in, must have been in the kitchen collecting another order. When she went to take their orders he spoke for all of them.

'One chicken dinner, one oxtail dinner, and two stew beef dinners.'

'Do you want any drinks?' she asked.

'You have any sorrel?' the lady sitting next to him asked.

'Yes maam.'

'Bring the ice separate,' she instructed. Customers asked for this when they wanted the full glass of drink. She didn't understand at first, but Jack Williams told her to give them what they wanted. It was the penny-pinching ones who asked for separate ice, but he wasn't going to turn them away for the sake of a couple ounces of sorrel, or ginger beer or any of the other drinks they made at the restaurant.

'Give me a beer,' said Mr White Suit.

'Make that two,' the other man said.

'Three,' the woman in the red dress and high heels sitting opposite him added.

There was nothing eventful about their meal, they ate, drank, talked, laughed, ordered more drink, happily getting ready for their night out. As they were leaving, Mr White Suit took her left hand in both of his, and pressed a note in it.

'You really know how to serve your customers.' He said aloud. Then, with his back to his friends he whispered, 'buy yourself something nice to wear. I would like to see you without your uniform.' Winking at her, he turned and joined his friends as they headed for the door.

Issy couldn't believe the size of the tip; it was ten times more than her biggest *ever* tip. She folded the note, sliding it into her pocket, before anyone could see. She wasn't going to share this one. She had earned this all by herself, he said to buy something nice to wear. She could make a whole wardrobe for that. The only problem was that she'd have nowhere to wear the clothes to, because Mavis hardly went out, even at weekends, she was always tired or broke. Even when Issy offered to pay for her, she refused.

She was a good saver though, and was accumulating more money every week, having nothing to spend it on. She had three dresses she hadn't worn, two pairs of high heels that were just begging for an outing, blouses and skirts hanging in the wardrobe craving an excursion, and at least a dozen pairs of stockings. Mavis said her job was insecure and she should put something aside for a rainy day, but she had enough to weather a hurricane.

She ran home that night, burst the door open and threw her tip on the bed next to Mavis.

'Guess what this is?' she asked excitedly.

'Them let you go, and pay you for the days you work already?' Mavis voice trembled with alarm.

'This is tonight's tip!' Issy declared proudly.

'Tip! You get this much for tip?' the suspicion was clear in her voice.

'Yes! From one table! The man said to buy myself something to wear.'

'Which man?'

'He was the one doing all the ordering, and paying the bill. He was in all white, even white shoes. He said I was a really good waitress.'

'That sound fishy to me.' Mavis turned away and continued to plait her hair, getting ready for bed.

'You don't think I'm a good waitress? Maas Williams think I'm good. I'm always getting tips from…'

'It's the size of the tip that's fishy.'

'You just jealous!' she blurted, stung by her sister's lack of enthusiasm and her suspicion, 'jealous because nobody tip you in your job.'

'You think you know everything don't you, little country miss, but let me tell you something; when a man give you this much tip and tell you to buy something nice to wear, it's not just because of how you serve him food.'

'What d'you mean?' This wasn't how she'd planned it. Mavis was going to be happy for her, she was going to offer to

33

buy them both a nice outfit and pay for them to go to a dance, or a party or somewhere other than this room which was beginning to stifle her, especially with a disapproving Mavis in it so much of the time.

'He might be just buttering you up for something else.'

'I don't know what you mean.' She folded the note and put it in her purse, before putting the purse in the drawer, where she kept it at night.

The silence hung like a fine steel mist between them, they could see each other but could not reach each other. They were too different. Mavis was a house rat, content to work and stay home, venturing out to a party or dance once a month when pressed. Issy wanted to be out at nights, enjoying the life she saw those who came into the restaurant enjoying. There was no point being in Kingston if all she was going to do was work and sit at home sewing clothes for the wardrobe.

It was a fitful night for both of them. The dawn had not thinned the steel particles between them. Issy resolved to find a way to have some fun, with or without Mavis.

It is often the way that when one makes a definite decision to do something, opportunities appear to facilitate their action. That evening one of the other waitress said,

'There's a new club opening down town on Friday night. Me and my friend going, you want to come with us. All you ever seem to do is work. You should come out and have a good time.'

'I'm not sure if I'm…' Issy began.

'I check the rota, you finish at nine o'clock. We not going till about ten, so you can come if you want.'

'Let me think about it and let you know tomorrow.'

'The thing is, my friend can get some cheap tickets, but she have to get them in the morning, so I would have to know tonight, otherwise you will have to pay the full price.'

With no way of checking with Mavis if it was OK, and

desperate for some excitement, Issy said, 'Yes, I'll come,' and decided to work out the finer details later.

All shift, she thought of how to broach it with Mavis. She couldn't see Mavis saying yes, not after last night, and they still weren't talking this morning. The dance was two days away, she would be nice to Mavis tonight, butter her up a bit, and then tell her. She was so preoccupied that Mr Williams called her over to ask if she was alright, as she had messed up two customers' orders.

'I'm sorry Sir,' she apologised, 'I won't do it again.'

On the walk home she still couldn't think of a way to tell Mavis, and decided not to say anything, but wait until the following day. She would, however, do whatever Mavis wanted tonight. She would apologise, which is what she knew Mavis was waiting for.

'I'm sorry Mavis.' She said as she entered the room.

'Sorry for what?' Her father always said that. He wanted to know that his children wasn't just apologising because they were expected to, but because they understood why they needed to apologise.

'Sorry for shouting at you last night, for saying you're jealous.' She tried to sound contrite, but inside she was still angry.

'Just so long as you understand, that all I'm trying to do is protect you from some of those devious and deceitful men out there.'

'Yes, I understand,' she said, but was thinking, 'how would you know anything about men, you never go out with any of them.'

The apology seemed to do the trick; Mavis relaxed as did the atmosphere between them. They chatted about their days, but Issy was careful not to mention her invitation, and still hadn't found a way to broach it the following night, afraid of upsetting the peace between them.

As she lay awake that night listening to Mavis' gentle snores, she hatched her plan. Mavis always left a little earlier than her in the mornings, having further to travel and more preparation to make before her store opened, it being so much bigger than Issy's. She'd take her clothes with her to work, and go straight to the club from work. Mavis wouldn't like it but she wouldn't be able to stop her, even if she was mad, at least she'd have had some fun. She would leave a note on the table to let Mavis know she'd had to work late. She wasn't sure what would happen when she didn't come home at the expected time but that's something she would have to play by ear. She'd be in the night club by the time Mavis realised she wasn't coming home; she'd face the consequences later. She just had to get out and have some fun.

Issy knew exactly what she was going to wear, having pictured it in her head a million times. The red and white polka dot dress, with the red sash that tied just below her breasts. It made her breasts look bigger and made her look older, more sophisticated. She saw other women who came into the restaurant in that style and knew it was the height of fashion. It was perfect with the black mock patent leather shoes she got from the market. You couldn't tell they weren't the real thing when they were new; it was only after a while that the difference in quality began to show. She wasn't likely to wear hers enough to show any wear and tear while she lived with Mavis. She had some red plastic bangles and a hair comb to put her hair up. She wore it in a pony tail most days for work but liked to dress it up for church and for their rare nights out.

The plan was perfect. At nine o'clock sharp she took her apron off and headed to the toilet to get dressed. It was a little cramped, even for Issy's slender frame, but she would have changed in a shoe box if she's had to. There wasn't a full length mirror in the toilet, and while she was very pleased with the way she looked from head to shoulder, she had to rely on her colleagues to judge the effect of the complete outfit.

When she walked into the restaurant clutching her tiny black purse where she carried her keys, money and lipstick; Mr Jack Williams, who was pouring a rum at the bar, seemed to forget he had to stop pouring as his eyes widened and his jaw fell open. It wasn't till the rum spilled over the edge of the glass and began to run down the counter that he remember the job in hand.

'Damn,' was the strongest expletive he allowed himself at work, as he reached for the cloth. He wasn't the only one to pause from his activity, almost every man in the restaurant, and most of the women, watched Issy walk across the room to her work mates waiting for her outside.

'Wish I was coming with you.' The men's stare said, while the women's clearly said, 'I'm glad you're leaving.'

Issy was oblivious to this, her main concern being to get the approval of her colleagues, which after tonight, she hoped would become friends. They were older than her by at least four years and she was praying they'd think her sophisticated enough to go out with them on a regular basis. She was still naïve enough to misread the look of disappointment on their faces as disapproval, rather than the envy of being outshone by her.

She looked around in awe as they stepped through the doors, into a large dome shaped room. A few feet ahead began a row of circular tables covered in white table cloths, on which sat long stemmed vases with a single red hibiscus in each vase. As she became accustomed to the dimmed lighting she saw that the tables curved around a central dance floor with a DJ's table to the far right of the floor. People sitting at the tables were being served food by waitresses in crisp black and white uniforms. The music was playing softly, at only a fraction of the volume it would get to later.

Issy was transfixed. She'd never seen anything like this before, neither had her colleagues by the look of it, as they all stood and stared at the pictures on the walls. Pictures of hummingbirds, of half open ackee plants, of the lignum vite flower, of things Jamaican, that looked at home in a place that could be in a film. Issy felt like a film star as they walked to the toilet to check that their lipsticks and clothes were still intact. It was a hot night but the club felt cool, almost cold. The air conditioning must have been on for hours.

The full length mirrors in the toilets gave Issy the first indication of what others had been seeing. She looked dazzling, and was pleased. She was bound to get at least one dance tonight. She was not to know that she'd be on the dance floor all night in the arms of one of the most sort after men in Kingston.

'Issy.' Her reverie was interrupted my Mass Joe.

'Yes, Sir.' She turned to look into his anxious eyes.

'Sorry to cut you break short but we're full in there and the customers getting impatient. You have to come back in. I'll give you the time back.'

'All right. If it's quiet later I'd like to leave early, because Ivan sick tonight.'

'We'll see.' Mass Joe didn't want to commit himself to anything. You can never tell how these nights can turn out. Sometimes it's quiet by 2 o'clock; other times it busy till 4 o'clock. He didn't want to make any promises.

Chapter 5

Easton Blackwell lowered his head as soon as he saw her. He'd been watching the door of the bar since he arrived just over an hour ago. He knew she would come out at some point, she always came outside for her breaks, she liked to see what was going on that she was missing, wanted to see who was out there, to watch the dancing, and even catch half an hour of it in her break. He knew so much about her, knew every curve of her body, every mark, every line, every dimple. He knew her moods, her cycles, her dreams, her fears. He knew these things, but he didn't know *her* anymore.

Not since Isaac's death. That's when she disappeared from him, or so he liked to believe. When he was been honest with himself though, he'd admit that she had disappeared way before that, had stopped being the girl he met. The girl who looked wide-eyed at him as she gazed at the note in her hand, the tip he's given her for good service. She was still too naïve to understand what he was saying. Someone older and more experienced would have asked him what he wanted her to buy and when he'd like to see her in it; might even have suggested that he come and help her choose. But she just thanked him and put the money into her pocket, almost skipping to the next table.

It was weeks before he saw her again. He'd intended to go back to the restaurant on his own, but hadn't found the opportunity before the Friday night when she walked into the club. He had a lot of women to take care of, and in his job he was meeting new ones all the time. He didn't recognise her at first. All he was aware of was the dazzling beauty in the polka dot dress and the beehive hair. He made his move before she was properly in the room; there were a lot of sharks out tonight, some looking to spend money on a sweet chick, some looking to have some money spent on them. He wouldn't mind spending some money on this chick tonight. He noted that she came in with two other girls, didn't look like they had any men. It wouldn't do any harm to introduce himself again.

'Good evening ladies,' he addressed all of them, not wanting to be too obvious till he knew what was going on. 'Welcome to the Kabana Club.'

They all spun round.

'Good evening,' they chorused.

'Are you going to take a seat or…are you the waitresses from Mass Joe's restaurant?'

'Yes,' they all answered.

'If you're all here, who running the restaurant. Don't tell me Mass Joe shut it for the opening of Kabana!'

'Mass Joe and his wife.' Marva giggled.

'So this is where you come on your night off. That man is paying you too much!' He laughed when he saw the worried looks on their faces.

'It's only a joke, in my opinion he should pay you more, especially for such good service,' he looked deeply into Issy's eyes.

'You here by yourself?' He asked.

'Yes.' They chorused again.

'Then I'll have to find somebody to look after you tonight. Lovely looking ladies like you shouldn't be on your own. Come and sit down at this table.'

He started to walk toward the nearest table and they

followed like sheep. They weren't used to this kind of place, and was grateful to be shown what to do.

'Do we have to buy food if we sit at the table?' Issy asked worriedly. She hadn't brought enough money to buy food in a place like this.

'No there's a show later, anybody can sit down but you must buy a drink.'

'Oh, we was expecting to do that,' Marva said. 'But I was worried bout the food too.'

'You can all relax now,' he reassured them. 'What's you names? I can't keep calling you ladies all night.'

'I'm Marva.'

'Issy.'

'Maxine.'

They all answered at once.

'Alright, Maxine, Issy, Marva, my name's Easton. When you make your mind up what you want to drink, I suggest one of you wait at the table so that nobody else sit at it, because the place filling up fast. I'll come back to check if you alright.'

As he walked away he could hardly believe it was the same girl from the restaurant. The other two looked nice dressed up, but there was something special about Issy. He was working as an usher so he had to keep circulating; he had to make sure all the important people were taken care off. The tables were really for people buying food, but he would buy the food for them if he had to. He really wanted to impress Issy.

He also had to find a couple of brothers to take care of her friends. That wouldn't be hard; there were plenty of men here by themselves looking for a good time. He found two willing brothers in no time, but told them to lay off the one in the polka dot dress.

'I see you net the lobster already, leave us with the shrimps,' grumbled Prince, a stocky young man of about twenty five, who used to be a fisherman and talked about everything in nautical terms.

'They're pretty good looking shrimps, and they have their own money, every single one of them working.' Easton winked at him.

'Can't complain too much then, I suppose,' mumbled Prince, while Ray weighed up whether it was worth spending his night on a couple of young girls. He preferred older women, being nearly thirty himself, they were less work.

The girls sipped on their beers from the long fluted glasses. Issy wasn't used to drinking. Her father was tee total, said he'd seen drink destroy too many men, 'make them turn fool, and they end up losing every thing, even them life.' No, he was no believer in drink. He wasn't happy about Issy working in a bar but when she explained that she only worked in the restaurant he relaxed. Given the price of the drinks they wouldn't be drinking many beers tonight.

As they relaxed they began to take in their surroundings. Everyone was dressed to the nines. A lot of the men had on suits, mainly linen or cotton. Some had on bow ties with shirts completely buttoned. There was a microphone at the back of the dance floor and a rumba box a few yards from it. The girls chatted excitedly about the night.

'Look like they have a band tonight.'

'That must be the 'entertainment' that was on the ticket.'

'I wonder who it is.'

'Must be somebody local. If it was international they'd have advertised it on the radio.'

'Must be a mento band.'

'What time they coming on?'

'Hope is not too late, I want to get some dancing in tonight.'

'What make you think you can't dance to the band?'

'If you think me going to get up on that floor in front of all those people to dance, you have another think coming.'

'Would *you* dance in front of all them people?'

'Me. You must be mad.'

'It look like is only rich people come here.'

'We're here, and we're not rich.'

'That's just because your friend get the tickets cheap.'

'Maybe everybody else get them cheap too. Sometimes they do that to full the place on the first night, then the newspapers can write that it was a sell out.'

'How you know so much?'

'When you live here long enough, you get to know things. You still have country water in you veins, still a breathe country air.'

'How long you live here?'

'Ten years.'

'And you?'

'Eleven.'

'How long you here now?'

'Six months.'

'You don't have a strong country accent, you sound like you here for longer.'

'Daddy make sure we talk proper English, and I went to a good school.'

'So how come you waitressing?'

'I'm waiting for something better to come up.'

'So waitressing not good enough for you?'

'It's alright but, I want something with a bit more prospects.'

'That's what every waitress say, even after ten years.'

'Don't look now, but there's two fellas making a grove to our table.'

'Hello ladies,' Ray greeted them, in his deepest most seductive voice. He was a little taller than Prince, slim with a long face and tight wirery hair cut short. His top shirt button was opened and the tail tucked into his dark pants.

'Can we sit down with you?' Prince's high pitched timbre chirped.

'If you want. You mind girls?' Maxine the oldest of them asked.

'No,' the others said in unison.

For the next half an hour the men's voices see-sawed as they tried to impress the girls with their ill-defined jobs from which they earned ill-defined large sums which were due to be paid at an ill-defined 'soon'. They mostly spoke to Maxine and Marva. Issy felt a little left out and contented herself with the fact that she was out, in a fantastic club with great friends. Maxine and Marva were now more than colleagues, they were people who'd invited her to be with them. It felt great to be with all these people. It was a shame Mavis wasn't here, she'd have enjoy it.

Mavis! There was only thirty minutes to go to the time when Issy would be home if she'd been working late. What would Mavis do? Would she go next door to ask if they'd seen her? Would she try and find out from her work? How? They didn't have a phone, and besides the restaurant would be closed and Mass Joe gone home.

'What you looking so worried about?' Easton said, sliding into the vacant chair by her side.

'Oh. Nothing.' Issy forced herself back into the room. No point worrying about something she had no control over. Mavis wouldn't know where to find her, and whatever problems there were, she'd deal with them later. Nothing was going to spoil tonight.

'That didn't look like nothing to me.' He insisted.

'I was just thinking about my sister. She couldn't come tonight.' Issy lied.

'Then you just have to make sure you enjoy yourself for the two of you.'

Issy gave him a nervous look and an anxious giggle.

'That's better. Now let me see a smile.'

'You know how to melt a man's heart,' he only half joked, because when she looked at him with her wide, innocent, trusting eyes, and smiled her soft nervous smile, he felt something inside him soften. She was like one of those dark skinned dolls they made in America, petite, tiny waist, firm breasts pushed up into the close fitting bodice of her dress, slim but strong legs. He couldn't see her feet, but remembered her high heels and the way she swung her hips as she'd walked to the table. She giggled, not knowing what to say. No one had ever spoken to her like that before.

'I see your glass empty,' he said leaning in close to her. 'You want another beer?'

'No. I think I drink that one too fast. I'm not used to drinking.'

'You want a soft drink? A Pepsi or root beer or something?'

'Maybe I could have a root beer, then it would feel like I'm still drinking beer.' She giggled again.

Easton bought drinks for her friends too, he drew the line at buying for Prince and Ray, who had not offered the women even one drink. He didn't mind buying for all the ladies. There was a tab on the bar for him to buy single women drinks. The management wanted a merry atmosphere, they didn't want lack of money to get in the way of creating it. Easton didn't mind, it made him look good. There were quite a few ladies he was working tonight, but he had a special eye on Issy. Little miss innocent, ripe for the picking.

It was always the same with these country girls, when they first come to Kingston. It's like them get let off a leash, they know nobody here watching over them like when they're at home and they become like leggo beast. There was something about this one though. She looked like she have some breeding, like somebody take time with her. Easton liked the way she talked, like she was always just out of breath. Like someone just give her a long kiss and she coming up for air.

45

'Stop it Easton,' he told himself. 'You have work to do tonight.'

It wasn't till much later that he got a chance to dance with Issy, and make the connection he'd been waiting for all night. The band had played a lot of Jamaica's favourite mento songs, *Nobody's Business, Hill and Gully Rider, Hold him Joe*. The very bold had got on the dance floor, and danced to every tune. Then, after the owners finished their speeches about how much they hoped everyone would enjoy the night, the floor was throw open again for general dancing, and more people, wanting to show off their clothes and their moves flocked to the floor.

He found her near the edge of the floor dancing with her two friends. Prince and Ray had disappeared, maybe looking for more lucrative pickings, women with more money than these waitresses.

'Where you learn to dance like that?' he asked as he stepped to dance in front of her.

'At home.'

'Where's home?'

'Brandon Hill'

'Brandon where?'

'Brandon Hill, in Clarendon.'

'So you not that much of a country girl then, you not so far down the road. What bring you to Kingston?'

'My sister live here. I begged Papa to let me come and live with her.'

'Where's you sister tonight?'

'I tell you already, she couldn't come.'

'Why? She don't like dancing?'

'It's not that, she have to work tomorrow morning.' Well it was partially true. Mavis did have to work tomorrow, but she probably wouldn't have come even if she didn't.

He reached out, took her hand and twirled her round. She was light on her feet and got straight back in to the grove.

'You like dancing?'

'Yes. I don't get to do it enough.'

'I can tell.'

She wondered if he meant he could tell she liked dancing, or that she didn't dance enough, but she didn't want to ask in case he thought she was being foolish.

'You want another drink?'

'You buy me two already.'

'You have a limit on how many drinks a man can buy you?'

'No, but…'

'All right. Soon come.'

He went to the bar and came back with four beers, giving one each to Maxine and Marva so they wouldn't feel left out, and he could be seen to be doing his job, keeping the ladies entertained.

The DJ played a lot of Calypso and Mento and Easton took it in turns to dance with Maxine and Marva as well as with Issy. Towards the end of the night when the DJ started to slow the pace down, Prince and Ray showed up like vultures to a fresh kill. They'd obviously not had much luck with anyone else, and were now coming back for the slow dances with the ladies.

Easton reached out and pulled Issy to him as the first notes of Calypso Quintet's *Night Food* begun. She stepped easily to him, and moved with his rhythm. She could waltz, and he enjoyed taking her around the floor. They were a handsome couple, him in his white linen suit and she in her polka dots and heels.

'You move good baby,' he said as he twirled her on the floor and reeled her in.

She giggled, but he could see she was enjoying herself. What *she* couldn't see was the envy in her friends' eyes. She was not aware of what a great couple they made, and how many eyes were on them. She was, however, aware that Easton was very handsome, a 'pretty boy' as her dad called men like him. She loved the ease with which he guided her round the floor and was a little unsettled by the way he squeezed her hands whenever he held them. She was very hot and wanted to go to the toilet to cool down, but the DJ kept playing great tunes and he kept asking her to dance.

Then, they took the lights right down low, and played some slow blues. It was the signal that it would soon be time to go. Easton manoeuvred her to the edge of the floor which was the darkest spot, and pulled her in even closer. She could feel his manhood hard against her hips as he slid from side to side. He made small circles in her palms with his middle finger, and breathed hot breaths in her ear.

'Issy, you one hell of a girl.' He whispered so she could hear him above the music. She didn't know what to say so she remained silent as he pressed her chest in hard against his. She felt her breast flatten against his chest, felt his heart beating against hers and wanted to hold him even closer.

She didn't want the music to stop, didn't want to leave the floor, didn't want to go back to the room with Mavis and her disapproving stares. If only Mavis knew what this was like she wouldn't be angry with me, thought Issy. Maybe she does know, maybe this is what she's been trying to keep me away from, maybe she's just being selfish.

Easton ran his finger from her neck, down past her shoulders, into the hollow of her back and right down to her coccyx. It sent a shiver through her, a delicious tingle to her nipples, and a dampness to her crotch. She was hot, like prickly heat, and her breath came in little gasps even though she wasn't talking. Easton had his arms wrapped round her, completely enveloping her. He was so much bigger than her, he made her feel wild and reckless. His hardness was pressing against her, but she didn't care.

'How you getting home tonight?'

'We getting a taxi.'

'You want me give you a ride?'

'All of us, or just me?'

'I'll take your friends home first, then you can show me where you live.'

'I'm not sure…' Issy hesitated, feeling anxious about Mavis again.

'You don't need to worry, me not going to do anything to you. I'm a respectable man. You can trust me.'

'I will have to ask them.'

'If them have other plans,' he said looking over Issy's head at Maxine in a serious grind with Prince, and Marva with her head on Ray's shoulder, 'I will drop you home by yourself.'

Not long after that, the DJ played the last song and the lights slowly came up again.

'Check your friends and wait for me at the door. I have to sort out some business with the boss.'

She watched him walk across the floor, the sweat showing through his white shirt like a map of Cuba. Marva wanted a ride back, but Maxine, who lived nearer the club, was going to walk home with Prince.

When he finally finished his business most of the crowd had gone, either to their homes, or to parties, or to blues.

'Come this way ladies,' he said bending his arm at the elbows for each to thread their arm through. He seemed very intent on making sure they were both looked after.

'What happened to Ray? Him tired already.' He asked jokingly of Marva.

'Him going on to a blues. Before you ask, some of us have to work tomorrow.' She retorted, with just a hint of resentment.

'Eeeasy, I was only joking,' he said to Marva, while squeezing Issy's arm with the fold of his elbow, and winked at her. She didn't know what to say. This wasn't something she was used to, and she was not to know then how rapidly she'd learn and how much a part of her life this would become. She was enjoying being on his arm, even if she was sharing him with Marva. She was also unaware of how much that sharing would come to feature.

Issy didn't know much about cars, but felt like a princess when Easton held the door open for her to get into the front seat, before guiding Marva into the back seat. Everything about him flowed, like molasses over the back of a spoon, nothing was hurried. He asked them about their night, did they enjoy it, would they come to the club again? Is it somewhere they would tell people about? Both women, a little tipsy from the free beers, were effervescent in their praise.

'Is just a shame it's a Friday night though,' said Marva, 'because some of us have to work tomorrow.'

'You mean later,' giggled Issy, as they pulled up outside Marva's house, which was just barely visible behind the high hedges of Crotons.

Easton got out to open the door for her.

'You didn't have to do that, I can open the door myself,' she protested, not being used to this treatment.

'Hope to see you back at the Kabana soon,' he said as he shut the door behind her, watched her walk up to the door, fumble with the keys and let herself in.

'Now it's just you and me,' he smiled at Issy as he kissed her.

She wasn't expecting it. Well she hoping that he would, but didn't think he would do it so soon, she thought he'd wait till they got to her house. She'd kissed boys before, back home, but they'd kissed on the lips. None of them had forced their tongue into her mouth the way Easton was doing now. He was breathing hard, searching for her tongue, licking it, making circles around it with his own. His hands were loosening the bow that held her dress together at the top, and cupping her beasts. She couldn't speak, could hardly breathe. He sucked hard on her tongue again, squeezed her right breast with his right hand while his left hand started to move up her thigh.

Gaining strength from the shock of his sudden onslaught, she placed both palms on his chest and pushed him hard. She thought he would rip her tongue out as he flew backwards, his shoulder hitting the door, his head the window.

'Get off me!' she screamed.

He lunged forward and clamped his hand across her mouth, fearing people would come running out of their houses. She pushed him again, this time with so much force he heard his shoulder crack as it hit the door again.

'God!' He gasped, reaching for his shoulder as she reached for the door handle, let herself out and ran down the street, her high heels clicking like ice picks on ice. He chased after her. He had to stop her, it was late and she said she didn't know this part of Kingston, besides, what would people think of him if she turned up at somebody's house in that state? Her friend just went in, what if she came running out?

She didn't hear his soft soles over the pounding of her heart and the roar in her head until he was a few feet from her. She tried to scream but her lungs were exhausted and her voice came out as a whimper. He held her from behind, pinning both her arms to her side; she tried to kick him with her heels, but being too close she couldn't get enough leverage. Her chest heaved as her lungs fought for breath.

'What you do that for?' He was incredulous.

'Let me go or I'll scream 'police.''

'If you do that I'll knock you out.'

'Pol…' she started.

He clamped his wide palm over her face, squashing her nose flat with his thumb. She couldn't breathe. She tried to bite him, but the pressure of his hand was too great and she couldn't open her mouth. She thought she was going to die. Her body sagged from lack of oxygen and he loosened his grip.

'Listen, Issy. I'm not going to hurt you. You can stop acting so crazy.'

She couldn't speak.

'I'm not going to do anything to you.'

'Then what was that in the car?' she found her voice.

'I thought you wanted it?'

'You didn't ask me. How you know I want anything from you?'

'All night you been acting like it was what you wanted.'

'Well you're wrong. I thought you were just being nice. Mavis was right after all.'

'I *was* being nice. Issy, I like you. I liked you from the night I see you at Jack William's restaurant. When I give you the tip I was hoping you would ask me to come and help you spend it, or something like that. When you come into the club tonight, and you look so pretty, I just wanted to spend the whole night with you, but I was working. Even the time I spend with you the manager complain about. That's why I was gone so long. He said he had to remind me that when I'm at work I can't have favourites.'

He was talking fast while he kept his hand loosely over her mouth. Her back was pressed hard into his chest, and she could feel his heart beating quickly.

'You can let me go, I'm not going to run.'

'Promise me you won't scream. Issy it wouldn't be worth while me doing anything to hurt you, especially tonight. Think about it. How many people see you leave with me? Even your friend Marva is just up the road. It would just be plain foolish to try and do anything to you that you don't want.'

'Alright,' she relinquished. It made sense.

He relaxed his grip. They both took two deep breaths before he turned her to face him. She tensed as he touched her shoulder, he dropped his hand.

'Look at me Issy!' He demanded, and she obeyed.

'I'm sorry about what happen in the car. I really believed you wanted it.'

'Even if I did want it, and I'm not saying I did, you didn't have to be so rough.'

'I'm sorry. It's just that some country girls… like it… a little rough. Think a man is a mamby pamby if him too gentle.'

'Well, I'm not one of them.' She said defiantly.

'I'm sorry.'

'So you keep saying.'

'Come on, let me take you home.'

Only as she turned to walk did she notice the pain in her ankle. He noticed her wince as she tried to put pressure on it.

'You foot hurting?'

'Yes,' she grimaced.

'Put your arm round my waist, and lean on me.'

It was only on the walk back that she realised how far she'd run. The pain in her ankle was excruciating, and she couldn't help the involuntary gasps of pain that escaped her lips.

'You'd better let me carry you.' Easton said.

'You can't do that.'

'Why?'

When she didn't answer he chuckled, 'You still frightened of me?'

'No. I just feel foolish.'

'Better you feel foolish than feel pain.'

He swept his hands under her legs and carried her like a child. She nestled into his chest, listened to his footfall on the sidewalk, and felt comforted.

'Easton.' She said quietly.

'Hmm'

'I'm sorry.'

'It's alright. I should've known you were not one of them girls.'

'What girls?'

'It don't matter. We here now.'

He manoeuvred her into the passenger seat and shut the door. Back behind the wheel he smiled at her.

'Time you was in bed.'

On the drive home, they sought solace in their own thoughts. He was even more attracted to her, she had fire, she had fight, she was nobody's push over. He had to find a way to pull it round. This wasn't over yet. She was thinking about how to explain her ankle, her messed up hair and where she'd been to Mavis.

'Your ankle still painful?' he asked as he switched the engine off.

'Yes.' It was throbbing like a plucked rumba box.

'You want me to carry you in?'

'No.' she snapped, picturing Mavis's face if she was awake.

'I'll come and help you out the car then.'

When she didn't reply, or made a move to leave, he asked, 'how you going to get to work tomorrow?'

'That's just what I was thinking about. I don't think I'll be able to get the bus. If I could get there I could hobble around the shop, and I'm not at the restaurant tomorrow night. I suppose I could get a taxi.'

'If you want...' he began carefully, 'I can come and pick you up later and take you to work... after all, is because of me why you can't walk.'

She thought about it for a while before replying 'That would get me there but I would still have to get home.'

He laughed out loud.

'The woman drive a hard bargain. What time do you finish?'

'Half past five.'

'Alright, I'll come and pick you up too.'

Despite everything, knowing that she'd be seeing him soon made it easier to face Mavis.

Chapter 6

Issy was so busy dealing with customers that she didn't notice that Lukan had come back to the bar. She *sensed* his energy before she saw him.

'What does a man have to do to get served?' he asked jokingly.

'Join the line,' she replied in her waitress voice, pleasant but not encouraging.

'Gimme a Red Stripe.' He said.

As she reached for the beer he added, 'why don't you have one yourself, you look like you could use it. Look like you been on your feet all night. Don't you get a break?'

She looked at him from under her long lashes. It was busy. It wasn't the first drink she'd been offered, but he was the first to notice that she was tired. If she wasn't going to get another break tonight, and it wasn't looking likely, not with the steady stream of people coming in, she may as well have a drink with him. At least he was good to look at.

'Thanks,' she said, smiling. 'I'll have a beer too. Sorry I can't stop too long, you can see how busy the place is.'

'It's a shame you won't get a chance to dance. They playing some good music.'

'I know, I can hear it.' Just because she couldn't see outside, didn't mean she couldn't hear the music. They played some of her favourite Blue Beat tunes, it's what was keeping her going.

'How comes you not out there dancing?' she asked.

'Because the only woman I'd want to dance with, is inside.' The words just flew out of his mouth, without any permission from him.

'Where?' Issy asked, looking round the room, but he kept looking at her.

'Oh,' she laughed. 'I'm a waste of time.'

'What you mean?' he looked puzzled.

'Nothing. Where you from?' she asked, changing the subject.

'Sav-la-Mar.'

'What you doing so far from home?'

'Building a couple houses in Chapelton.'

'By yourself?'

'No, I work with a man name Vincent...I'm a carpenter.'

'Oh, you good with your hands, then.'

'I have to be.'

She carried on talking to him while she served.

'How long you been down here?'

'Two months now?'

'You don't miss home?'

'Yes, but I'm getting used to it now.'

She had to go to the other side of the bar to serve, and was over there for a while. Lukan couldn't take his eyes off her. He liked the way she moved, her quick but graceful movements. She knew where everything was, was quick at working out the prices in her head, didn't have to write it down like the other barmaid, and she was always right. He liked the way her voice tinkled like ice in a glass, and the way she looked at him from under her lashes. She had long lashes like Darcie's. He liked her wide hips, narrow waist and full breasts. He liked the way she twisted her hair into the nape of her neck. He liked her neck, and her slender shoulders. Liked the way she dropped her head from side to side to loosen the tight muscles in her neck. He wanted to massage her shoulders for her, to relieve any tension she was feeling. He was a good masseuse, and could always make Jez relax. He took a swig of beer. He didn't want to be thinking about his family. It was the first weekend he hadn't gone home on his days off. Mass Vincent paid, as he agreed, for the first two trips home, but the last one he had to pay for himself. It was always good to see Jez and the girls. He thought he would miss them a lot more in the first week, but everything was so new, and the hours were so long, that when he went back to the lodgings at night he was in bed by nine o'clock.

When he got on the bus to go home on the first Friday evening, he couldn't wait to tell everybody about his two weeks in Chapelton. Jez met him at the bus stop. He spotted her straight away, her pale face amongst the dark outlines waiting in a jumbled mass at the stop, waiting for somebody they knew to get off the bus, somebody they longed to see, or just had to meet. There was no great show of emotion, they smiled at each other, and fell into step as they walked back to their house.

'Where's the girls?' he asked immediately

'With Miss Inez.'

'Them alright?'

'Yes, them miss you though. Darcie wanted to come with me.'

'She don't gone to bed yet?'

'She wouldn't sleep. From the time she know that you coming back tonight she asking for you every minute. She miss you so much Luke.'

'What about you? You miss me?'

'Of course me miss you.'

'You going to have to show me how much you miss me when we get home,' he said pulling her to his side with his free hand and kissing her fully on her lips. They were out of sight of any passers by now and he felt safe to kiss her.

'We have to get the girls first.'

'I know, and I have to go and see Mama.'

The veranda was empty, so they made their way into the small living room where his mother sat with Darcie in her arms.

'Sshhh,' she put her fingers to her lips. 'She just drop off to sleep.'

'I'll take her,' Jez bent to relieve her mother-in-law of her daughter.

'Let me take her,' Luke said. He hadn't seen his daughter for two week and he wanted to hold her. He hadn't anticipated the emptiness he'd feel each morning when he woke up and realised that she wouldn't be coming to jump on him. Hadn't anticipated either, how barren his nights would be without Jez, or how much he'd miss his mother, whom he was used to seeing every day.

Standing there with Darcie in his arms, with Gloria asleep on the chair in the corner, with his mother and with Jez, he felt complete. He couldn't imagine anything in the world more fulfilling, more worthwhile. He could not know how soon this would all change.

'You want me to keep the children tonight as they sleeping already? It don't make any sense you taking them out in the night air now.'

'We only have to walk across the yard Mama.' Luke said looking down at Darcie like he was seeing her for the first time.

'You look tired Luke, and you two don't see each other for a long time. Let me keep the children and you can get up whatever time you want tomorrow without Darcie waking you up.'

Luke looked at Jez.

'That's alright with me,' she said, thankful for a night off from the children.

'Alright then.' Luke agreed, handing his daughter back to his mother and giving her a brief hug in the process. He wasn't very demonstrative, hadn't yet been shown how. He went to the chair where Gloria slept and stroked her face lightly, as she breathed deep, even breaths.

'Thanks Mama.'

'You don't have to thank me, and don't rush to come for them tomorrow.' She was giving them opportunity and permission to spend time together. She knew too well what separation can do to couples, especially young ones like Luke and Jez. They thanked her again before they left.

'Oh, by the way, Dudley want you to come and see him tomorrow.' Inez said as they were leaving.

'What time?' Luke enquired.

'He didn't say. But he won't be expecting you too early.'

Which was just as well as Jez and Luke got very little sleep as they spent the night riding the rapids of their pent up passion. The initial wild frenzy giving way to a gentler more thoughtful love. He told her about his land lady, about the other men he was sharing with, she told him about the girls and the things they'd done. They made love. He told her about the work, and the district, about Mr Vincent and his exacting ways. She told him about the new words Darcie had learnt. They made love. He told her about the bus journeys, about his travelling companions. She told him that his Uncle Dudley seemed very happy that he'd taken the job. He told her about the pay, and how he was thinking of building another room onto the house so they could have a living room. She held him tight and made love to him. The cocks were crowing when spent, yet filled they fell asleep.

The pounding on the door woke them up.

'Sun hot out here and you two still in there.' Dudley's words clambered in through the slats in the louvered windows.

'Just coming, Sir.' Luke scrambled to find his pants as

Dudley knocked again. Still half asleep he opened the door and blinked hard as the sunlight assaulted his eyes. He stepped out onto the veranda pulling the door closed behind him. Jez was still asleep, there wasn't a living room yet; he only had the two bedrooms and the kitchen.

Dudley had a sour look on his face.

'What's the matter Sir?' Luke asked, afraid he may have done something to upset his Uncle.

'That gal still sleeping in this hot sun?'

'She didn't go to sleep till late.' Luke said sheepishly.

'And leave the pickney with Inez?'

'Mama wanted to keep them. In fact, she beg us to let her keep them.'

'But I bet she didn't expect to have them till this time of day.'

'What's the time Sir?'

'Half past eleven.'

We can't have had more than six hours sleep, thought Luke. He knew his uncle didn't like Jez, and would find any reason to run her down, so he tried to change the subject.

'Maas Vincent is a hard task master.' He ventured.

'That's what I've come to check with you.' Dudley said, skilfully redirected to his original purpose. 'What you mean by hard?'

'He want everything done at top rate, but in the time it would take to do half as good a job. Everybody have to work twice as fast as normal. Some people complaining bout it already.'

'What about you?'

'I can do it, but I'm just dead by the end of the day. But the truth is, I like it that everything have to be tip top. It make me proud when I stand back and look at a door frame where all the joints are perfect.'

'That's what being a journeyman is all about bwoy,' he said looking excited, despite his outburst of a few minutes earlier, 'learn from the best. That's why I wanted you to go with him. Everybody talk about what a good reputation him have, and how people don't complain about his work.'

'They would be making it up if they complain. Him don't leave any stone unturned, always checking and double checking. I don't know where him get the energy.'

'When is your own business and you care about your reputation, you find the energy. Learn that bwoy, and learn it well.'

'I miss Jez and the girls though.'

'Don't let them worry you. They will always be here. The likes of Jez will *always* be here.'

'Uncle, give her a chance. She's a good mother.'

'But she don't know how to help a man build a life. She don't have any ambition.'

'She a good mother, and… and… she love me. I don't care if she don't have what you call ambition.'

'That's because you don't meet a woman with ambition yet. Give yourself a chance; don't come running back here every weekend.'

'Uncle, I love my children, I want to see them, and… and… I love Jez.'

'Like I said, give yourself a chance.'

With that, he stood up to leave. 'Anyway, come and see me before you leave on Sunday,' and, holding Luke's shoulder with a firm right hand he said, 'I'm proud of you bwoy. I didn't think you had it in you. If you got through this first couple weeks, you will get through the rest.'

'Thanks Uncle.' Luke allowed himself to feel his uncle's pride.

'Remember, Sunday.' He said over his shoulder as he walked away.

All this went through Lukan's head as he watched Issy bend and stretch for glasses, watched her unscrew bottles, pop corks, wipe the counter, do mental arithmetic and make change. Effortlessly, like it was second nature to her. Jez would be lost behind a bar like this. She wouldn't be so easy with people, wouldn't know how to smile at them, and make them feel special, while calculating how much money they owed her. She didn't have Issy's curves, couldn't walk so well in high heels, didn't know how to style her hair like Issy's. But she was a good mother, and she loved him. She was the only woman, apart from his mother that had ever loved him.

He took another sip of his beer. This was probably the kind of woman his Uncle Dudley was talking about. That first Sunday, and every week before he left Sav to come back to Chapelton, his uncle reminded him that he should 'broaden his horizons'. Repeated that he was a very skilled young man and could do better for himself. Every week he defended Jez, and felt justified, because of what he was seeing in Chapelton.

As he became acclimatised to the work, and being away from home, he had some energy left to go out some nights, to drink a soda, or a root beer, and eat a piece of jerk pork in a bar. He didn't like to spend too much, because he wanted to put a room on the house, and he was helping his mother with money every week. He was meeting women, he even stayed over one Friday night to go to a party that the land-lady of the lodgings was giving, and met quite a few that night. Some were definitely interested in him, but he was too shy, and too bound up with Jez to pursue any of them. He was very flattered, but looked forward to getting home to Jez and the girls at every opportunity. That was, until he came into this bar and met Issy two weeks ago. Since then he hadn't been able to stop thinking about her. He'd felt something the first day, when she handed him the bottle and their fingers touched. He'd felt something when she looked up at him from beneath those long lashes, when he couldn't tell what she was thinking but knew he wanted to look into her eyes again.

Watching her now, he realised that he'd memorised everything about her. He didn't know anything about her other than what he saw, but she filled his thoughts every moments break he got from his work. She was taking over the space that had always been for Jez, and was even encroaching on the places he'd reserved for Darcie and Gloria. He was too afraid to ask anyone about her. He didn't yet have the sophistication or the skill of finding out about women before approaching them, didn't yet have the confidence, or the charm to ask outright for what he wanted, and laugh it off as a joke if he was rebuffed.

He didn't know he was staring till she winked at him from the other end of the bar, and smiled. He smiled his gappy endearing smile for her. He didn't know that she was staying on that side of the bar because she didn't want to get into any more conversation with him, because she had made a resolution to keep away from pretty boys. Didn't know how much he resembled her children's father and how many memories he was evoking for her. Memories of waiting home at nights, listening for Easton's key in the door, waiting for him to turn the handle and come back to her bed. He didn't know how many nights she'd cried herself to sleep and woken up to an empty heart, and an empty bed. How was he to know that she lived in terror that he would walk in the door at any moment, disregarding his ban, and try to persuade her to take him back? He wasn't to know that Easton was outside right now, thinking of doing just that, and taking another swig from his bottle to build up his courage.

If he'd known he might have walked away, gone back outside and try to find someone else to dance with, to focus his attention on for the night. But he didn't know, and so he stayed there all night, having one beer after another, watching her, grateful for the crumbs of conversation she threw his way from time to time, and she was strangely comforted by his presence.

Neither of them knew that Easton continued to take courage-building swigs in vain. He sat on the bench under the tree all night, thinking about what was, and what he'd hoped he could get back, while someone else made plans to walk Issy home. He went home before the end of the dance, while he could still walk, and because someone had offered him a ride back to Frankfield.

'It looks like it's quietening down now.' Issy observed as she pulled herself up on a stool and sat opposite him at the bar. 'You miss everything, and didn't even get one dance. Poor old you.' She teased.

She was exhausted, and could do with a laugh to lighten up the rest of the night.

'I was happy enough in here.'

'So where you been hiding yourself since the first time you come in here?' she pried. She hadn't intended to let him know that she remembered him, but there, it was out.

'Just working solid.'

'Even at the weekend?'

'Weekends I go home.'

'To Sav-la-Mar?'

'Yes.'

'Every week?'

'Every other week. I was working half day every other Sunday.'

'To your wife and children?' Any working man who go home that often is going back to a woman at least and more often children. They were the lucky ones.

'I'm not married.' He said innocently, not understanding her meaning.

'Living with?'

'Well we…'

'That means yes. Children?'

'Yes.'

'How many?'

'Two.'

'Boys? Girls?'

'Girls.'

'How old?'

'Two and one.'

'Busy. So why you not with them tonight? What you doing leaning up on a bar all night?'

Again he didn't get her meaning, took her literally.

'The guys that I come with said they were staying till the end, if I wanted a ride back with them.'

'I mean, why you not in Sav-la-Mar tonight?' she giggled. When he knew her better, he would recognise that giggle as a sign of nervousness.

'My uncle...' he began, then thought better of it. It wouldn't sound right telling her that his uncle said he should find someone with more ambition and he'd been looking at her all night wondering if someone who looked like she looked, could have ambition as well.

'You uncle?' she said, when he didn't continue.

'My uncle wanted me to tell him what the dance was like, because they planning to have another one, and he wants to know if he should travel to come.' It wasn't a lie, but it wasn't what he was thinking.

'Then you're going to have to make up some story.'

'What you mean?'

'Because you didn't see the dance at all.'

'I see enough. Anyway, how you getting home tonight?'

'Why? You offering me a ride?'

'There was two spare seats in the jeep.'

'But you don't know if your friends, who was out there all night, don't fill those seats already.'

'I'm sure we could squeeze....'

'It's alright. I have my transportation sorted out. You don't think I'd be waiting for a ride home from just any man sitting on a bar all night, do you?'

'I'm sorry, I just wondered if…'

'Thanks for the offer, but like I said, I'm alright. Anyway, I have to start clearing up now,' she said sliding off the stool. 'Thanks for the beers and the chat.'

'Can I see you again?' He blurted.

'You know where I work, you can come and see me any time.'

'I mean, can I take you out one night?'

'You mean, you, me, your wife and the two girls? Or did you mean just me?'

'Just you.'

'No thank you. I'm not looking to give any woman grief. Don't want anybody to go through what I've been through.'

'Would you say yes if I didn't have somebody… I mean wasn't with some…' he trailed off realising his position. He'd told her everything, not skilled enough yet to hide the truth.

'There wouldn't be any point. You're a good looking man, but you couldn't give me what I'm looking for.'

'How you know that? How you know I can't give…'

'Because you don't look, or sound like the marrying kind to me. You look like the kind that I just got rid of. I don't want any man who don't done his running round yet, and you look like you just starting. I want a man with ambition, somebody who want to better himself. I want somebody I can work with to make life, and I'm not looking at him.' She was breathing heavily, wondering where all that came from. All the man was doing was asking her for a date, but she knew it wasn't just about him. She needed to stop herself getting pulled into another Easton.

'What if I was the marrying kind and all of those other things you said. Would you see me?'

She laughed out loud, throwing her head back.

'How would you even know, you look liked you not too long out of nappies. How old are you?'

'Twenty-two.'

'See. That's what I mean. Not even started your running round yet.'

'I'm not the running around type. I've been with the same girl for three years, and she's the only one.'

'So tell me, Mr Faithful, what you doing now? Where does she think you are tonight? Does she know you're asking someone you've spent all night staring at to go out with you?'

'Would you say yes if I wasn't with anybody?' He couldn't believe he said that. Things were just flying out of his mouth tonight without any consultation with him. He was with Jez, had always been with Jez. He didn't know what would happen if he wasn't with Jez and the girls, and hadn't had to think about it until this moment. Could he leave? What would he tell her? It wasn't strictly true that he'd come to the dance for his uncle's benefit. When he heard where the dance was he wanted to come to try and see Isabell again. He'd figured that with such a big night they'd have their best barmaids on. It was a gamble, and it had paid off. He had chosen to be away from Jez tonight, and he hadn't missed her, not like he used to, and he had enjoyed tonight.

'Come back when you're free, and if I'm still here, I'll tell you what the other conditions are.'

'But what if I get free and I can't meet the other conditions?'

'Then you back to square one. The point I'm making Mr Lukan...what's your surname by the way?'

'Levy.'

'The point I'm making Mr Lukan Levy, is that you shouldn't be leaving one woman for another. You should be leaving because the relationship done, because it's too big a weight for the other woman. I don't want any man to tell me how him leave somebody for me, like he would expect me to be grateful.

I'm done with that. That's why I'm looking for a man in the church, who will respect the vows of marriage. So you see Lukan, there's no point starting something that you can't finish. But don't feel bad. I enjoyed your company, and thanks for the drinks.'

Chapter 7

This was the day Dudley had prayed for. Luke wanted his advice, wanted to know if he should leave Jez in the hope of being with somebody else, or if he was being foolish, because there was no promise that if he did leave Jez, that the other person would have him. He might not match up.

'You see, is just the kind of thing I've been trying to tell you.' Dudley almost rubbed his hands with glee that his nephew was finally seeing sense.

'This Isabell seem like someone with ambition, somebody who want something better than just having pickney.'

'So what would you do, Uncle?'

'Your problem Luke, is that you don't know what you want. You see how she could just tell you what she looking for? You need to do the same. Work out what you want out of life, then you can tell her. If she still turn you down, there will be other women willing to snap you up.'

And that's how Luke, at the tender age of twenty-two, made the plans that were to secure him a bride, and a change of life.

Four months later, after three more requests, and three more refutation, she relented and said she would go out with him. They went to a bar that served food. The black belt around the waist of her orange dress matched her black shoes and bag. He wore a white shirt and brown pants and well polished brown shoes. They looked good together as they walked into the small eating house on David Street.

'You said you wanted someone with ambition. I didn't really know what you mean so I asked my uncle.'

'You talk to your uncle about me?' She was surprised.

'Yes.'

'When?'

'The weekend after you tell me what you want and how I couldn't give it to you.'

'What did he say?'

'He said you sounded like the kind of woman that wanted a man with a plan, and I didn't have a plan, because I didn't know I needed one.'

'And you have one now?'

'Yes. I talked to him about it, and I want to talk to you about it.'

'All right then. I'm listening.' She leaned back and crossed her arms, and although he was feeling nervous, he started.

'Weell,' he began slowly as she continued to stare at him. 'There's four things I want.' He paused, wondering which one to start with first.

'Go on, I'm listening.' She was impatient to hear what he had to say. Easton didn't have a plan. Not even after she got pregnant with Ivan and wanted them to start putting their money together to try and buy a little plot of land to start building a house. He said his money wasn't regular and he couldn't commit himself to any long term bills like paying off for land. She struggled to look after her son in that little space she shared with Mavis, but with her sister's help she managed to hold down her job at the restaurant, and, because she had so much savings put by, she could manage on just the one job for a while. Mavis was mad as hell with her, but when Ivan was born she fell in love with him. Issy looked after Ivan in the days and worked at night. Mavis looked after him at night. Easton gave her money when he could, but it wasn't regular and she couldn't always rely on it. He loved his son though, always wanted to show him off to people. The two most beautiful people in his life he would tell them. He'd bring Issy beautiful cloth to make something for herself and something for Ivan. He loved it when they were dressed up.

'The first thing is; I want to build a house, a nice house with three bedrooms, a living room, a kitchen, a bathroom and an inside toilet. I want to build a house like the ones I've been working on for Maas Vincent.'

Issy sat up, unfolded her arms, leaned forward onto her elbows and almost snapped, 'Where?'

'I don't know yet.'

'So it could be anywhere in Jamaica?'

'Well, it would be where my wife is.'

'I thought you didn't have a wife? You mean you going to marry her after all?' Issy's heart sank a little. Just when he was getting interesting.

'I don't have a wife yet. But when I have one I want to come home and see her sitting on the veranda, waiting for me.'

'Go on,' Issy urged. He was beginning to sound really appealing.

'One day I want to be a contractor like Mass Vincent. I want people working for me. I want to be the one who check over everybody's work, and be the one to pay people. I want to pocket the big money.'

He leaned back, as though finished, watching her face for clues about what she was thinking of his plans. She searched his face, waiting for him to continue.

'You said there were four things; you've only told me three. What's number four?'

'Oh, I don't want that anymore, because I have it already. That was the easiest one to get.'

'What was… is it?' Issy was trying to hide her excitement.

'I wanted to accept Jesus as my personal saviour.'

'And?'

'Two months ago, I decided to do it. I went to church, and when the pastor called sinners to the alter, I found myself up there, begging God to forgive me and to save me from my sins.'

Issy was speechless. She couldn't believe what she'd heard. Could God have had a hand in this? Could he really be delivering her wish packaged as a pretty boy? Could she really have everything? There had to be a catch. Maybe it was a cruel joke and Lukan just wanted to tell her that he'd decided to marry his baby mother after all, that it was what God was showing him, and he just wanted her opinion. She scanned his face, looking for clues, but it was his turn to sit back. He smiled at her, barely showing the gap in his teeth.

'Which church?' she asked, not trusting herself to ask about the wife.

'The Church of God.'

'Where?'

'In Sav, but I talk to the pastor here and he says I can worship down here if I stay here at the weekend.'

'What made you do it?' She knew it was a crazy question to ask, because the answer should be obvious. He had seen the errors of his ways and turned to God, but why now? Did it have anything to do with what she said about wanting someone in the church? Would he go to those lengths, and if so, how genuine was he? If he was, he couldn't still be living with his baby mother, he would have to move out or get married, those were the rules of the church, they were the teachings of Jesus, not fornicating, and living in sin was fornicating.

'It was time. I want to be free; I want God to guide me now.'

'And what about your baby mother, what does she think of this?' Issy was still a little sceptical.

'She understands. It was hard at the beginning, because when I moved out, she thought it was because of another woman, but I only moved into Mama's house. I still see my daughters at weekends. It's hard seeing Jez so upset, but at least she know I didn't leave her for somebody else.'

Issy thought about how she'd begged Easton to come to church with her. He could barely drag himself there when the children were christened, saying churches was for christenings, weddings and burials, only to be attended on rare occasions. He said all the people in these churches were hypocrites, praising God on Sundays and back-biting the rest of the week. She remembered begging him to come with her after they buried their son, told him it would help to ease the pain. He said he couldn't trust a God that would take a child's life for no reason, not to fuck with his head. She could go if she wanted, just don't drag him there. That's when he sought solace in the bottle, and he was still there even though it had failed to deliver the comfort he sought.

She didn't think about Isaac's death every second, of every minute, of every day anymore. The tight knot that was in her stomach since that day had moments of slackness, but was always present, but life had to go on. She still had two children to support without any help from Easton, who didn't work anymore, and couldn't hold himself together long enough without a swig from a rum bottle to function in the clubbing world. In any case, no one trusted him around liquor. It was ironic, that she was selling to others what was destroying her man.

'Tell me something, Issy,' he leaned forward, eyebrows pulled together in a puzzled furrow, 'are you saved, or do you just go to church?'

'Why you asking?'

'Because I can't understand how you can be saved and be working in a rum bar, when the bible strictly forbid liquor.'

'Weell… I believe in God, and serve him in my own way.'

'But have you actually accepted Jesus as your personal saviour? Have you given your heart to God? Because Pastor Jacobs say once you give your heart to God you have to give up the things of the world, and liquor is one of them.'

'Look Lukan, I didn't know you were going to go and get saved. I wasn't expecting to…'

'But you said you wanted a man in the church, how can you ask for that if you're not saved yourself?'

'I will get saved when I meet somebody,' she said quietly, burying her head in her root beer.

'So what now Issy? I do all this for you and you not even off first base yet?' He was annoyed. Over the last four months he'd worked at everything in his life, trying to be the man that she wanted, putting Jez out of his life, going to church every week, even planning to get baptised, and she not even saved yet. Now he was in the church he couldn't marry…

'I didn't ask you to do anything for me!' Her angry voice cut into his thoughts. 'That's what I mean about men thinking you should be grateful when they think they do something for you!'

'You confusing me Issy. I thought this is what you wanted.'

'Lukan, if you want to get saved you have to do it for *you*, not because you think that's what I want.' Despite what she was saying she was flattered that he'd gone to all that trouble.

'So what happens now?'

'I don't know what you mean? What do you want to happen?'

'I want you to marry me Issy. I want to see you sitting on my veranda when I come home at night, I want to sit down and eat with you. I don't want you working in that bar anymore. I want to look after you and Irene. I want you to bring Ivan to live with us. I know you not happy with him living at his grandmother's. I want to go to church with you on Sunday mornings and worship with you as my wife. I want our children to be blessed in a marriage. That's what I want to happen now.'

She stared at him, astounded. This was all happening too fast. She didn't know he was going to do all of that. He didn't tell her any of what he was doing, not when he came into the bar and they had a drink together. She didn't think anything of the fact that the last time he drank root beer, not his usual Red Stripe.

It was all making sense now. His questions about her children. Why didn't Ivan live with her? Would she like him to live with her? Because she'd written him off as marriage material, she'd told him everything. How she couldn't afford to look after the two of them, how Easton's mother had taken Ivan and was raising him. How she missed seeing him every day and couldn't wait till she could bring him back home.

On another of his visits she'd opened up to him about Easton, about how he'd fallen apart when their youngest son Isaac died from a fever. About how he was so drunk at the funeral he couldn't carry the coffin. Everybody forgave him, said it was a hard thing for a man to have to bury his baby boy, but they were less forgiving when months later, he was still drunk.

She'd confided in him, as the friend he was becoming, that she wanted stability more than anything, wanted a permanent roof over her head, not to have to answer to landlords. She longed for an inside toilet because she hated insects.

She recalled now how he'd joked about a man needing to wear stilts to measure up to what she wanted, how, when he let himself go, his laughter rang out clear and crisp. She remembered asking him if he sang, because she was sure he could, from the sound of his laughter.

'No, not really.' He'd replied bashfully, but she'd persuaded him, and had been surprised when he sang a hymn;

'*Rock my soul in the bosom of Abraham. Rock my soul in the bosom of Abraham. Rock my soul in the bosom of Abraham. Oh rock my soul. Oh Lordy.*'
and how she'd laughed, and laughed as he did the rocking actions with his arms and dipped down into the ground on the *Oh Lordy*, how he'd continued till she almost peed herself and had to beg him to stop, tears streaming down her cheeks.

She didn't know how much he'd enjoyed those times, how he had fallen in love with her, how he longed to make her dreams come true. She didn't know how he fantasised about kissing her, making love to her, being the father of her children. She had no idea how jealous he was of Easton, and how foolish he thought him, for giving her up. Yet, how grateful he was, because if Easton hadn't left her, she wouldn't be talking to him. Didn't know that the age difference between them only made her more attractive to him, because she was so sure of what she wanted, and had so many skills that would help them, as a team, to achieve them.

As she continued to stare at him, she realised how carefully he had crafted his proposal, how well he had worked her out, how he left her no room to manoeuvre.

'What about love?' she finally asked.

'You never said anything about love, but if it's love you want, I have plenty.'

She looked into his face, trying to find some reason there to say no, but all she saw was the gap in his teeth as he smiled at her, as if to say, 'there, I've told you everything now.'

'Let me think about it,' she said eventually, 'this is all so sudden, and you're so young.'

He reached across and grasped both her hands in his.

'Issy, say yes, and make me the happiest man in the world.'

'Let me think about it,' she said again, her voice a little unsteady.

Chapter 8

Easton Blackwell experienced the news of Issy's and Lukan's engagement as a heavyweight's body blow, the kind that lands in the stomach, but is felt first in the groin before radiating down through the legs, and up to the head. He felt dizzy and had to hold on to the back of a chair to stop himself from crumbling to the ground.

'Who tell you?' he croaked at his friend Mikey.

'It all over the place, everybody talking about it,' he replied with compassion.

'You know how people talk nonsense.' When his friend didn't reply, he added, 'I won't believe it till I hear it from her.'

'Well, maybe she'll come and tell you herself, but I just thought you should be prepared.'

Dudley Levy on the other hand was jubilant.

'Well done bowy.' He'd slapped Lukan vigorously on his back. 'Things going to change for you now.'

'I know Uncle. I can't believe she said yes.'

'Don't start thinking she doing you a favour bowy. The woman have sense, she know that she's getting a good bargain.'

'You make me sound like a piece of furniture.'

'When you going to bring her to meet me?'

'Uncle, I think you should come and meet her. I think it will be difficult bringing her here with Jez living so near.'

'You don't have to bring her here, just bring her to town and me and Inez will come to meet her there.'

'I will have to ask her.'

'That shouldn't be a problem bowy.'

'I want her to meet Darcie and Gloria too, but I don't know how Jez will feel about that.'

'They're your pickneys too. It's not like you ever disown them, you're a good father to them, she will have to get used to it sooner or later.'

'I don't want to rub her face in it Uncle, she's a good mother, and this is hurting her bad.'

'Not so bad that she want to get off her backside and go and look for something to do. Issy have pickney too, but she still work. Jez have it too easy, sit down all day minding two pickney, and don't even have to cook and wash for a man. You spoil that gal.'

Lukan didn't like to listen to his uncle talk about Jez like this. He couldn't forget that she was the only one prepared to love him when he was disfigured. He couldn't cast her aside. Yes, he did want better than living in a two-room house next to his mother, but he didn't want to do anything that would hurt her, any more than she was hurting already. It wasn't like he was walking away from her for good, she was still his children's mother, and there was a part of him that still loved her. In truth, the only reason he'd left her was because Issy had made it plain that she wouldn't tolerate another woman. If he could have had them both, he wouldn't have left. He still wanted to hold her, to love her. There were many nights when he had to force himself to stay in his mother's house, and not walk the few short steps to her bed, where he knew he would be welcomed. Many nights, even since he got saved, that he started to think about Issy while he relieved himself, but at the crucial moment found it was Jez on his lips. For him, the sooner he got married and moved away, the better.

One evening, after he'd eaten with her and the children,

she leaned over him to move the plate. As her breast accidentally touched his arm, he felt an instant tug in his pants, so violent and unexpected, he caught his breath. She shot him a glance that said, 'why are you doing this? Why are you denying yourself?'

All she knew then was that he was abstaining for the salvation of his soul, not to enhance his eligibility for someone else. All that was about to change now, he was going to have to tell her the truth. He wasn't looking forward to it.

He chose his moment well, did it while they were sitting on his mother's veranda. He didn't want to be alone with her in case he couldn't handle her reaction, in case she attacked him or broke down, or smashed up things. His uncle had warned him that women can take this kind of news badly; he wanted his mother in the next room, just in case.

'Jez,' he began, 'I have something to tell you.'

She didn't answer, didn't look at him, continued to stare out in front of her. Her silence disconcerted him. Had she responded, he may not have just blurted out, 'I'm getting married.'

His heart was beating fast to pump blood to every tense muscle in his body, every cell braced against the tirade he was expecting. Without moving her head, she asked so softly he barely heard her, 'When?'

'I'm not sure of the exact date yet, but in about six months time.'

She said nothing, didn't move, kept her head straight.

'Jez?'

She didn't answer.

'Jez, say something.' Her silence unnerved him. He used to know her so well, used to be able to tell what she was thinking, but not now. When she didn't answer he began gabbling to hide his nervousness, and assuage his guilt.

'You don't have to worry about the girls. I'll still give you money for them, and I'll still make sure the house is repaired and I'll make sure I paint it before…before… and you know I love the girls, and Mama say she will help if you need it like always, and Uncle Dudley will help with the girls too and…'

The look of pure contempt on her face as she turned to him stopped him in his tracks.

'I suppose him happy now, him finally get what him want. I know him never like me, always think you was too good for me. Well, just tell him I don't want any help from him. And as for you, you think because you have nice skin now that you better than me, and I was foolish enough to believe that skank you pull about the church. I was just waiting for you to get fed up of it and come back, and all the time you sticking your wick in some other woman's candle.'

'It's not like that,' he tried to defend himself. 'I haven't been with her.'

She laughed out loud, looked at him as if he was stupid.

'So, you going to buy the goods without opening the bag? Maybe them turn you fool in Clarendon. Maybe she put something on you.'

'Jez, it's not like that.'

'Then how is it. I've been with you… I have your two pickney… I live in your house… I open my legs to you whenever you want, never say no to you, and never once you even mention marriage to me.'

He didn't know what to say, didn't know how to explain the difference between her and Issy.

'Tell me Luke. Because I don't understand.'

She was crying now, great marbles of tears rolled down her face, chasing each other as if in a silent race. He wanted to hold her, to tell her it was going to be OK, he'd never seen her like this, she always took things in her stride, never placed too many demands on him. He didn't know how to handle this high emotion. As he moved towards her, she stepped back.

'I'm telling you Luke,' she pushed the words out through clenched teeth, 'if you leave me and marry this woman, you will never be happy. You hear me. YOU WILL NEVER BE HAPPY!' She turned and ran down the steps, her skirt flying behind her.

As he slumped onto the bench, he felt a chill slide from the top of his head, down the back of his neck and lodge somewhere in his lower back. He rubbed his eyes, trying to erase the raised and pulsing veins in her neck, the fingers digging deep into the palms of her clenched fists and the look of pure hate in her bulging eyes.

His mother poked her head round the door.

'You alright son?' concern coated every word.

'I don't know what get into her Mama, she look like she hate me.'

'I did warn you son. Sometimes Dudley's way is not always the best way.'

'What can I do Mama?'

'Make sure you do right by her... and son, be careful.'

Chapter 9

'Do you, Lukan Calder Levy, take Isabell Hannah Elmers, to be your lawful wedded wife, to have and to hold from this day forward, for better or for worse, for richer, for poorer, in sickness and in health, to love and to cherish; and promise to be faithful to her until death parts both.'

'I do.'

'Do you, Isabell Hannah Elmers, take Lukan Calder Levy, to be your lawful wedded husband…'

As Issy whispered 'I do.' She felt she could finally thank God. He had delivered on his promise, she had trusted him, given her life to his son, Jesus and had been rewarded handsomely.

The sisters and brothers in the church, the pastor, her father, brother, sisters all turned out to witness her enter into the guild of respectability, to be the first to call her Mrs Levy and to wish her well for a long and happy life. Luke had fewer representatives. His Uncle Dudley stood by his side as his best man, Luke not having many friends. His mother looked timid in a pale blue shift with a matching hat and black patent leather shoes. She clutched Darcie's hand, the two looking equally bewildered at times. They had travelled down that morning, and not wishing to be away from home too long, were returning that evening.

There were no bridesmaids, no page boys, no ushers. Issy's priority was paying for the land and building their house. The rush to marry was so they could, in the eyes of God, fulfil the passion that threatened to engulf and overwhelm them, whenever they met. The anticipation of which, kept Luke hard throughout the whole day. He wondered at times during the ceremony whether anyone noticed.

Issy looked beautiful in the ivory taffeta dress she'd made herself. A full dress with: small puffed sleeves, scooped neck line, fitted bodice held together by a row of buttons down the back and a wide skirt kept in place with a stiff crinoline underskirt. She carried a bouquet of red roses held together with white ribbon. A short veil framed her face and rested gently on her shoulders. Lukan's hands trembled as he push it back and kissed her plumb lips, devoid of the lipstick she wore before becoming saved. Her hair, piled high on her head was the only thing she was not responsible for that day. She had turned herself over to the hands of Mavis who had worked wonders with it. It was her way of apologising to Mavis for the grief she's caused her all those years ago. Mavis was happy to see her sister settled at last.

Luke's deep navy linen suit was a wedding gift from Papa Elmers. The jacket sat relaxed across his broad shoulder and the pants clung to his long legs. His shirt, the same ivory as Issy's dress, was held together at the neck by a thin navy tie. His wavy hair was slicked back with pomade, and when he smiled, he oozed happiness.

Weddings are places where healing can happen, where wars can break out, where old scores can be settled and where new quarrels can begin. Issy and Lukan were blessed with more of the former, and less of the latter. Their day ran smoothly, everyone was fed, Papa Elmers made sure of that, and everyone went home at a respectable hour. Being a church wedding there was no dancing after the reception. Issy missed this, dancing was one of the things she regretted having to give up. Dancing, lipstick and the odd tipple of rum. But they were a small price for the gifts she got in return.

Dudley and Inez were the first to leave, as they had a long way to go, then one by one the elders of the church went home, until there were only a few of Issy's and Luke's friends, and a few of his work mates left in the hall where the reception had been.

As Pastor Morgan, a man of about forty with twelve years marriage under his belt, prepared to leave he put an arm on each of their shoulders and wished them God's blessing. He charged them to be an example to those in and out of the church, of a match made in heaven. Those who were not yet interested in having their match made in heaven, left to attend a dance in May Pen.

Finally, Issy and Lukan were alone together. They had the room to themselves, the children were at her father's house, being looked after by her sisters. He held her at arms lengths, and beaming from ear, because he could scarcely believe his luck, and said, 'Mistress Levy, I have Mistress Levy to myself at last.'

'Luke, I have to take off these shoes, they're killing me.'

He could see she'd have difficulty bending over in the wide crinoline dress and immediately dropped to his knees.

'Pull up your dress, let me help with the buckle.'

'I wish I had a slip on pair, I couldn't even slide my feet out for a second all day.'

'I don't think anybody noticed, you didn't show it.'

'I can hide a lot of pain, I know how to smile even when my feet are killing me.'

'Well you could fool me. Take them off now.' He said and she stepped down off the heels, unusually high for her.

When he stood up again he was surprised at how low she'd shrunk.

'But bwoy, Issy you not bigger than a pint pot. How you shrink so?'

'I don't shrink, you've just never see me without my shoes.'

'Well, if I did know you was such a little pint size I wouldn't bother marrying you. Is how you think me and you going to fit?'

'Help me take off this dress and I'll show you.' She laughed.

His shaking hands fumbled to undo the row of buttons at the back of her dress.

'Don't rush and rip it.' She cautioned, feeling his tugs at her back.

'It's a nice dress Issy, but I wouldn't want to have to take it off you every night. There!' he sighed as he undid the last button and slid the dress off her shoulders from behind, to reveal her smooth round shoulders and her soft, slightly damp skin. The bits she began to keep covered after she got saved, which he'd waited till now to savour again.

His flag, which had never really been lowered all day, only ever got as low as half mast, was flying high as he ran his hands from the top of her hair piled head to the small of her back. She sizzled with excitement. It was a long time since she felt the touch of a man's hand like that on her body. She spun round to kiss him, forgetting the dress around her ankles and began to fall, reaching out to steady her, he lost his footing and tumbled with her into the billows of her wedding dress, laughing and kissing.

'Let me take off your shirt' she offered, already unbuttoning him. She was quick and sure, which surprised him, made him feel a little awkward for how long he'd taken, but he soon forgot as she slid it over his shoulders and allowed it to mingle with her dress. She reached down and found his zip, pulled it down in one easy move and deftly released the button from its anchorage.

While still kissing him she reached into his pants, found his upright mast, slightly bent from the angle he was half sitting half laying at, and pulled it out like a mongoose who found its rat. His mind flashed to that first time with Jez.

Breathe, he reminded himself, breathe deep. It was his remedy for holding his shot and not firing off too soon. It had been so long, and he was so hungry for her, that he was afraid he wouldn't be able to hold it. Closing his eyes he thought of running water, pictured the water rippling over the rock on the river bed and felt calmer. He wasn't aware of the deep guttural sounds he made as she worked her hand up and down his shaft, wasn't aware of his body gradually getting rigid as he watched the water flow over the rocks, wasn't aware that he'd spread his legs wide to make it easier for her, wasn't aware any more that he was lying on her dress. He fought hard to stay focused on the river, tried to breathe deeply, yet his breath was as shallow as the river and as rapid. Then there was no more room in his lungs for breath, the river tumbled over a ridge and turned into a waterfall, spilling onto her ivory dress.

Too ashamed, he lay with his eyes closed for a while. He opened them as he felt her tugging at the dress beneath him.

'Looks like the dress get the first shot,' she laughed, 'I hope you have some more where that come from.'

'I'm sorry Issy,' he muttered into his chin.

'What you sorry for?'

'You know, for shooting so quick.'

'Let me tell you Luke. I'm glad you did that. It show me that you been waiting for me. But as soon as you catch your breath, I want mine.' She leaned over and kissed him full on his lips, parted his tongue and slid her tongue round and round his. He grabbed her, held her to his chest, as he felt himself stirring again.

'Get up off my dress,' she said tugging it from under him. 'let me wipe it out before it stain.'

That night she taught him things he didn't know a man was supposed to do and he was happy to learn. She straddled him as he sat on the edge of the bed, lifted her still pert breasts to his mouth by arching her back, encouraged him to slide his tongue round her nipples instead of just sucking them, like he was used to doing with Jez, move his head from one to the other as her body rocked back and forward with excitement. She panted and moaned in a way that Jez never did. Then in a flash, she was off him and lying on her back on the bed, legs wide apart.

'Come on big bwoy, come and give you baby some juice, but stir it good before you spray it.'

He didn't know where the sensible Issy had gone, the Issy who'd taken control of the planning, who'd sat him down and given him the wisdom of her years, and the energy of her ambition. The Issy who'd been appalled at how frivolous he'd been with his money, and had worked out a plan for them to build their house as quickly as possible. Issy who had negotiated a deal on a quarter of an acre plot of land right there in Chapelton, paid a deposit, and worked out a payment plan which would give them ownership in less than six months, while making sure he maintained his commitment to looking after his children. Issy who worked out a fair rate for Jez to be paid, which he'd presented to Jez with some trepidation. Issy who he kept in his head to face Jez's anger, not in the emotional way of the night of disclosure, but in the steely look she gave him, and her, 'she start run your life already? You better be careful' warning.

He didn't recognise her as this Issy, who was opened up to him like an alter offering, calling him big bwoy and inviting him to stir her up. He just prayed he could live up to her expectations.

She guided him into her oven of warm sweet potato pudding, let him taste every ingredient, the slippery butter, the sticky eggs, the sweet currants, she sprinkled sugar all over him. She bucked and stretched and arched and twisted. For someone so small, he had to hold on hard to stay with her, and when she was ready she pulled him in, tightened her muscles, flexed and squeezed till he had to let go, and she let go with him, with just a hissing sigh, her whole body sagged beneath his. He propped himself up on his elbows, afraid he would flatten her. Putting her hand up to his chest she gently pushed him off, giggling a little as his withdrawal slurped, like a bursting bubble of boiling molasses.

He wanted to check if it was good for her but he wasn't sure if he was supposed to ask or wait for her to tell him. In the event, neither happened as they both fell asleep.

It's likely she conceived that night as nine months later, during the height of the independence anniversary celebrations she gave birth to Lennox. She wept when the midwife gave her the tiny seven pound bundle, and she saw his creased up prune like face. She wept as many mothers do, from the exhaustion of a fourteen hour labour, from the strain of pushing, from sheer fatigue. She wept too, from the joy of bringing safely into the world another life.

But unlike most elated mothers, she didn't stop. What began as a snivel, turned, despite Luke's proud and comforting arm around her, into a blubber. None of his, 'Issy it's alright, he's alright, he's a fine baby,' made any difference. None of the midwife's 'Come on Issy, the baby's alright, you did a good job,' stemmed the flow. Not even when the midwife lost her patience and yelled, because she was also tired from the long labour, 'For God's sake Issy, stop the bawling!' did Issy cease the body wracking sobs, which, from time to time were accompanied by an ear piercing wail.

'It's a good thing there's so much noise outside already, otherwise you would wake up the whole neighbourhood,' the midwife, a woman in her fifties, who had delivered at least as many babies as her years, reprimanded Issy. 'At least stop the noise so your baby can get some sleep, even if *you* don't want any.'

Luke looked on anxiously, holding his son for comfort and support. He didn't know what to do. He wasn't there when Jez had Darcie and Gloria, both times he was out on jobs and didn't see his daughters till he got back in the evening, by which time Jez had rested, and the babies were asleep. This was new to him. This was a new side of Issy he'd never seen.

She was always so confident, so sure of herself. She almost always got her way when she bargained for anything; like the way she persuaded the man who sold them the land to let them start building on it before the last payment, because she was pregnant and wanted to have their first child in their own house. She'd persisted, pleading her case, pointing out the benefits to him of having work started because he would know they were staying and not going to sell the land to people who could be bad neighbours, and when that didn't work she'd reverted to emotional blackmail asking him, with the full seduction of her big wide eyes, 'Mr Bennett, do you want to see me have my first child with my husband in someone else's rented room, for the sake of one payment?'

Mr Bennett had given in, and Luke was able to begin building straight away, because she had paid for the architect's drawings from her own money.

Even during the last weeks of her pregnancy she was a little dynamo, finishing work at the hospital and coming down to the house to help out. She started to make curtains as soon as the window frames went in, even before they were glazed, because she wanted the house, or at least two rooms, to be ready by the time she had the baby. Sometimes when Irene was at Papa Elmers they would be there till late at night, well after the people who were helping him had gone home. The other men envied him, couldn't understand how a fine looking woman like her didn't mind getting her hands dirty.

He'd never seen her cry, not even once, since they got married. Now, here she was, looking like she was never going to stop. He wasn't used to this, didn't know what to do when the midwife looked at him as if saying, 'she's your wife, you shut her up.'

Recognising that she was expecting him to do something, he gave her the baby to hold and sat down on the bed beside Issy. Taking her face in both his hands, he turned her to look at him. She gazed back like she'd never seen him before, then looked past him, as if he wasn't there. He wasn't to know that she was seeing the face of another baby as it lay wasted and lifeless on her bed. He could not know, for she had never talked about it. He didn't know that she had never mourned her son's death, had never forgiven herself for not knowing sooner that his fever was more than one that could be cured by rubbing him down with Bay Rum. She didn't know how quickly the diarrhoea would have dehydrated him, she thought that because he slept, he was getting some rest from his pain; not that the disease had so totally claimed his body that he could not fight it any more. How was Luke to know the times she'd reproach herself for not acting sooner, for letting her pride get in the way of seeking help?

It was Easton who'd noticed that Isaac had stopped breathing, had screamed her name to come and look. It was she who had opened his tiny eyes looking for the life of his soul, and, not finding it, had checked his pulse. She'd picked him up and tried to shake life back into his limp body, held him tight and tried to infuse her own energy into him. She'd given him life once, she could do it again. If only she could go back, start again, put him inside her and pay the penance of her neglect with the pain of his rebirth.

She remembered Easton's twisted face, ugly with agony, as he dropped to his knees and clutched her ankles, shaking his head in disbelief.

'Issy, no. Issy, no. Issy, no. Issy, no.' He'd whimpered as she tried to extricate herself from his grasp. They stood there, mother, father and son, in a most unusual pose.

She lost them both that day, her son and his father, who tried to blot out the image and memory of his dead son with a bottle of rum, leaving her to do all the practical arrangements. She'd had to put her own grieving on hold, and had never returned to it, till now. Now she had another son, and could not look at him while she felt the pain of the other ripping through her, sending more waves though her body than the contractions she'd just experienced. Another son to miss, another son to die?

She couldn't see Luke, didn't want to see the baby. Pulling her head away from his hands she turned onto her side, curled her knees up, like the baby she'd just delivered, and cried herself to sleep. As he watched helpless, the people outside celebrated the anniversary of Jamaica's independence from Britain. Another year of jubilant self congratulations of the bold step the nation had taken. Lukan looked at his sleeping wife and baby and felt a million miles away from the revelry outside his window.

Chapter 10

The celebrations Lukan had planned, had to wait. He had to draw heavily on Issy's family for help as she took no interest in her son, herself, or in him. They had to wake her up to feed the baby, and this she did reluctantly. Her sister Daisy, who was not working at the time came to stay with her in the days, making sure she fed Lennox when he cried, which is all Issy seemed capable of doing. They took care of all his other needs.

Under intense pressure he begged his new family's favour for one weekend so he could go to Sav to visit his other children, who had not seen him for over two months. His Uncle Dudley was at his mother's house when he arrived.

'You don't look like a man who just have him first son,' he said as he watched Lukan's weary steps up to the veranda.

He flopped onto the bench in answer, worn out from the last month, and from the journey on the crowded bus. He remembered the first time he'd made that journey back, Jez had been waiting for him, waiting to take him to their bed. Tonight there was no one, just the dark inky night which swallowed him, leaving no trace as he moved about in her. Things were so much simpler then.

'I don't understand it Uncle.' He said, unable to keep the fatigue out of his voice.

'Dudley,' his mother interrupted, 'let the bowy have something to drink and eat. You can see how tired him is.'

'I just want some water, Mama.' His mouth was dry and the dehydration was affecting his ability to think.

'So, what happen?' Dudley began as soon as Inez's back was turned, ignoring her requests to give Luke a break.

'I don't know Uncle,' his body slumped even further into the bench.

'The baby alright?'

'Yes, he's alright,' he mumbled, unable to muster any of the enthusiasm he felt for his beautiful son.

'Then what's the problem?'

'Issy.'

'Now look here Luke, I hope you not doing anything to…' he stopped as Inez returned with the glass of water.

'Didn't I tell you to leave the bwoy alone?' she looked reproachfully at Dudley. 'Can't you see him tired?'

'But I come all the way over here to talk to him.'

'Then come back tomorrow.' She'd always been able to tell when things wasn't well with Luke, and had always tried to protect him. She hadn't always agreed with some of the things Dudley said, or some of the things he got Luke to do, but he was the only man Luke had around while he was growing up, and Dudley had steered him well with his trade, recognising his skills with wood when Luke was only a boy and persuading him to become an apprentice. Luke was doing well for himself now, but Inez was still uncomfortable with the way he treated Jez, because she liked Jez, and Jez didn't do anything to Luke, other than be herself, which Dudley convinced Luke wasn't good enough for him.

She wasn't saying it was wrong for Luke to have what he had in Clarendon, she just felt uneasy with it. She had to see Jez every day, and couldn't just forget about it the way Dudley and Luke did. And she helped to look after the girls now that Jez had a little job as a maid for the family at the big house down the road. Dudley and Issy, between them persuaded

Luke that he was giving Jez too much money, and that if Issy could work to help support them, so could Jez. Jez wasn't happy about it, but didn't have any choice if she wanted money to buy things for herself, because the money Luke was giving her now was just for the children.

She wanted to hear from Luke, why he looked so haggard, before Dudley had a chance to get to him. Wanted to see if she still had any influence over him or if that was all with Issy now, he looked like he could use a mother's ear, and a mother's touch. They were not a tactile family, but sometimes, when he was hurting badly, Luke would put his head on her lap and she would stroke it. It's what he used to do when the other children called him mapface or sidewinder. It's what he did when Issy told him he wasn't good enough for her. She didn't know if he would do it tonight, but he looked like he needed it. She never initiated it, never touched him without his permission, but was always eager to respond when he approached her.

'Alright! I'll come over about nine o'clock in the morning,' pronounced Dudley.

'Come at eleven,' asserted Inez, 'nine o'clock too early. The bwoy need a rest.' He heard the rare authority in her voice and acquiesced.

'Alright. I'll come at eleven.'

'You want something to eat?' she asked when Dudley had gone.

'No Mama.'

'I'll go and get you a bit of soup.' She turned and went back inside, aware that he was following.

Inside, he leaned on the kitchen doorframe and studied her as she used a tin cup to scoop up the soup from the large metal pot on the stove, and pour it quickly into an enamel bowl.

'You want to go back outside?'

'No, I'll eat it here.' He wanted to talk to her and didn't want to run the risk of being overheard.

Placing the bowl with a spoon in it on the small table in the corner of the living room, she pulled up one of the two chairs and sat down, waiting for him to do the same. In the dim lighting of the oil lamp, wick turned down to economise on the fuel, she watched as he took his first sip from the spoon. She was in no hurry, not like Dudley, he could take all night if he wanted to.

'I don't know what happen to her Mama.' He said eventually, halfway through his soup.

'Issy?' She knew it had to be about her, if it was the baby he would have told Dudley. There are some things he checked out with her first.

'Yes.'

She waited for him to continue.

'It's over a month now since Lennox born, and she don't seem to take any interest in him, or in me, or in anything.'

He went on to explain his predicament, how ashamed he felt because his wife wasn't even getting dressed in the day, how he would leave her in her nightie and come back and find her still in it. How she hardly seemed to notice him, would just take the baby when he needed feeding, feed him and lie down again. The first week wasn't too bad, but it wasn't getting any better.

'Was she happy when the baby was born?'

'Mama, when Lennox was born she put down one piece of bawling. I thought it was the pain, but the midwife say most women forget the pain afterwards, say they too happy to have a live baby to remember the pain.'

'She still crying now?'

'Not that loud bawling like that night, but almost every day I see tears running down her face. She won't talk about it to me, or to anybody in her family. Mama, I'm worried. She not going mad, is she? I know that some women go mad after they have a baby.'

'Sometimes women just have the blues.' Inez muttered under her breath, but she wasn't thinking blues, she was thinking of the conversation she'd overheard between Luke and Jez the night Luke told her he was getting married.

'How was she before she have the baby?'

'She was fine Mama, getting everything ready, she made the house look really nice, almost killing herself to get everything ready so the baby would have a nice home to come into. Everybody was so impressed with what she did.'

'Did you tell Jez when the baby was due?'

'What that have to do with it?' he was bewildered by her diversion, why would it matter whether he'd told Jez, he couldn't remember.

'Did the baby come on the day it was due? Was it early, was it late?'

'No, I mean yes, him came when him was due. I remember the midwife saying that is not many babies so considerate. She thought it was because Issy was sure exactly when she got pregnant.'

Inez got up and slowly paced the small room, scratching her head and frowning. She knew how hurt Jez was by what Luke had done, the way he treated her. Could she be carrying out her threat, could she have a hand in this? She liked Jez, felt sorry for her, but her first priority was to her son.

'What you think it is Mama?'

'I think it might be something called Baby Blues, some women get it sometimes, it will pass after a time.'

'How long? I can't take this much longer.'

'It shouldn't be long now.' She reassured him thoughtfully. 'What about the church, them been praying for her?'

'Yes, but it don't seem to be working. They going to come and have a prayer meeting at the house next week.'

'That should help son.'

'But what if it don't, what if she don't get any better? I can't keep relying on her family to look after Lennox, and Irene too.'

'Don't worry son. Get some rest tonight. I'll go and get the children from Jez tomorrow, she working in the morning anyway. We'll talk about it in the morning.'

Confession brought relief and Lukan fell into the kind of deep sleep he'd not had since Lennox's birth. While he slept Inez got down the small grip she kept on the top of the wardrobe, opened the metal clasps quietly and slowly lifted the lid. Inside the case lay rows of jars and phials, neatly wrapped in cream calico cloth, some pieces yellowing with age. She extracted three phials, unwrapped them and stood them in a row on the kitchen table, now devoid of dish and spoon. Into an empty jar she carefully measured equal portions from each of the three phials, shook it, held it up to the dim light, examined it closely, shook it again before screwing the lid on tightly. Putting the jar in a corner of the wardrobe she carefully wrapped the others, replaced them exactly, and returned the grip to the top of the wardrobe.

As she lay on her back thinking about the situation, she was glad that they'd arranged to have a prayer meeting. It's always better when they think it's prayer. It was much easier to explain Lukan's skin clearing up with prayer. Much safer. She was going to have to rely on him to apply the treatment, but she couldn't sit by and do nothing. She was going to have to keep a close eye on Jez, she was only supposed to use this thing to do good. Still, maybe it wasn't her, maybe Lukan's wife did just have baby blues, but there wasn't any point taking chances.

Lukan awoke much brighter, less worried, more relaxed, and eager to see his children. He brought two dresses for them that Issy had made before she went into labour, she said it was cheaper for her to make them than for Luke to give money to Jez to buy them, money that they needed to pay for things on the house.

'How you sleep last night?' Inez asked as he came out onto the veranda.

'Good. Man, I needed a good night sleep. Where're the girls?' He was impatient to see his children.

'They still with Jez, she not working after all this morning. She say to let her know when you wake up.'

'There's no point her bringing them, I can just walk over there.'

'No Luke!' he looked up at the sharpness in her voice. 'You eat your breakfast while I go and get them.'

'OK' he said weakly, taken aback by her asperity. He knew, just like Dudley did, not to argue with that tone.

'It's on the table. I'll go and get them now.'

She knew Jez wanted to come and see Luke, but she wasn't taking any chances with her till she could put her mind at rest that she wasn't involved in Issy's sickness. She'd sprinkled some of the mixture over Luke last night and he woke up much better this morning, she would put some in his clothes before he left.

'Jez, me come for the girls.' She called as she approached the veranda. She didn't have to announce herself but as Jez was expecting to bring them over; Inez thought it was polite. All three of them appeared at the door at the same time. Jez holding Gloria on her hips while Darcie forced her way out from behind to come running to her granny.

'Daddy come! Daddy come!' She cried as she tumbled down the steps.

'Darcie, stop it.' Jez reprimanded her, but she took no notice, just kept running to her grandmother.

'I was going to bring them over.' Jez looked at her perplexed.

Yes, thought Inez, I can see you make a special effort with your dress and your hair, but he's a married man now, you have to let him go. He made his choice.

'Change of plans,' she said out loud, 'him just get up and still eating him breakfast.'

Jez didn't even try to hide her disappointment, not much point with Inez, she knew her too well.

'Him bring the baby?'

'How him fi bring the baby when him mother still feeding?'

'Oh, I forget it's only a month.'

Inez held out her arms to take Gloria from Jez's hips.

'Tell him he don't have to hide from me.'

'Him not hiding Jez, him just want to see the girls by himself for a while. Him will most likely bring them back.'

'I'm not working today,' she looked on wistfully as Inez took her children to the man she still loved, only a few yards away, but who may just as well have been in England.

Luke was on the veranda waiting for them. His heart swelled in his chest as Darcie came running to him, and laughed as he picked her up and swung her around, careful not to hit her legs on the bench. Gloria was always much more serious, he felt he was losing contact with her, being away a lot more from her during her baby years. She put her arms around his neck.

'Hello Gloria,' he greeted her.

'Hello Daddy,' she replied as though she was being introduced to a distant relative, which is exactly what he felt he was becoming.

A little panicked by this growing distance, he was eager to try and bridge it with the gifts he'd brought for them; the dresses, the Bustamante sweets, peppermint balls, and the two elastic bangles Issy had bought.

Inez watched as he played with his children, become their horse, tried to play jacks with the set she kept for when they stayed at her house. When he was out of breath from all the frolicking, Inez tried the dresses on the girls so he could see if they fitted, and could report back to Issy. He wanted to take them into town, to show off his girls in the pretty frocks. He could walk to Dudley's house, save him a trip, kill two birds with one stone.

Inez sprinkled some of her mixture over the girls when he went to the toilet. Better safe than sorry, if it wasn't Jez it could be somebody else jealous of his success.

Jez watched as her life walked past her house on their way to display themselves to the town, and felt her heart break. She would do anything to have him back, but each time she saw him, he seemed to be slipping further away. There was something different about him this time. He held his head higher, his back straighter, his strides were longer, his steps surer. Marriage seemed to agree with him. She hadn't found anyone to replace him, wasn't even looking. He may have become Mr Handsome, Mr Desirable, Mr Successful, but she was still plain and gangly Jezmine. She hadn't gone anywhere and remodelled herself. She had stayed and looked after the two children he so proudly displayed, in clothes she hadn't bought. She hoped with all her heart that his marriage would fail, that he would come back to her, and that she would join her daughters when he took them walking.

Chapter 11

What a friend we have in Je-sus, all our sins and grief to bear, what
a privilege to car-ry, all our sins to God in prayer.

So began the first song at Issy's prayer meeting. The brothers
and sisters stood around her bed and raised their hands and
their hearts to heaven, sincere in their wish to have their
sister's body and spirit made whole again. Lukan stood with
them; looking down at his wife, longing for the vivacious,
energetic, sexy woman he'd married to come back to him.

Oh, what peace we often for-feit, oh what needless pains we bear, all
because we do not car-ry, every thing to God in prayer.

He listened to the drone of the chorus of the six people present
and wished they'd chosen something a little more uplifting.
He silently asked forgiveness for not doing much praying
since the baby was born. He was too tired. He hadn't been to
church either, too busy looking after Issy, Lennox and Irene at
the weekends. He'd had to give up overtime at a time when
they needed it most.

One or two church sisters had dropped by in the day to
pray with Issy, but it didn't seem to have done much good,
he'd requested prayer at church, but that didn't seem to have
worked either. It was Pastor Morgan who'd suggested the
prayer meeting and he'd leapt at the opportunity. Planned for

the Monday after his visit to Sav, he was in much better shape to host the event, though in truth he was not a shadow of the hostess Issy was, is – he caught himself, she will come back to herself. He hadn't needed to worry though, because the sisters, both Issy's and the church's had rallied around to make sure everything was arranged. Made sure Issy was bathed and dressed in church clothes, not in the nightie she seemed to love. Made sure the house was clean, the children were fed and dressed properly and made sure there was lemonade for everyone if they wanted it and iced water for those that didn't.

Are we weak and heavy la-den, cumbered with a load of care, precious saviour still our re-fuge, take it to the Lord in prayer.

Luke's eyes were fixed on Issy. She didn't seem to be taking too much notice of the people around her, she picked at a bit off fluff on her dress and tried to brush it off. What was wrong with her? She hadn't rushed to welcome the brothers and sisters when they arrived, had barely shaken their hands when they came into her room. When she wasn't picking at her dress she was staring past the small shiny head of Brother Tulloch, the meeting leader, at the wall behind him.

Do thy friends des-pise forsake thee, Take it to the Lord in prayer. In his arms he'll take and shield thee: thou will find a so-lace there.

As they drew the song to the end, Brother Tulloch invited the brethrens to pray with him for their dear Sister Issy.

'Holy Father,' he began, head bowed as he'd invited the others to do, 'we come here tonight to pray with you daughter Sister Issy. You know, Dear God her condition, there is nothing that is hidden from you. Oh God only you can bring about a quick and complete healing…'

Luke's mind wandered to the whimpering Lennox being

looked after by Daisy on the veranda, hoping he wasn't hungry again. They'd made sure Issy fed him before people started to arrive, but sometimes he didn't go the full three or four hours before he needed feeding again.

'Please, Dear God,' he said a silent prayer of his own, 'don't let him get hungry till this is over.' He couldn't face the embarrassment of everybody having to stop while Issy fed Lennox. He was probably less comfortable, through his lack of experience, than any of the elders in the room.

'…and Dear God we pray for our dear Brother Lukan,' Luke tuned in again at the mention of his name, 'who has been given this cross. Keep him strong Dear Lord to be a help mate for our dear sister. In Jesus' name. Amen.'

'Amen.' They all chorused.

There were more songs and more prayers, each person adopting a slightly different slant on the theme of Issy's healing and support for Lukan. It was only in the final prayer that Brother Tulloch laid his hand on Issy's forehead and called for Jesus Christ to cast out whatever demons were occupying her body, to remove any unwanted spirits from their dear sister and to bring her the 'peace that passeth all understanding', that she could once again be whole, and once again praise the Lord with all her heart, with all her mind and with all her soul. He called on God to strengthen her faith in the healing power of prayer and to give their Brother Lukan strength and patience to keep this new and precious family together.

'We ask all of this in Jesus' name, in Jesus' name, in Jesus' name,' and his hand shook on her forehead as he said his final 'Jesus' name.'

They didn't linger long, leaving the young couple to feed their baby and get a good night's sleep. Most of them were parents themselves and understood this young family's needs. Before he left Brother Tulloch took Lukan aside and cautioned him to trust in God's timing for healing, warned him that not all miracles were instant, and that the important thing was for him to trust God's timing for Issy's recovery. Lukan felt he was just covering his back because Issy had shown no change from beginning to end of the meeting.

'I will Brother Tulloch. Thank you,' Lukan said, shaking his hand goodnight.

When everyone had gone, when Issy had fed Lennox and was once again in her nightie and asleep, Lukan removed the jar his mother had given him from his bag, opened it carefully and sprinkled some of the clear mixture over Issy's sleeping body. He then did the same to Lennox before putting it at the back of the cabinet in the kitchen. He used about a third of the contents. Inez's instructions was to use sufficient but not to drench them, and to do it after the prayer meeting, if there didn't appear to be any change in Issy. He crept into the bed beside her and curled himself around her back. There was no response from her, there hadn't been since Lennox's birth, but he found her body, however unresponsive, comforting.

Lennox's crying awakened him. Half asleep he threw one leg out of bed and willed the other to follow. He went to pick Lennox out of his crib in the corner of their room; the crib he had built himself with such anticipation for the joy they were going to share with their new baby. He woke up fully when he realised Lennox wasn't there, and he couldn't hear his crying anymore. Was he dreaming, had he imagined the cry, maybe he'd been in a dream and Issy hadn't had the baby yet? He looked across at the bed expecting to see her curled up in her usual shape, but she wasn't there. An instant power surge of panic flooded his body. Where were they? He stopped in mid-stride as he entered the living room and saw Issy sitting in the chair, Lennox at her breast, stroking his head and smiling down at him.

'Did he wake you up?' she enquired thoughtfully, 'I'm sorry. I tried to get to him as quick as I could so as not to wake you.'

She mistook his dazed look for lack of sleep, not for the transformation in her he was witnessing.

'Just go back to sleep, I'll be quiet when I come back to bed.'

He staggered back to bed, too dumbstruck to argue or to try and figure out what had happened to make her switch back, if indeed she had switched back and this wasn't just some flash and she was going to revert back to being the sloth in the bed. He lay there, unable to sleep, listening to her billing and cooing to Lennox, telling him what a glutton he was, how he was sucking her dry, how he was just like his father once he latched on to her breast, 'just like your daddy,' she joked with her son.

Lukan was still awake when she came back to bed, having laid a sleeping Lennox gently back in his crib.

'Luke, you still awake?' she whispered.

'Yes,' he whispered back.

'That little boy so greedy. Sorry he woke you up.'

'It's alright.' She was speaking as if she always got up to attend to him, like it had not been Luke's job for the last month. Then she snuggled up to him, threw her arm across his chest, yawned and said, 'I'm tired too.'

He tentatively tried to embrace her, and to his surprise and delight, she reciprocated.

Chapter 12

'Come in Miss Inez,' Issy proudly welcomed Lukan's mother into her newly finished and furnished home. 'Let the girls come in too.'

Inez stepped cautiously into the living room clutching her small brown grip. 'Careful girls,' she said to Darcie and Gloria who were less than cautiously pushing past her into the room.

'Where's Irene and Lennox?' Darcie asked excitedly looking up at Issy.

'Where your manners deh girl?' Inez chided her. 'Say good day to your step-mother.'

'Good day Miss Issy, where's Irene and Lennox?'

Inez raised her eyes to the sky with a look of 'what can I do with her?'

'They're in the yard,' Issy replied light-heartedly, patting Darcie's head as she ran past her calling, 'Irene, Lennox, we come!'

'That pickney getting wilder and wilder every day,' muttered Inez.

'Never mind Miss Inez, she's just happy to see her brothers and sisters. And what about you Gloria?' Issy bent to look into Gloria's solemn eyes. She always had an air of seriousness about her, and a permanently quizzical look, like she never quite believes anything she hears. It could be quite disconcerting at times, and, coupled with her naturally reserved personality, made her harder work to have around than her sister. But Issy loved them both, and was convinced that if they spent more time with her and Luke that she would drop her guard and allow a little more trust into her eyes.

'Good day Miss Issy,' she looked into Issy's eyes without any change of expression.

'I didn't mean how about you saying good day, I mean how you doing?'

Gloria's look said, you can see how I am, why are you asking? If it wasn't for the fact that she was only seven years old Issy would have sworn that she was mocking her.

'She's fine,' Inez answered for her, 'just tired because she wouldn't sleep last night. She always don't sleep the night before. I tell her to do like her sister, but the pickney ears too hard, now she a suffer because she tired.'

'Do you want a drink Gloria?' Issy asked, not wishing to embarrass Gloria further.

She nodded.

'Speak up child.' Inez interjected.

'Miss Inez, why don't you come and put your grip down in your room, and I'll get Gloria some lemonade. Do you want some too?' Issy steered her mother-in-law to the bedroom. 'It's a shame Maas Dudley couldn't come.'

'Him coming tomorrow, him had some business to take care of today. That will be good because him can help me with the girls, them getting harder to manage these days, especially Darcie, and as you can see, me not getting any stronger.'

That was one of the reasons Issy suggested bringing Inez down to stay with them. Her health had been getting steadily worse, she had high blood pressure, and although she was doing what the doctor suggested, eating less salt, less hard foods, yam, dashine, coco and the like, it was still high. It wasn't like she was overweight, she was, and always had been a slip of a woman, but the pressure was beginning to affect her breathing and her eyesight. Issy's seven years as an auxiliary nurse gave her some understand that stress could be contributing to Miss Inez's pressure. She wasn't sure what could be stressing her, but sometimes she looked as tight as a ball of steel wool.

Issy took the case from her and put it on the bed while Inez looked around the room as if seeing it for the first time.

'You do something different in here?'

'Just moved the furniture around to make more space for the children, especially with so many of them now. You don't like it?'

'It looks alright. Is just that I knew where everything was before.'

'You'll soon get use to it this way. I'm just going to get Gloria a drink. I'll bring one for you too. Sit down, you look tired'

Gloria was sitting on the edge of the sofa when she returned with the drink.

'Thanks Miss Issy,' she reached both hands up to take the bright yellow plastic glass, and drank steadily without a pause till she got to the end and handed the glass back to Issy.

'Do you want to go out in the yard?'

She shook her head, just as the baby began to cry. 'Lilly-Mae wake up. You want to come with me to feed and change her?' Gloria nodded and stood up to follow Issy as the newest member of the family began to exercise her lungs in earnest.

Inez sat on the side of the bed and looked around the room slowly. It would make things more difficult if Issy was going to keep moving things around. It was better if the bags stayed in one place after she set them. If they move around it might upset the balance and make them less effective. She'd have to have a word with Luke, try to get him to persuade her not to keep changing up the rooms.

She clutched her chest, and nearly bent double with the sharp stabbing pain that shot through her. She feared for her health. She was having to use a lot of energy to keep Jez under control, each day she seem to get stronger. She had young energy, and a lot of anger. The problem Inez had was that she liked Jez, and could understand the way she was feeling, because it was the same way she felt when Luke's father left her, dropped her and her son for another woman with more class and more money. History was repeating itself, but now she had to watch another woman go through the same suffering, and at the same time try to protect the man who was causing it.

Jez have a lot of natural ability, Inez reflected. She'd been testing it out bit by bit and was getting more confident. Inez knew the signs, the bits of cloth soaked in chicken blood, the burnt twigs left under the house. Since they had the prayer meeting Inez had been supplying Luke with enough mixture to use on him and his family. It was helping to keep away anything Jez's was doing to get at them, but it was taking a lot of her energy to keep Jez in check. Moreover, Inez knew she would be no match for Jez when she came into her full power.

Inez didn't know for sure who was training Jez. Since she started the little cleaning job she was away from the house a lot more, and although the girls usually came to *her* house, she was free to come and go in Jez's house when she was looking after them. It meant she could untie some of the knots Jez was using to try and bind she and Lukan together. But her health was going down further and further every day. It was good to get a break; at least she wouldn't be fighting any battles for the next few of days.

Winded by the pain she lay back on the bed to catch her breath as Issy and Gloria came in with Lilly-Mae, her youngest granddaughter.

'Come on Lilly, let Granny hold you while I go and get her drink, then I'll feed you too.'

'Granny can't hold her right now,' Inez wheezed.

'Inez, you don't look alright at all,' Issy was alarmed to see Inez wide-eyed and gasping, 'I think you should lie down as you already on the bed. You look like you need to see a doctor.'

'I don't need a doctor, is just the travelling, I'm getting too old for them long distance.'

Issy was about to point out that it's only sixty miles between Savanna-la-Mar and Chapelton, but thought better of it. Inez needed to lie down.

'Gloria, go out into the yard and tell Irene to come here.'

'What you want to drag the pickney away from her game for?' she rasped, struggling to push out each word.

'I want her to come and turn down the bed so you can get into it.'

Inez wanted to protest but she really needed to rest, and Issy's hands were full. It comes to something, she thought, when a child have to come to put her to bed.

She drifted into a fitful sleep in the hot airless afternoon, and dreamed that her mother was bathing her forehead with a damp rag. She was gentle in a way that her mother had never been. It wasn't that her mother didn't care, she just didn't know how, never been given any example, but Inez always knew she cared. She showed it in small ways, the way she patted her head after combing her hair for church on Sundays, the way she'd put an extra dumpling on her plate, the way she oiled her legs at night.

Her mother began unbuttoning Inez's blouse, slowly pushing it over her shoulder leaving her breasts bare, open to inspection. Inez knew she should feel embarrassed; try to cover herself, or roll onto her belly to hide herself, but she welcomed the freedom, welcomed her mother's closeness.

'Sshhh,' her mother said, as Inez groaned from the pain that shot through her heart, 'you'll wake everybody.'

Inez groaned her reply.

'Hush baby.' Her mother dabbed at her temples, raised her

head up and put a cup to her lips. Inez felt the cold water against her lips and wanted to take big gulps, suddenly she was very thirsty and very hungry.

'What you doing here Mama?' she asked, as she lowered her back onto the bed, 'I thought you'd gone for good.'

'I've come to help you Inez, if you want to come, I want to help you.'

'But… but what about Luke and the children? I can't leave them, not yet.'

'Then show him what to do, the way I showed you what to do before I leave, show him or show him wife.'

'I don't have not enough time.'

'There's always enough time.' As her mother slowly faded Inez felt naked and tried to button her blouse, but the more she tried to pull the two sides together, the smaller the blouse got. She couldn't get them past her sides. She tugged and pulled but each tug made the blouse smaller. She tried to roll onto her stomach fearing somebody might come in and see her nakedness, but it was hard to move her body, her right hand wouldn't move, lay like a wasted staff by her side. Rolling from the left, gasping and wheezing she finally made it onto her belly. That's when she felt the hand on her back, pressing her hard into the mattress, squeezing the air out of her lungs.

She moved her lips to tell her mother, 'Mama, you pushing too hard, I can't breathe.' Although no words came out, Jez must have read her mind and answered. 'Is not your Mama Miss Inez, is me.'

'Take your hand off me.' Inez tried to shout but the words came out like bubbling guava jelly, thick and hot and slow.

Jez's disembodied voice floated above her head before settling on the tips of her ear.

'I don't have my hands on you, I'm not touching you Miss Inez, I don't have to touch you.'

'Why you doing this Jez?'

'Because you getting in my way.'

'Jez, don't do this. Remember all I do for you.'

'But it didn't work, him still leave me, and him don't come back.'

'Let him go Jez, for God's sake, let him go.'

'It's too late, you shoulda think about God before.'

'No, no, no,' she struggled to push herself up. There was no way out, exposed on her back, stifled on her front.

'Miss Inez, Miss Inez,' Issy was shaking her. 'Miss Inez, wake up. We're going to eat now, the food's going on the table.' It was the long mahogany table that Luke made three months after them moved into their new home. He wanted a table big enough to seat all his family, for all the children to have their own chair, so he made eight of them, now it looked like he was going to need more, but for today they were using a stool.

'Miss Inez, you're sweating badly, do you want to take a shower before we eat.'

'Luke!' Issy shouted as Inez's body went into an involuntary twitch, a spasm that looked like someone had cattle prodded her.

'Luke! Come here quick!' she called again as Inez mumbled and babbled, unaware of Issy.

'What's the matter?' Luke asked as he walked into the room? 'What's Mama doing in bed, didn't you tell her we're going to eat,' he was clearly annoyed.

'I can't wake her, she looks sick. You might have to go and get the doctor.'

'What do you mean?' his annoyance turning to concern as he reached the side of the bed.

'Look at her!' Issy insisted.

Sitting on the edge of the bed he looked into his mother's face just as she opened her eyes and looked straight through him. When her lips moved he waited but no sounds came out, instead a long line of saliva dribbled down her chin and onto her neck. For a moment, one fraction of a second her face looked like his grandmother's, then she was back to being herself, or not quite herself because he'd never seen her like this.

'Lord God, don't let anything happen to her. Please God she's my mother, I don't want anything to happen to her.'

'Nothing's going to happen to her Luke.' Issy tried to reassure her.

'Pray with me Issy, pray for her.'

'Dear God, we know that you have your eyes on us all the time, we know that you are our protector, our guiding light.' She tried to remember the prayers she'd heard for the sick. 'Put your healing hands on her Oh Lord and… where're you going Luke?'

'I soon come back.' He was in and out of the room in a few seconds, in time to hear Issy begging the Lord to reach down and touch his mother.

'What's that?' she asked as Luke began to mop his mother's forehead with a wet cloth smelling faintly of cloves.

'It's what Mama use sometimes. Keep praying Issy.'

'We place Miss Inez in your hands, Oh God for safe keeping and… Oh God Luke, she open her eyes.'

Inez had indeed opened her eyes, this time looking *at* Luke, not through him. Issy saw the bewilderment turn to fear as she recognised where she was.

'You alright Mama? Thank God you alright!' he added not waiting for an answer.

Issy answered the question she saw on Inez's face as she turned her head and looked up to her.

'We couldn't wake you up. We were just a bit worried.' She tried to play down the fact that they were very frightened. Maybe they'd been worried over nothing, Issy told herself, but something inside her knew that Miss Inez had been in danger.

'You don't have to worry about me. I was just tired from that long journey, I'm not as young as I used to be,' she tried to reassure them, while rubbing her right arm which was now moving quite easily. She smiled a weak, watery smile. 'Just help me up.' Luke grasped her outstretched arm and pulled her into a sitting position.

'The food's nearly ready Miss Inez, but if you not ready to eat now, I can put yours to one side for you, or I can bring it in here for you on a tray if you don't want to sit at the table,' Issy didn't want her to feel obliged to join them at the table, especially with the children being so loud and excitable.

'I'm just going to the bathroom, then I will come to the table.' She said with more firmness than her legs portrayed as she stood up.

Issy and Lukan watched as she took a weak first step, Luke was ready to catch her if she fell.

'Mama, you sure you don't…'

'Don't fret Luke.' Her voice, and her next step were now much firmer.

'OK,' he said, still a little uncertain but knowing that there was nothing else he could do, 'come to the table when you ready, we have something to tell everybody.'

Inez was quite prepared to hear that Issy was pregnant again; she and Luke were producing some fine children, pretty and bright. They could probably afford another one too, as they were earning good money between them. Luke was never out of work, everybody said how skilled he was, and he was being paid top rate because everybody wanted him. She supposed she had Dudley to thank for that, for making sure he got a good trade.

Issy had her job at the hospital, and on the side she made and sold sweets to the shops, to her work mates at the hospital, and to some of the higlers. She made their money stretch by sewing a lot of their clothes, she said she got that from her father. If Inez had any grumble about her, it was the way she shut out anything that didn't come from the church, that didn't come out of the mouth of Pastor this or Deacon that, or Elder the other.

Inez tried to warn her once to be careful about who she let into her house, when she took on a maid to help with the children. Inez had a feeling about the girl when she met her and, one night, taking Issy to one side she had suggested she look for someone else as her spirit didn't take to the girl. Issy had told her, in that oh-so-certain and dismissive way she have about her sometimes, that the girl was good at her job and she wasn't going to let her go, just because Inez didn't take to her.

She'd let it drop with Issy, but had suggested to Luke that he should find a way to get rid of the girl. If he couldn't, because he was so much under Issy's frock tail, and she wouldn't, because she was too stubborn, then he should make sure he soaked the little bags of herbs once a week in the mixture she gave, and make sure he hang them back in the same place. She made sure she brought an extra supply today, because Issy still didn't get rid of the girl, she was still working there. What she didn't want to tell Issy or Luke was that the girl knew Jez. There may be nothing in it at all, but Inez didn't like it, and she didn't like the girl and her quiet, sneaky ways.

Inez wiped her face with the towel. The water was cool on her face, but as she stared at her reflection in the mirror she could see that the water had failed to refresh her features. She looked old, much older than her fifty years. It had been a hard life and now it was showing in her face. She wasn't sure what happened to her in the bedroom, but she knew something wasn't right. She'd never had that feeling in Luke's house before, and she wasn't as strong to fight it off, and what was her mother doing here? Why was Jez stifling her? There were answers to these questions that she didn't want to contemplate, she'd better go out and hear what the news was.

Issy looked up from serving one of the children and smiled at her, as she made her way to the table.

'Miss Inez you look much better.'

'She look the same as before,' piped up Darcie, glancing over her shoulder and seeing no change in her grandmother.

'Be quiet child.' Luke admonished her, seeing the remarkable change in his mother, the strength in her step and the freshness in her face, no trace of the woman who a few minutes earlier had stared through him without recognition.

'Good afternoon Granny,' Irene and Lennox said in unison, with Ivan following a split second later.

'Bwoy, everybody grow so big.' She responded.

'How can you tell if we're sitting down,' Lennox wanted to know. He was an inquisitive child, never taking anything on face value, and always wanting answers.

'Sit here Granny,' Irene indicated the chair next to her. She liked her Granny, like the way you always knew what you were getting with her, her predictability, her consistency. She always brought them Bustamantes, and mints, and drops. Even though her mother made drops, the ones Granny brought were bigger and had more sugar in than her mother's. Her drops had a skirt of sugar around the clustered tiny chunks of coconuts, and she always had little bags of flower petals and herbs that she hung around the house. They smelled lovely, and just when the smell was wearing out she would either bring some more or send some with her daddy when he went to visit. Granny or her daddy would remove the old ones and put up new ones.

She said she wasn't rich, and couldn't buy them big presents, but she could work with her hands, and make something for the whole house. She promised to show Irene how to make them when Irene came to visit her, but she had never yet visited her Granny's house in Sav-la-Mar. Both her parents said there wasn't much room, and it was better that her sisters came to them in Chapelton, where they had a bigger house, now complete with three bedrooms, two living rooms, a kitchen, and inside toilet.

She was the envy of her friends, because, not only did she live in a big house, she didn't have to do much work in it as they had a maid, and she could concentrate on her school work. Her mother believed in schooling as the way to success and was always saying she wished she'd paid more attention at school, wished she'd learned a profession sooner, because, although she was an auxiliary nurse now, she could earn much more if she was a real nurse. She wanted her daughter to do better than that, to have a real profession, and told her almost every day that she was bright enough to be anything she wanted.

Her Granny hadn't had much schooling but she seemed to know things, like which bush to boil for bellyache, or fever, or what to mix together to put on a cut. She knew how to get rid of a headache without any tablets, just by pressing parts of your forehead. Irene wanted to learn how to make these things but her mother said she had to concentrate on her school work, if she wanted to cure people she would make more money by aiming high, and perhaps become Chapelton's first woman doctor. Inez sat next to her step-daughter and squeezed her hand.

Everybody ate the feast Issy had prepared. Inez had to give it to her, she could cook. It wasn't expensive food either, callaloo and saltfish, fry dumplings, belly pork cooked down in a sweet gravy, hard food, and fried plantains. The children were hungry from all the playing outside; even Gloria had eventually gone out to join the others. They ate heartily, and chatted noisily. Issy and Luke passed Lilly-Mae between them so that one could eat while the other fed her. Well, if she was pregnant again, they would both have their hands full.

'We have something to tell everybody,' Luke said when they'd finished eating, and the children were beginning to get restless. 'We wanted to tell you all at the same time.'

Here it comes, thought Inez.

'I'm going to England.'

'What!' Inez exclaimed. This was news to her. 'What do you mean you going to England!'

'England! Are we coming too?' Irene was excited.

'Where's England?' Lennox asked puzzled.

'You should listen in school, then you would know.' Irene quipped.

'Are you joking Luke?' Inez looked at him in disbelief.

'No joke Mama. I'm going.' Sitting back with Lilly-Mae on his lap he beamed at her. 'Mass Vincent say they looking for people in the building trade in England, paying big money. He get somebody to sponsor me and I can go anytime in the next three months.'

Inez couldn't speak; it felt like someone had hit her hard across her face with a cricket bat, deafening her, like her father used to do. She didn't hear the children's excitement at the prospect of having a daddy in England; that would just be the icing on the cake for Irene who only knew one person whose father was in England, and she got all sorts of clothes, and toys, and things sent in barrels. Inez was so wrapped in her own shock that she didn't see the worried looks on Darcie's and Gloria's face, or hear Darcie's tentative question.

'Will we still come here when you gone?' Or Issy's and Luke's reassurance that Inez would still bring them down, or even their Uncle Dudley when Inez couldn't make it. A baby would have been far less disruptive, Inez thought.

'Granny, you look tired.' Irene was the only one who noticed Inez's lack of contribution to the discussion.

'Yes, I'm still a little tired. I think I'll go and have a lie down.'

'Granny and Lilly-Mae are the same,' observed Lennox.

'How?' questioned Ivan, who, as an outsider, didn't think he would feel the loss of his step-father as acutely as his siblings. He'd never moved back to live with his mother. His

Granny Blackwell had put up a fight to keep him, and in the end, Issy had agreed, because Ivan had said yes. That was the only home he knew, and as the only other person living there, he felt responsible for his Granny B, but he agreed to visit his mother every week. He saw his mother more often than the girls saw his step-father, but he still lived on the periphery of the family. He didn't know how Maas Lukan's move would affect him, and added little to the discussion.

'They're always sleeping, and Mama and Daddy always worry about them,' said Lennox. It was news to Inez that she was being worried about.

'Don't be stupid Ivan, of course Granny and Lilly are not the same. Granny's just tired tonight,' Irene rebuffed him.

Whether it was the effects of the incident Inez had earlier in the day, or the news of Lukan's impending departure, she was not able to leave her bed the next day, or the day after. By Sunday when she was due to take the girls back home she was in no state to travel. They'd called the doctor, at great expense, who said her blood pressure was sky high, and that she had to rest; she definitely couldn't travel till the pressure came down.

'You'll have to take the girls back, Luke. It's a shame Dudley couldn't make it this weekend. Do you think it was the news that sent her pressure up?'

'I don't think so, remember she had that spell earlier in the day.'

'Well, it's probably a good idea anyway for you to take the girls back.'

'Why?' He couldn't see how it was good to do all that travelling in one day, and go to work the next.

'Because you can tell Jez about going to England. It will be better coming from you than from Miss Inez or the girls.'

Lukan didn't share Issy's belief. He wasn't looking forward to telling Jez.

Chapter 13

'So, what we going to do now?' Jez lay by his side in the dark.

'What do you mean, what we going to do?'

'Well, you have to tell her.'

'Tell who?' She wasn't making any sense.

'You going to have to tell her that you and me back together now.'

'What do you mean, back together?' He knew he was sounding like an echo, but she couldn't mean what it was dawning on him she could.

'Luke, you can't pretend that what just happen, didn't. We're supposed to be together. All that happened is that you come back home.'

He propped himself up on one elbow and spoke to the soft outline of her body, etched in the shimmer of the moonlight beaming in through the naked window. They hadn't pulled the curtains in their haste to get into the bed.

'Jez, what happen tonight shouldn't have happened. I was only trying to comfort you as a good Samaritan should. It shouldn't have gone that far.'

'So now I'm a charity case. What make you stop tonight when you been walking on the other side of the road for years? I don't remember anywhere in the Bible where the good Samaritan took anybody home and fucked them, and tell them how much him miss them. I don't remember that'

Lukan winced at her language. He'd forgotten how coarse she could be, he was moving in a different world now.

'Jez, it was a mistake. We shouldn't have done what we just did. We have to forget it…'

'It wasn't a mistake for me Luke. It's what I've been working for since the day you tell me on that same veranda out there, that you leaving to get married. All that work was not…'

'What do you mean 'what you been working for' Jez?'

She heard the suspicion in his voice.

'I mean, what I've been hoping for.'

'No Jez' his voice was getting harder, 'you said all that work… what work?'

She caught herself quickly.

'Luke, I clean people's houses to keep your pickney them, and I don't mind doing it because I know it's just a test… '

'What kind of test? Jez you talking rubbish, you not making any sense.'

'I know it's just a test to see if the two of us belong together. Every night, God knows, I go to bed and think about this night, this night when you and me get back what we had.'

'I don't think God had anything to do with this. This was pure sin.'

'You can call it what you want, but I was your first wife in the eyes of God, if anything, is you two sinning.'

'Jez, you talking crazy. You're not even saved, what you know about God?'

'About as much as you know, because the two of us in this fornicating bed together.'

Looking at her silhouette in the darkening room, as the moon moved on, no longer willing to shed light on their dark deeds, he felt repulsed. How could he have been so weak? How was it an hour ago he could not say no to her, and now, he couldn't bear to look at her, to touch her. He should have ignored her knock at the door of his mother's house, should have pretended he was asleep and let her go back to her bed. Instead, he'd gone to open the door and she had thrown herself at him weeping and begging him not to leave, that she couldn't stand the thought of not being able to see him for years, it was bad enough that she only saw him every one or two months, but that was enough, because she still loved him, that he couldn't pretend he didn't see it every time he looked into her eyes, because everybody else could. She blubbered that she had tried to stop loving him, but she couldn't deny what was in her heart. She was prepared to give up ever being with another man, because she was waiting for him to come back. If he was determined to go at least love her one more time. He must still feel something for her, she challenged him, she saw it when he wasn't trying to hide it.

She was pressed hard against him, her face buried in his bare chest, he felt her hot tears on his skin, her breasts, unfettered by a brassiere were still pert despite the two children. She was not voluptuous like Issy but… he didn't want to think about Issy, not when Jez turned her head up to his and he found his mouth on her lips. She opened her mouth and let him into every crevice. It came back to him in an instant, the feel of her, he knew every part of her body, she hadn't changed, hadn't got fatter or thinner. She was saying his name like she never did before, telling him she missed him, telling him she wanted him to fuck her just one more time.

'Luke, no other man's been in your place. I don't let anybody else touch me, I know you would come back,' she said as he pulled her blouse over her head, too impatient to undo the buttons. 'Luke you're the only man for me. I miss you Luke, I miss what we used to do. I want you to do it to me tonight Luke.'

He ran his hand inside her panties, she was wet, she was ready.

'Take them off,' he whispered hoarsely.

She bent over, and while she was down there, pulled his underpants over his erect pole. They were still in the living room of his mother's house. He was too impatient to take her to the bedroom; in case he changed his mind. He had to take her now. Lifting her skirt up over her hips, he backed her up against the wall.

'Open your legs,' he instructed her.

Lowering himself till he got the angle right, he hoisted her over his hot rod, and allowed her to slide onto him. She felt good, tight, stimulating every nerve ending, electrifying his body. His brain was an un-fused mass of exposed wires. He pulled her up and down on his pole moving with her like a pestle and mortar.

She cried out from the pain but he didn't stop, couldn't stop, he was in too deep and he couldn't come up till he hit the bottom. He felt the roof of her cervix hit his exposed tip and knew he was close to exploding.

'Come, let's go and lie down,'

Wrapping her arms around his neck she allowed herself to be carried to his single bed. Laying on his back he kept her on top astride him and instructed her to ride him, rocking backward and forward, guiding her where he wanted, thrusting into her when the pressure eased and he felt less like shooting. She moaned, called his name as though she was meeting him for the first time, but this was so much better than the first time. The bed creaked and groaned adding to the clamour in his head.

He wanted to make her come, to please her, in a perverse way to show her what he'd learned, how much better he was now. Easing her onto her back, he took full control, thrusting hard, pulling out and teasing the mouth of her hole, then in again. She held him tight, tried to pull him in, flexed and squeezed her muscles till he got faster and faster like a runaway train on her open inviting track, building speed, building power, heading for the collision that would exploded like starlight in a forming galaxy. They held each other, waited till the dust had settled before he rolled out of her and onto his side.

'I think you should go Jez.'

'Why, the girls will be alright. Them just next door.'

'No Jez. You can't sleep here tonight. It wouldn't be right. I'm a married man.'

'Is a pity you didn't think about that an hour ago.'

'I was doing you a favour Jez. I could see how distressed you were.'

'No Luke, you were doing yourself a favour, trying to make yourself feel better because you leaving your children to go and look money.'

'That's the problem with you Jez. You don't have any ambition. Why do you think I left you?'

'Because your Uncle Dudley hate me, and because you was too weak to stand up to him. That's *your* problem Luke, you too weak. You let that little woman wrap you round her little finger, have you working all hours and now she sending you off to England to make more money. How much money she want? If you was my husband, Luke, I wouldn't let you go to England, because I wouldn't trust you. Is how many other women you do this with?' She was ranting again now, like she did that night on the veranda.

'None. I've never done this before.'

She was quiet for a moment before telling him slowly, 'but now you know how easy it is, you will do it again.' She was letting him know he'd crossed over a threshold that he would cross again and again. He didn't believe her. He loved Issy, he had a great life with her, why would he want to put all that in jeopardy?

'No Jez, you wrong.'

'I'm not wrong Luke, and I'm not worried, because you will come back to me.'

'You can think whatever you like, but this thing is over between us Jez. This was a mistake, and I'm going to ask God for forgiveness. I'll get baptised again if I need to, but this won't happen again.'

'You might have to live in the water then. And how you going to explain to your wife, and your pastor and all your brothers and sisters who think they better than everybody else, why you have to be getting baptised every three months. No Luke, you won't get baptised, you will just become a hypocrite like the rest of them. But that's all right. I won't turn you away because you're a hypocrite. I know what you are already.' She was picking up her clothes and getting dressed as she spoke. Now ready, she turned to him, still craving his long lean legs, his broad chest, his gap tooth smile. 'Make sure you come and say goodbye to your pickney them tomorrow before you leave.'

He heard the click of the door as she left. This was not how he'd planned it. If only his mother had been here there would have been no opportunity and he would not be lying here full of regret, full of doubt that she could be right, that he would come back to her.

Chapter 14

Issy, sewing a new pair of pants for Ivan and humming a hymn to herself, didn't hear Inez come into the room over the whirring of the sewing machine, didn't become aware of her till she was right next to the table, making Issy jump, lose concentration and run the needle through her finger.

'Jesus Christ Miss Inez, why you have to creep up on me like that?' her voice muffling a little as she stuck her finger in her mouth.

'Sorry, I didn't mean to frighten you. The needle go through your finger?'

'It's not too serious.' Issy replied, aggrieved at being interrupted and injured. She was trying to finish the pants so Ivan could get it to wear to church on Sunday, as he needed a new pair. With Luke going away and having to save up the plane fare she was doing everything to keep the spending down. She was even putting in some overtime at work. It's true she had to use the maid more, but the difference between her wages and the maid's, made it worthwhile. And it didn't help that they just had to pay out for the doctor to come and see her.

'Mek me see it.' Inez held out her hand to receive Issy's finger.

'It's not too bad. I'll put a plaster on it.'

'I have something to rub on it before you put on the plaster.'

'What is it, Miss Inez?'

'Just a little ointment I made.'

'Miss Inez, what do you put in those ointments and mixture you bring here?' she couldn't hide her annoyance. Every time her mother-in-law visited she brought a bagful of tonics, ointments, and body rubs. She never explained what was in them. Luke was the one that used them the most, and now Irene was beginning to use them, instead of asking Issy for advice.

'Is just herbs and things.'

'I'm a nurse you know, I need to know what's in these ointments and things you bring here…'

'Well… I use the usual things, shame-mi-lady, guinea hen weed, rose petals, and a little nutmeg and cloves.'

'You don't need to keep bringing them you know. I know it must take you a long time to make them, and I can get almost any kind of medicine from the hospital. Especially now you're not well, you need to rest and not waste your time making all these things.'

'It's not a waste of time for me Issy. In fact, I wanted to talk to you about why I keep bringing them, and what Luke using them for.'

'I know you think they're helping Miss Inez, but you can get almost any medicine from the drug store without the effort you have to use to make these things.'

'Issy, I need to talk to you!' The force in her voice made Issy look up, like Inez had pulled an invisible string in the top of her head and yanked it skywards. 'There's things you need to know, because I don't know how much longer I can protect you.'

'What d'you mean protect me, protect me from what?' She was indignant. She liked Miss Inez, but she could be a bit strange sometimes. What did she think Issy needed protecting from? Maybe her pressure had gone up again.

'People… some people…maybe one or two people…' Inez stumbled through Issy's hostile stare. She offered no help or encouragement, just watched her with the impatience of a parent waiting for a child to tie her shoe laces when they're already late.

'…might want to harm you, and I…'

'Who in the world would want to harm me?' she was incredulous. Miss Inez's pressure must be high. 'Why don't you sit down, Miss Inez, I'll go and get you some water.'

'I don't want any water,' she said as she sat down, grateful for the invitation, and realising that she felt more confident sitting down.

'Issy, remember when you had Lennox and you wasn't… well? I remember Luke telling me that one night you was your sick, sick self and the next morning, after him sprinkle the mixture on you, you just changed back to normal.'

'You mean the night after the prayer meeting?'

'Yes, but they'd been praying for you for weeks, and none of it made any difference, till him used the mixture.'

'So what you telling me is that me getting better didn't have anything to do with prayer, and everything to do with some water Luke throw on me,' Issy sneered. The woman was losing her mind.

'I know you think I'm just some old country woman who never go anywhere and don't know anything, but there's things, Issy, that can hurt you if you don't know about them.'

'You'd better tell me what these things are Miss Inez, because you're not making much sense at the moment, but you need to make it quick, I'd still like to finish Ivan's pants before I go to work.'

Taking a deep breath Inez began, her voice a little shaky at first because she'd never told anyone the whole story before, not in one go. She'd shared snippets with Luke over time, tried to get him to understand what was in some of the bottles, the phials, the sachets. She told him that Jez had a lot of natural abilities with this work and that she was helping her to develop them.

Then, they were a family, Jez, Luke, Darcie and Gloria were all her family, it was like she was passing on her skills to her daughter, and Jez was a quick learner. But when Luke decided to marry Issy; it changed everything. Jez took it badly, convinced herself it was just a passing thing with Issy, said it was just part of the excitement of Luke living away from home, maybe, she thought, Luke was just saying it to punish her because she didn't try to stop him going to Clarendon to work. But when it was clear that Luke was going to get married; she began to get malicious. She told Issy how she'd overheard Jez tell Luke that if he married Issy he would never be happy with her.

'Well that's rubbish straight away. Even you can see that me and Luke are happy…and successful,' she added for good measure.

'That's because I've been putting up a shield between you all down here and her, but she's getting stronger and it's taking too much of my energy to hold her off. Issy, she's trying to get into your house. I've already told Luke that your maid is one of Jez's distant cousins, she might be working with Jez to do harm to your family.'

'Miss Inez,' Issy pointed out patiently and not without a little sarcasm, 'the only person in this family who's sick is you, and you're the only one who believes in all this hocus pocus.'

'Listen to me Issy,' a measure of desperation was evident in her voice as she reached out and gripped Issy's wrist. 'I'm going down, I can't hold her off much longer, you and Luke need to work together to keep her out of your life. I know her. She just waiting for an opportunity.'

'So even if I was to believe you, what do you want me to do?'

'I want you to let me teach you what I know, let me teach you how to make the ointments and tonics so that you can use them to protect yourself and your family.'

'Miss Inez, what you're asking me to do goes against the teachings of the church, and of God. You can believe what you want, and I'm sorry that you're not well, but don't expect me to go against the teachings of the Bible, that God is our *only* protector, *my* only protector. I don't need any herbal water or any ointments or any more of your little bags to hang round the house.'

'Issy…' began Inez, desperate to make her see sense.

'The subject is over Miss Inez, if you want to stay under this roof till you get better, I don't want to hear another word about Jez, or your protection.'

Inez could feel her blood pressure rising. Issy was leaving them completely exposed. She wished she had more time to make her see sense, she wished Luke wasn't going away, at least she could've continued to work through him. She wished Issy would listen. It was a pity she wasn't around when Issy too, wished she'd listened.

It was a full two weeks before Inez was fit enough to go back home, before she was ready to admit that there wasn't anything else she could do to change Issy's mind, but not before she had used every night that Issy worked a late shift to show Luke what she knew, to explain what to put into the bags, how to make the ointments, how to make the tinctures. They didn't write anything down, Luke didn't want to take the risk and Inez didn't know exact quantities anyway. She'd been doing it for so long, she just knew.

Luke didn't say much, he didn't like to hear his mother say that she didn't have long left on this earth. Not knowing how to answer her after his numerous attempts at contradiction, he fell silent, listened and tried to remember what she was telling him. There were so many unspoken things between them. She wanted to tell him that she knew, the instant he walked into the house on his return from Sav, that he had been with Jez. He knew by the way she looked away from him and avoided his eyes, that she knew, and he felt a heavy sense of double betrayal. Not only had he betrayed his wife, he had also betrayed his mother who had been working so hard on his behalf. Inez felt wearied by his actions. Luke had given her adversary strength, had sided with Jez against her, not knowingly of course, he didn't know, but Jez did. She knew that this would weaken Inez, but there was no point burdening Luke with this. He would have enough to fight when she was gone.

Luke was also feeling the guilt of betraying God and the church by taking his mother's instructions. He knew that he should dismiss her in the same way Issy did. As a God fearing man he had no right to be listening to how to make what was tantamount to spells and curses to ward off evil spirits. He should leave all that to God; but there was something in him that could not yet forget that no amount of prayer, or medicine, had helped to heal his skin, but his mother's poultice had.

He was walking a tightrope between Issy, God and his mother, and at the same time making preparations to leave all of them. He'd suggested to Issy that they delay his departure because of his mother's illness. She'd been emphatic in her rebuttal. He had to go, Miss Inez would get better. Couldn't he see she was getting better every day? She had Dudley and Jez right there in Sav-la-Mar to look after her if anything happened, and the girls were not so demanding anymore and could even help her around the house if she needed it. No. Luke had to follow through with his plans and go.

He hadn't told her about him and Jez. She didn't act as if she knew anything had happened, didn't seem to pick up on it like his mother, and he was beginning to feel he could relax with her.

'OK,' he said, trying to inject some enthusiasm into his voice.

'I'll book your fare on Thursday, on my day off.'

'Mama say she is strong enough to travel home this weekend. I'm going back with her, and I'll get to see the girls again, seeing as how I'm not going to see them so often when me gone.'

Chapter 15

'Come on Luke, your uncle's ready, if we don't leave now you might miss your plane,' Issy urged him to get into the car.

'Coming,' he said putting Lilly-Mae down, and ruffling Lennox and Irene's hair. 'Be good for your mother, I don't want to hear that you give her any trouble.'

'No daddy,' the older two said. Lilly-Mae was aware something important was happening, but was too young to understand what.

Lukan was buying himself some more time. He had this same feeling in his belly when he left Savanna-la-Mar all those years ago. The same alternating tightening and loosening, like someone was clenching and releasing a fist inside him. He needed the toilet again, but he knew there'd be nothing when he went, just like there wasn't ten minutes ago and the ten minutes before that.

His last sweep of the room took in all that meant so much to him, the dining table and chairs he'd made himself, the dresser, table with the vase of plastic flowers where he'd taken the photo Issy had insisted on, so they would have something to look at when he was away. He'd grumbled about the price but she'd been relentless, and he'd agreed. He scanned the wooden floor. He knew every board, every nail, every joint, remembered every drop of sweat that fell in the laying of it. The pale green paint on the walls, a darker green from a left over tin from one of Maas Vincent's project that he'd watered down with white to make it paler for Issy. The dark green and maroon patterned curtains that Issy had made and that they had hung together, the green and white check plastic table cloth that Issy used to protect the table, the rush matting on the floor to protect the varnish, the transparent plastic on the sofa to protect the cloth.

'Come *on* Lukan,' Issy called again from outside. He knew she was getting impatient; she only called him Lukan when he'd upset her in some way. When she was trying to get round him to agree to something he didn't want he was Lukey, otherwise it was plain Luke.

'Coming,' he said again as he stepped to take one last look at their bedroom, the room in the middle of the house directly off the living room. It wasn't the biggest room, or the one they had originally built for themselves, that was the end room where Irene and Lilly-Mae slept. Issy wanted to be in the middle where she could hear what was going on in Lennox's and Ivan's room as well. He hadn't protested, he was just happy to be in the same one as her.

'Stop the coming and come,' she oozed frustration.

He pictured them in the bed the first night they had finished the house, how they'd celebrated, how she'd buried her head in a pillow to muffle her moans, so that she wouldn't wake the children, how he'd tried to be gentle but how she'd urged him to ram her like the bull he was, a Taurean born under the zodiac sign of the bull. It was such a turn on for him when they had to be quiet and she had to whisper his name. He remembered the tension of silenced passion and the explosion as he gave in to a force that rocked his body.

He saw all that in one sweep of the room; saw his clothes, the ones he wasn't taking with him, hung in the wardrobe whose door had been left ajar in the haste to get going. It wasn't like Issy to leave it open. He also saw her dresses hanging on the other side. Each of them had a memory for him.

'Lukan.' She sounded exactly like his mother on those rare occasions when she spoke with authority, when her voice nailed your feet to the ground because it was so unexpected.

'Coming!'

He turned and walked out to the veranda, down the steps and into the yard where everyone had gathered to say goodbye.

'At last!' An exasperated Issy rolled her eyes to heaven. 'God knows it looks like you're trying to miss the plane.'

'Come on Luke.' Uncle Dudley coaxed.

'Goodbye Mass Luke,' a couple of the neighbours' children said, mimicking their parents and a few of his colleagues who'd come to wish him well. It was almost a replica of the weekend scene in Sav when he'd said goodbye to Darcie, Gloria , Jez, and some of his neighbours, only there were more people here, and Issy and his uncle would be getting into the car with him.

People in Sav said he was lucky, that it looked like Clarendon agreed with him and that they hoped he would find as much luck in England. They said not to forget them, a euphemism for 'remember to send me something.' It was a sentiment being echoed here as he stood outside his house, shaking hands and embracing. He smiled, promised he wouldn't forget anyone, and hoped they couldn't see on his face the terror he felt in his heart. This was more than a trip forty miles away, or even a hundred and forty miles. He had never been off the island, had never travelled to anywhere closer like Cuba or Cayman, and now here he was going nearly five thousand miles away. He couldn't come back every weekend to see his family, to see Issy, to play with Lennox.

What if he never saw them again? Like he knew he would never see his mother again. What if something happened to them, or to him? He went around and gave all the children another hug, and squeezed them tightly. Then he got into the car in which Issy and his uncle were already waiting. Sliding into the back seat next to Issy, he ignored the 'I thought you were going to sit up in the front with me,' look on Dudley's face. This would be the last time he'd see his wife for six months, maybe even a year, because they'd agreed that if things worked out well, and they could stand the distance, he would stay for a year, to recoup some of the losses from the plane fare.

As the car pulled away, he turned to wave to the cheering crowd as they called out 'Good bye Mass Luke, good luck Mass Luke, good bye Daddy.' He held down the lump that had pushed its way up from his stomach and into his throat, held Issy's hand tightly, and tussled with the tears that threatened to embarrass him in front of his uncle. No one spoke as the houses and shops of Chapelton slid by and the car gathered speed.

'How're we doing for time?' Issy broke the silence, addressing Dudley.

'I'm going to have to step on the gas as soon as I hit the open road.'

'You think we'll get there in time though?'

'We should do, if we don't face any hold up.'

'Let's pray for no hold up then.' Lukan thought she was about to start praying, but it was only a figure of speech. Maybe she felt there had been enough praying already. There had been praying in church on Sunday, prayer for his safe travel to the shores on the other side of the world, prayer for keeping him centred on God, for bringing Christ into everything he did, prayer for him to find work quickly to continue providing for his family, prayer for the family he was leaving behind, that God would protect them, shower them with blessings and keep them from all harm. At the prayer meeting last night, there was a special prayer that God help them to keep their marriage vows intact, a reminder to both of them that God's vision knows no time or space, that he sees and knows all, and that it was to him they would both be accountable for any thoughts of straying.

They'd sat side by side in the dining room as Brother Tulloch put his hands on both their heads and asked for God 'to shine his light on these two people who were trying to walk in his footsteps, and to guide their steps every day that they may never stray from his divine path.' Luke said his own prayer, asking forgiveness for the times he had veered from the narrow and difficult path God had laid out.

Brother Tulloch continued, 'you know God the trials and tribulations that this couple has gone through in these last few months, I am asking you to give them strength Oh Lord, to remind them to call on you when they are feeling weak, when temptations get in their way, remind them that you are the way, the truth and the light, that you know the seductive ways of Satan, and that you will shield them from Satan's wickedness if they just remember to call on you.' Luke had a most uneasy feeling at the mention of temptations, and without any warning his head filled with Jez and the times he'd been with her since his marriage.

'Dear Lord,' continued Brother Tulloch as he placed both his hand on Luke's head, 'bless our Brother Lukan as he prepares to take this journey. Guide the pilot that he may deliver our brother safely to the other side, calm all winds, part the clouds and guide them to a smooth landing Lord.'

He looked out of the window at the trees, the flowers, the rickety old shacks and the newly built and painted houses standing side by side. Some of these houses he'd helped to build, he could go up to them and see where he'd spliced a joint, where he'd built an architrave, laid a floor, crafted a window frame. It wasn't just the building, he could enter most of these houses and find a piece or maybe two of furniture that he'd made.

Since independence everybody seemed to want to build or to buy. The bauxite in Clarendon had suddenly shot up in price, and now that Jamaica had control over what it got for the sales a lot of people were better off. He'd considered himself lucky, being in the right place at the right time. So why was he leaving it behind? Issy, as always, was planning ahead. She said that he was young now, but couldn't work that hard all his life, that he needed to start saving, putting something aside for later on. She also wanted them to build a house and rent it out, so that they would have some income later, so that they wouldn't have to work so hard, and if things went well in England, they might even be able to build two. His Uncle Dudley agreed with her, reminded him that this was the difference between Issy and Jez. And yet he was being increasingly drawn to Jez.

After that night when she came to him, he made a vow to never go there again, and he meant it. He went to the alter and begged forgiveness, began afresh with Issy, even though she was unaware of her part in this new beginning. But when his mother died, and he needed someone to comfort him, and Issy was in Chapelton, Jez was there, holding his head close to her bosom and weeping with him. That night she'd made love to him, gently and tenderly, like she was comforting a child. He had woken in her arms the next morning, filled with remorse, but she'd soothed him into making love to her again. It would be good to get away from her. That was another reason for going. He didn't feel he could keep the promises he'd made to Issy as long as he had to see Jez.

'You alright?' Issy asked squeezing his hand, pulling in close to him, and bringing him back to the present.

'Hhhm hum.'

'You're very quiet. You frightened?' she was keeping her voice low, so Dudley couldn't hear.

That was the thing about Issy, she sometimes knew exactly

what he was feeling. They'd even developed a silent language that they used when the children were around. He was going to miss that. He didn't answer, didn't have to; she knew his signs, sweating palms, tight muscles.

The rest of the journey passed in relative silence, each one deep in their own thoughts. For Dudley, this was a dream come true. Luke was taking that step he'd never had the courage to take, but, he reflected, he didn't have somebody like Issy behind him, pushing him, and he didn't have anybody like himself when he was young to show him which way to go. He was proud of where he'd got to, but Luke was going further; Luke was going to England where the big money was, he was going to make it big. At least one member of his family was going to make it big.

Issy was thinking about his passport and his ticket, she felt for them a hundred times. She was concerned about how he was going to manage without her to organise him, but he'd be living with her Uncle William till he could get himself sorted out. They were meeting him at the airport and would help him to find work. Luke didn't know William, he went to England years ago on the Windrush with 500 other Jamaicans. Issy had never really taken much notice of the letters he sent to her father until she had the idea for Luke to go. She'd started to write to him herself, explaining her husband's situation and asking if he would be able to help.

'If he's good with his hands, he will find work here' her Uncle William had written back. Issy was convinced. All she had to do was convince Luke that it was a good idea. She was thinking of the first time she made the suggestion, one night after they'd made love and she was snuggled under his left arm pit. He was in a very mellow mood.

'Lukey,' she'd begun.

'Hmmm,' he was beginning to doze.

'I wish we didn't have to work so hard.'

'I know, but we doing all right. In fact we doing better than all right. Anyway, it won't be forever, as soon as we finish paying off the money for the house you can drop to part time, or even give up the job altogether'

'How would you like to build another one?'

'What for, we have a nice house already, what would we want with another one?'

'Well, we could rent it out and get regular money.'

'And where you think we going to get the money from to build another house when we don't even finish paying for this one yet?'

That's when she'd suggested going to England, and he'd laughed so loudly, she had to shush him in case he woke the children. He thought it was a stupid idea, leaving his wife and family to go and live thousands of miles away. It took six months of constantly dripping the idea to him, and the help of his Uncle Dudley doing the same, before he finally agreed. By the time they told his mother and the children, the plans were well advanced.

She feared Miss Inez's death would derail the plans, but with some careful management by both her and Dudley, it merely delayed it by a couple of months. She didn't want to be uncharitable, but more than once the idea crossed her mind that his mother purposefully died to try and stop Luke from going. He'd felt so guilty about not being there for her, he lost weight running backward and forward to Sav to take care of things, even though Dudley told him he was looking after the funeral. Until then, Issy hadn't really understood the bond between Inez and Luke. She had underestimated too, the effect Inez's death would have on Irene who cried every time her name was mentioned. She regretted all the things she would never be able to do with her grandmother; visit her home, listen to her stories of strange happenings in the bushes in Sav, learn how to cure people without medicines. She was inconsolable. So too, was Luke.

He closed in on himself, kept her at bay, held himself together till the day of the funeral. As they begun to shovel the earth onto her grave, as the graveside mourners sang *in the sweet by an by, we shall meet on that beautiful shore* his shoulders shook, and sounds like a choking dog shot from his mouth. He looked into the grave, rigid with grief, then suddenly grabbed the shovel from one of the men and shovelled furiously, at three times the speed as everyone else, tears streaming down his face. He later told her how ashamed he felt that he couldn't control himself, how he should have been more of a man, set a better example to Ivan and Lennox. She said that when she died, she hoped they would cry for her, and let everybody see that they loved her enough to bawl out loud. She would be proud of them. She was sure, she told him, that Miss Inez was proud of him.

That's when he said he didn't want to go to England anymore, didn't want to lose her or his children, didn't want Lennox or Ivan to experience what he had just gone through. She had to persuade him that he would not be losing them; in fact, a few short months away would mean that they could spend more time together, that they would be able to send the children to good schools, and eat good food and employ a maid more often so they could spend more time together.

Eventually, he agreed to set the wheels in motion again and now here they were, on the way to the airport, making it happen. In two hours he'd be gone and she would be back on her own, but this would be different. Being on your own because your husband is in England was a different matter to being on your own because your baby's father was a womaniser and a drunkard. Issy was now a very respectable woman in Chapelton, the six months, or the year would pass by quickly, as quickly as this journey to the airport. Dudley was parking the car, it was time.

The woman at the BOAC counter looked him up and down, squinted at his picture in the passport and swept her eyes up and down him again. Lukan began to sweat, was there something wrong with the passport?

'Are you travelling on your own Mr. Levy?' she glanced from Luke to Issy.

'Yes.' His throat was dry; his voice shrill and weak.

'To Birmingham?' she enquired, looking at his ticket.

'Yes.' The same dry weak voice. Why was she asking him if she could read what was on the ticket? Did Issy make a mistake when she booked it?

'Just the one case Mr Levy?'

'Yes.' That's all he seemed able to say, but that's all she required. He'd never done this before.

She checked the label Issy had carefully written out and tied onto his case, then peeled off another label and stuck it on the side.

'Hand luggage?'

'What?'

'Do you have any luggage to carry onto the aircraft Mr Levy?'

'Yes, this.' Issy answered, holding up the brown canvas bag in which she'd packed the bush tea, bammies and bulla cakes her uncle had asked her to send, things he couldn't get easily in England, and when he could, they were very expensive. She'd also put in some of her sweets, grater cakes, drops, robin red breasts. She made sure there was a suit of clothes and a pair of pyjamas in his hand luggage in case anything happened to his main case and he had to wait for it, she'd heard that had happened to some people. She'd made a small album of photographs of him and his family, glued them into the small book and put it in to surprise him when he opened up his bag.

He was all checked in now, it was real, he was going. The

three of them sat in a row of seats watching others arrive with their cases, wearing the same bewildered look that was their own just a few minutes earlier. Saw them locate their desks and hand over their documents. Some people were accompanied by what appeared to be the whole village. Men wore suits, despite the heat, but there was more variety in the womens' dress. They seemed more concerned with whether their clothes would be fashionable in England and less about being warm enough when they got there.

Then his flight was called.

'Will all passengers travelling on BOAC flight... to Birmingham, England please make their way to the departure lounge. '

'That's me.' Luke shot up like a popped cork, followed by Issy and Dudley.

'Bwoy, me proud of you,' Dudley said, his eyes misting over, as he shook Luke's hand. More than anything he wanted an embrace from his uncle, to take some strength from his solid manliness, but Uncle Dudley wasn't into hugging... or crying.

'I'll leave you to say goodbye to Issy,' he turned and headed to the door.

It was from Issy he got the embrace and the strength, but was mindful to leave her with enough to fight her own rising panic. Their hearts banged against their ribs and he longed to kiss her, to feel her soft lips on his one last time, but it was too public and he was too self-conscious. So he whispered into her ear, 'look after yourself Pint Size. I'll be back before you know it.'

'Write to me.'

'Yes.'

'Promise?' She knew he didn't like writing letters.

'I promise.'

The tannoy announced the flight again.

'You'd better go,' she whimpered, trying to wipe away the tears before he saw them. She was determined to be strong, she didn't want him worrying about her. She needed him to concentrate on what he was going to England for.

'I'm going to miss you, Issy.'

'Me too, Lukey.'

'I love you,' he whispered, afraid someone may overhear him in the noise of the concourse.

'I love you too. Forever.'

'Forever.'

She watched him walk through the doors to the departure area and went to find Dudley. They planned to wait till the plane took off before going home, to be able to report to everyone that they saw him leave.

They were both preoccupied with their own thoughts as they made their way to the viewing gallery. Issy and Luke brought the children once on a Sunday to watch the flights take off and land, not knowing then, how soon one of them would be sky borne.

'You think he'll be alright?' Dudley asked as they sat down on a bench.

'I think so,' she answered, trying to convince herself. She got up and began pacing, he joined her. He couldn't settle either till he knew Luke was in the air. He'd come a long way, and had a lot further to go.

'We might as well talk about Inez's house and what you want me to do with it while we're waiting,' Dudley suggested.

'Didn't Luke talk to you about that already?'

'No, him said that him had too much on him mind, and to talk to you about it when him gone. Him say him will go along with whatever you decide.'

Issy hadn't expected to be talking about this now, but it would help to pass the time and take her mind off his impending departure.

'We talked about renting it out.'

'Yes, I know, but if you want to rent it out you will have to fix it up a little. Miss Inez never bothered too much with the way the house looked, she was just grateful for a roof over her head, but now people want them house to look good.'

'I think it would be better if I come and have a look at it, see what I can do without having to spend too much money, because until Luke start working we just going to be living off our savings and the little that I'm earning.'

'If you want, depending on how much it going to cost, I can lend you a little money to fix it up, and you can pay me back out of the rent, better for the house to be bringing in money than sitting there idle.'

'Let me come and see it first.' Issy didn't like being indebted to his family, she had seen it cause too much bad feeling and falling out. When she wanted something she preferred to throw her hand of pardner till she had enough. That's how they bought the furniture in the house, and fridge, and stove. People wondered how they did it so quickly, but it was none of their business.

They watched planes take off and planes land while waiting for Lukan's. Eventually, it was his time. The propellers began slowly, before gradually becoming a blur as the plane began to taxi down the runway, inching along at first, like a baby taking its first tentative steps, then, gaining in confidence, began picking up speed, running. Confidence turned to pride as it dipped its tail, lifted its nose, and took off. Not a backward glance as it hurtled away from the green, lush land and the turquoise sea into the unknown.

'Bye bye Lukey,' Issy said under her breath assured that, above the roar of the engine, above the whirl of the propellers, above the chatter and the excitement of the crowds, above the anxious bellowing in his head, her heard her.

Chapter 16

Dear Issy,

I just want you to know that I arrive safely. Your Uncle William and his wife was at the airport to meet me. They are really nice people, and I'm settling into their house. I get a job already. The first week after I get here, William (him say to call his William, I'm not being disrespectful) take me to his site manager and they take me on straight away. They ask me to make a few joints and put a cabinet together. I didn't even have to make all the parts, just put them together. The manager say him impressed with my work, but because I just come him have to start me on the lowest wage, but I can work my way up quick, because he can see that me good.

William say not to worry about it, that's how everybody start off, but Issy, even the bottom level is more than twice what I was earning over there, and because them have so much work, there's a lot of overtime. Your uncle is helping me to open a bank account, because him say it's not good to carry your money around with you, especially when is not you one living in the house. They have two boarders (they call them lodgers here) apart from me.

I know it's only two weeks but I miss you already. I miss the children too. Kiss everybody for me. Write to me soon, let me know what's going on with Mama's house.

Your husband,

Lukan.

Dear Jez,

I just want you to know that I arrive safely. I'm sorry I didn't get a chance to come and see you the week before I leave but everything was so busy. I'm staying with one of Issy's uncles. They're nice people and they looking after me like I was one of their own. I get a job, so I will be able to start sending money soon. Issy will send the money for the girls every month. It will be easier that way.

England isn't what I was expecting. Everybody live inside their house, people don't know the people in the next house even though a lot of the houses join up together. I'm going to sign off now as I have a lot of letters to write.

Kiss the girls for me, I miss them.

Lukan.

Dear Uncle Dudley,

I just want you to know that I arrive safely. Thanks for taking me to the airport. The flight took over nine hours, my legs was stiff as board when I get off. They make the plane seats for shorter people. Issy's uncle and his wife are decent people, they treating me like one of their family. I get a job already, working on a building site. They paying good money, but after a few month, if I keep up the standard of my work I could be on more. It shouldn't be hard because a lot of things come ready cut and we just have to put them together. It's easy work, but I'm not used to the cold yet.

William take me to buy a donkey jacket to keep warm, but my fingers feel the cold badly. William say it's not so bad in the summer. They build a lot with brick here, so it take longer for a house to go up. Is the brick layers I feel sorry for, because they always working outside, at least I get to work inside sometimes.

Keep an eye out for Jez and the girls for me please Uncle.

I miss everybody.

Lukan.

Dear Pastor Morgan,

I just want you to know I arrive safely. I made contact with Pastor McCullough a few days after I arrive. Thanks for sending to tell him about me. I went to church on Sunday and was warmly received by the brethren, two of them are from your parish, Brother Thomas Barclay, and Brother Edward Rickard. They said to say hi. That's what everybody here say, 'hi'.

I want to thank you for your support and the support of the church members over the last few months. I never got a chance to thank you properly for travelling to Savanna-la-Mar to take the service for Mama. Me and Issy are very grateful. Please give my regards and blessings to Brother Tulloch and the prayer meeting band for their support and for the goodbye meeting they had for us.

Pastor, I am in a strange land miles away from home. I know God is with me but can you also remember me in your prayers? Can you please ask God to take care of my wife and children, as I do every day?

Yours truly,
Brother Lukan Levy.

Dear Lukey,

I was so happy to get your letter. When we didn't get a telegram I knew that God had delivered you safely. Lukey, I miss you a lot, and the children miss you too. Lennox keeps asking when you coming back. I'm still trying to get used to sleeping alone, at least you got some practise when I was working nights at the hospital. I've had to cut back on the amount of overtime that I do at night to make sure I'm at home for the children. I didn't realise how easy it was with you here. Elaine sleep in when I have to work nights but I don't like leaving her in the house by herself with all the children. I think she getting more experienced though, I just worry whether she would know what to do in an emergency.

I had a long talk with your Uncle Dudley after you left. I went up to have a look at Miss Inez house because he suggested that it would be good to do some repairs and dress it up a little before renting it out. He said we would get more money for it if we just paint it and put a few shelves in the kitchen and fix up the veranda a little. He said if we didn't have the money now he would pay, and we can pay him back when you start earning. Although I don't like to borrow from family, what he said made sense. I didn't want to worry you with all of this as soon as you land, so I tell him to carry on. He's going to do some of the work himself to try and keep down the price.

When I went up to Sav, Jez offered me a drink, she invited me into her house. I felt a little funny going in there, but I couldn't refuse. Lukey, I was so surprised to see how she living, and how Darcie and Gloria living. It's not right that two of your children should be living in those conditions while the others live so well. I think we should get your Uncle Dudley to fix up her house too. I didn't say anything to him or her about it, because I wanted to know what you think. There's more I want to tell you but I run out of space. These air mail letters don't hold half as much as I want to write. God bless you.

Your loving wife,
Issy.

Dear Lukan,

Thanks for you letter. I'm glad to know you get there safely. I'm happy that you get a job so soon. Remember to look after your money and don't forget why you over there. If other men want to squander what they earning, mek them. You don't have to join them. I talk to your wife about your mother's house. She agree with me to fix it up, but I'm sure

149

she write and tell you that already. I start work on it straight away and finish the work in two weeks flat. I get one of the boys that's not so busy to help me. I have to add his money to the total bill, but it was better to get it finish quick and get somebody in there. I find a tenant straight away, and he move in three days ago. I'm getting a lot more for it because of the little fixing up.

When your wife came up she spend a good hour with Jez in her house. I know she trying to be friendly but I'm not too happy with her spending time with that woman. I don't trust her. It would be wise to tell her not to get too heggs up with Jez.

Once I've taken out my bill, I'll start giving the rent to your wife. It should be a tidy little sum to start putting down for the next one. Your wife tell me about her suggestion and I think it's a good one. She have a wise head on those shoulders Lukan. Don't forget it.

I'm sure you will soon get used to the cold, everybody who go to England complain about it at first, then they get used to it and you don't hear no more complaining, especially when the money start coming in. Just bide your time. It's not forever.

Your Uncle,
Dudley.

Dear Issy,

I was happy to get your letter too. I'm missing everybody too, but like I said in my last letter, I'm keeping busy. It remind me a lot of when I first leave Sav and was boarding out. The only difference is I can't come home every two weeks to see you and the children. Anyway, I was happy today because I get another pay packet. That's why I'm sending you some money. I know you will know how to use it, but just let me tell you that Uncle Dudley write to me and say he will take what we owe him from the rent, so don't worry about sending him any money. He didn't say if you meet the tenant but I expect you gave him permission to appoint somebody in there.

About Jez and the house. I don't know if there will be enough money to fix up her house as well, maybe you can talk to Uncle Dudley. I will write to him as well. Have you seen the girls since I leave? I don't hear from them yet.

I want to get this money in the post to you quickly so I'm going to sign off now.

Your loving husband,

Lukan.

Dear Lukan,

I'm sorry it's taken me such a long time to reply to your letter. I'm pleased that God made it a safe journey for you. There is no need to thank me for the support. As brothers and sisters in Christ it's our duty to support each other, I'm sure you will do the same for your brethrens when they need it.

Your wife and children are attending church regularly and the Lord is blessing them. Yours is a blessed family Brother Lukan, and I pray that he will reunite you all as soon as he sees fit. Please give my regards and blessings to Pastor McCullough, and Brothers Barclay and Rickard. Till we meet again may God watch over you and richly bless your soul.

Your sincerely,

Pastor Morgan.

Dear Jez,

I write to you nearly two months ago now and you don't reply yet. I hope everything is alright. Did you tell the girls that I miss them? I know things are a little more difficult with transport now that I'm not there, but Uncle Dudley say he will take the girls to Issy every two weeks if you get them ready.

Issy suggested to me that I should get Uncle Dudley to fix

up your house like he fix up Mama's. I think it's a good idea. If you want it done, talk to Uncle Dudley, he will sort it all out. Issy say that if you want a couple pairs of curtains she will make them for you, but you have to tell her what colour and give her the measurement, and send a sample of the cloth and she will try and match it as close as she can.

How are you getting on with the new tenant in Mama's house? Write to me soon.

I'm missing all of you.

Lukan.

Dear Lukey,

Thanks for the money. I was surprised by how much there was. I was able to make it stretch quite far, and what with the money coming in from Inez's house we should be able to pay off your Uncle Dudley in the next couple of weeks. He said he talked to Jez about fixing up the house, and she agree. She don't want me to make the curtains for her though, she said she will get her own curtains, but she want us to pay for them. I don't mind that if she keep the cost reasonable. It's the girls I'm more concerned about. I only see them once since you leave. It seem like she not so interested in sending them. Dudley said when he went to pick them up the last time they were still outside playing. She said they weren't going, because she couldn't see the point of sending them to go and spend time with somebody who wasn't their parent. Even though he explained that it was their brothers and sister they would be spending time with, she wouldn't budge. Luke you need to write to her and tell her to let the girls come.

As for our children, they are still missing you, but Lennox has stopped asking me every ten minutes when you coming back. Now it's about every two days. I have to tell Irene not to get too angry with him. They all doing well at school, especially Irene, she get the scholarship for Clarendon College. I wanted to tell you as soon as we got the letter. It's times like that when I miss you so much, and when I have to get into the empty bed, night after night. Lilly-Mae put out another teeth last week, everybody saying you can tell she your daughter, you have the same gap teeth, only Lilly's bigger. You should see how proud she look when people call her Lukan's daughter, like she understand. All Lennox talk about when he's not asking when you coming back, is that his Daddy in England, and he's going to England to see him. I don't know where he get that from but he seems convinced and I don't want to upset him by telling him anything different.

The only thing bad I have to report is that Ivan have a sore on his foot that isn't reacting to any treatment. They thought it was ringworm at first but now they're not sure. Anyway, I'm trusting God that it will clear up soon. Take care and write soon.

Your loving wife,

Issy.

Dear Lukan,

I hope these few words reach you in good health. I know from talking to Issy that things are going well. I'm writing to let you know that I finish doing the work on Jez's house, it look a hundred times better. If it alright with you I'll take my pay back from the rent for Inez house.

Lukan, I just want to ask you if you ever sort out who own Jez's house. I know you build it and was living there, but did you ever draw up any deed of ownership? I didn't want to ask Issy because I don't know how much you tell her about you and Jez. If you didn't sort out ownership I think you should do it now. The house is worth a bit of money now I've fixed it up, and you married now, you can't leave these things hanging. If you want, I'll start looking into it for you.

Your sincerely,

Dudley.

Dear Issy,

I hope everything alright with everybody. How is Ivan's foot? I still don't hear from Jez. I hear from Uncle Dudley this week but him didn't mention if Jez letting the girls come to visit. Him say that him finish her house. Did you go up to see it?

I'm sending the money as usual. Uncle Dudley say him will take the money for Jez's house from the rent, so you don't need to pay him anything. I'm feeling tired. All I do since I come here is work, sleep and go to church. Sometimes I'm so tired I fall asleep during the sermon. I don't think I can take a whole year of this, of not seeing you and the children. Let me know which bills still leave to pay when you write next time. Remember to tell Irene congratulations.

Tell Uncle Dudley thanks for the house for me, and that I will write to him soon about the other matter. I miss you.

Your loving husband,

Luke .

Dear Jez,

I'm writing to you again to beg you to let the girls go and see their brothers and sisters. Uncle Dudley say him talk to Darcie and Gloria and they want to go, but you stopping them. I don't know why you doing it Jez, when all I ever do is try to be fair to you and them.

I hope you like the house.

Luke.

Dear Lukey,

Thanks for the money. It seem to be one disaster after another. No matter what we try with Ivan, his foot not getting any better, and now Lilly-Mae have some kind of pneumonia. I have to ask Irene to stay home with her a couple of days because I couldn't afford to take any more time off.

As regards the money, almost everything paid for now, and I'm expecting a hand of pardner in three weeks time. That means we can start banking money again, that's if your uncle is still alright with taking his from the rent. In a couple of months we will finish paying him back and that money will be going into the bank too.

Luke I can't believe how quickly we manage to sort things out, but with all the overtime and the backwards and forwards to Sav, and looking after the children by myself – I'm tired, and I miss you. The children miss you too, and now that Lilly-Mae sick, she ask for you more. Maybe you should think about coming home, even if it's only for a few months. And by the way, Darcie and Gloria don't come to visit since you leave. The only time I see them is when I go up to Sav to see about the houses. They're missing you too. Think about it Luke.

Your loving wife,
Issy.

Dear Issy,

I nearly cry when I read your last letter. What's the point of the money if you there and miserable and me here and miserable. Don't get me wrong, I like living with your uncle but not as much as I like living with my wife and children. I talk to William about the situation and he suggest that I come home for a few months. There's still plenty work over here, so if I save up for a couple more months I can afford the plane ticket, but it would mean I wouldn't be able to send you any money. Can you manage on what I'm sending now if I don't send any for a couple more months?

How is Ivan and Lilly-Mae? Did you ask for a prayer at church? Maybe you should ask for a prayer meeting.

I finally hear from Jez. Just one line she write. *If you want to see your children come and get them yourself.* I really don't know what's wrong with that woman, after everything I've done. Let me know what you think.

Your loving husband,

Luke.

Dear Brother Levy,

I hope this letter finds you strong in the Lord. I am taking the trouble to write to you because I think you are needed with your family. I don't interfere in my members' life unless I think there is some detriment to them. The church has been praying for your step-son for weeks, and now for your daughter. Your wife is trying her hardest but she is struggling. She's probably not telling you that because she doesn't want to worry you. I don't want to worry you either, but one of the visionaries in the church said she saw a dark cloud over the house. We are praying to lift the cloud, and I trust that God will work miracles and wonders, but I think your wife needs your support. I would urge you to try and come back home as soon as possible.

Yours in Christ,

Pastor Morgan.

'Telegram for Mrs Isabell Levy.' The post man announced.

'I'm Mrs Levy.' Isabell came onto the veranda, heart pounding the instant she heard the word telegram. Something's happened to Luke was her immediate thought. As if she needed anything else to go wrong.

'Sign here please.' He held out the paper and her hands shook as she signed.

'Do you want me to wait till you open it?' he enquired cordially, fully prepared for his invitation to be declined, but most times people receiving telegrams wanted somebody around to share the bad news, as most of his deliveries contained bad news.

'Oh my God,' she said dropping like a dead weight on the bench and bursting into tears.

'Sorry, Mrs Levy, is it bad news.'

'No, it's not bad news, Lukey's coming home day after tomorrow,' and she sobbed even harder.

The telegram man looked on perplexed, he didn't get it. Good news usually made people happy, jump up and down even lift him off his feet and swing him round. Bad news made them sit down and cry, but she was laughing and crying at the same time.

'Do you need any more help?' he enquired, not knowing if his services were required for condolences purposes.

'No, no thank you Sir, I need to go and tell my children, their father is coming home. Thank you Sir, God bless you.'

It was a good job when it was like this. He liked to leave people happy. He just hoped his next one would be as welcomed.

Chapter 17

Dudley saw him first.

'See him deh.' He was almost as excited as Issy. It hardly seem like six months since they dropped him and his bags off, and watched him walk through the doors on the other side of the room with a bewildered look on his face. He could hardly believe the tall confident man striding toward them, grin spreading from one side of his face to the other, his gap in full view, was his nephew, who, a few years ago didn't want to leave Sav-la-Mar.

Issy couldn't believe it either. Six months had changed him. He looked broader, his skin was paler, like he'd drunk too much milk and it had diluted his pigment. His hair had grown, it was the longest she'd ever seen it, and curly, no, not curly, wavy. He was wearing a cream pair of pants and a pale blue and white striped shirt. For a split second he reminded her of Easton, the same confident walk, the same head up in the air, the same long sure strides, like he knew where he was going.

He saw them waving, and as soon as he was through the barrier Issy threw herself at him. He had to drop his bag to catch her. It didn't matter that it was public, he held her soft body against his, lifting her clean off the floor like a child, only she was no child, and if his Uncle Dudley wasn't there he would have suggested they go somewhere, find a room or something, and get to know each other again before he had to account to the children or anyone else. He was as stiff as a clothes line pole. He'd been dreaming of this moment for months, and since he made the decision to come just three days ago, it's all he could think about. He was rigid almost every waking moment. Issy's head was on every nail he picked up, on every screw, every plank of wood, every hinge, every bracket. He saw her smile in anything that reflected light. He saw them tangled up in her wedding dress, laughing and getting ready for the next round, saw her the night before he left, her wide eyes as he thrust deep inside her and she tried not to moan out loud, or to scream, trying hard not to make any sound that would wake the children. He felt her damp thighs around his waist, and her wet cave suck him in like quicksand, felt the roundness of her buttocks as he cupped them in his hands and drew her in even closer. He saw her breasts, which got bigger, rounder, and fleshier with every baby, shimmer and tremble when he licked her nipples.

'Oh my Pint Size Beauty,' he'd said over and over coaxing her to her total fulfilment. What started as a joke was now firmly part of their lovemaking. She knew that when he started with the Pint Size Beauty that he was beginning to build to his peak, it was his five minute warning, his indication that he had climbed to the top of the waterfall and wanted her to join his as he crashed over the side, falling and tumbling into the foaming waters at the bottom.

'Issy Baby, Issy Pint Size, Issy Beauty.' He'd mumbled and muttered, almost incoherent in his fall.

She'd arched her back and travelled to meet him. They'd met in the middle and fell, rolling and tumbling and spinning as they crashed, wet and spent into the torrent of the waterfall. He remembered how they'd held each other, fearing they would drown if they let go, realising that they were agreeing to give this up for a long time.

Now that wait was over. He was back and she was in his arms.

She felt his chest like a wall as she flew into him. As her feet dangled off the floor she felt the change in him. He was more solid, had become a man of more substance, there was something different about him, something she would have to get to know for the first time, but there was something the same. She knew what he was feeling, she always did, he could never hide it from her, even when they were in church and he was kneeling down to pray she could tell. She would mockingly chide him later on, tell him he needed to ask God for forgiveness for thinking lewd thoughts in his temple. He'd wrap his arms around her from behind and say, 'But I'm not in church now. How about it?' Once in a while, when none of the children were home they would head to their bedroom and make as much noise as they wanted. She loved it when she could just let go. There was something special about those times.

She forgot about Dudley patiently waiting his turn to be acknowledged, until he coughed. Luke looked up and allowed her to slide slowly over his protrusion to the floor.

'Lukan!' Dudley exclaimed shaking his hand with one hand and slapping his back with the other.

'Uncle,' Luke greeted him, feeling the love that flowed from his uncle.

'Look like England agree with you. You look good.' He stood back and looked at him; like he'd just finished sculpting him and was admiring his handy work.

'Thanks Uncle, must be the cold,' he laughed as Dudley picked up his bag and started to walk back to the car.

'Where's the children?'

'They're at home, I let them have the day off school, they wanted to come to meet you but as there wasn't enough space for all of them, so I said none of them could come.'

160

'I can't wait to see them.'

He blinked as he walked out into the bright sunshine. In six short months he'd forgotten the intensity of the Jamaican sun, the way it bathed your skin before gently seeping into your bones, warming you from the inside out. The sun in England was like an imitation of the real thing, there was light, but very often no heat. Stopping for a second to take it in, he noticed several other doing the same thing, looking up to the heavens as if thanking God for their safe return. One middle aged gentleman stretched his arms out to the sun, as though he wanted to draw it down from the sky and hug it close to his chest. Lukan wondered how long he'd been away.

Issy and Dudley wanted to hear about the flight, about what it was like being up there, about the food, the other passengers, about take off and landing. Lukan tried to answer them, while appreciating for the first time the colour and vibrancy of his home, the brightly painted houses, such a sharp contrast to the monotony of brick and stone and slate in England. He'd never again take for granted crotons, frangipani and hibiscus, or the Aloe that lined the streets as his uncle drove deftly around the potholes in the road.

As they strolled up the steps to the veranda Issy was surprised that no one ran out to meet them. Walking into the living room she saw Irene with Lloyd over her knees slapping his back hard, the other two watched anxiously.

'Daddy!' Lennox was the first to see them.

They all turned to look at Lukan, just as a genep seed flew out of Lloyd's mouth, and landed on the floor in front of them. He gasped, flew off Irene's knees straight into his father's arms, holding on to him as though Lukan had personally plucked the seed out of his throat.

'What happened?' Issy was shaking. 'I just turn my back for two minutes and this…' the rest of the sentence was lost as she looked from one to the other, as if counting them and mentally checking that they were all OK. 'Irene, why d'you give him the genep?'

'I didn't give it to him Mama, it was Ivan.'

'I didn't give it to him,' Ivan defended himself, 'he took it off the table.'

'How many times I must tell you not to leave geneps and peanuts in their reach. You see what I mean now. You could've killed him.'

'I put them out of his reach, he climbed up on the chair to get them.' Ivan defended himself.

'Ivan you have an excuse for…'

'No point arguing about it. Lloydy's alright,' Luke tried to calm the situation. 'It's a good job Irene knew what to do.' He looked from Issy to Irene, who was rightfully aggrieved for not being praised for saving her brother's life.

'You see what I have to deal with?' Issy appealed to Lukan, eyes wide open, on the verge of tears. This was not how she'd planned his homecoming.

Lukan wanted to comfort her, to hold her and take the concern out of her eyes, but Lloyd was clinging to him like a leech. He put his arm out to his other children who each took up their place in the formation of the twisted and entwined tree trunk. Issy and Dudley looked on, relieved that the danger had past.

Chapter 18

'Daddy!' Darcie saw him first, flying down the veranda steps two at a time to him. Gloria, not one to rush at anything, followed more slowly, giving her sister time to get her embraces out of the way, so she could have her father to herself. He noticed this about Gloria, she didn't like to share him, didn't like to sit on his knee if Darcie, or any of the other children was on the other one. He'd worried about her the most, thought she would miss him the most. She was quiet, private, like he used to be at her age.

Like his other children they'd both grown, and he was just marvelling at their height, when Jez appeared on the veranda.

'You come back,' she said, as though he'd just gone down the road for some flour, instead of halfway across the world.

'Yy…ee…s,' he stuttered, stunned by her transformation. He started at her head, hair out of plaits and piled up in a kind of beehive style on top of her head, making her look taller. She was wearing a deep red sleeveless dress, with a deep neckline that just showed the top of her breasts. Tightly belted at the waist, with a wide white belt, it hovered just above her knees. Her long, smooth legs ended in a pair of white sandals with a small heel.

He couldn't hide his surprise or his appreciation. He'd never seen her looking like this. There was something else, though, other than her clothes and her hair. It was her skin. It had lost that ghost like transparency, it now had depth and body. Following his eyes Darcie said, 'See how Mama change?'

'Yy…ee…s,' he stuttered again, rooted to the spot but wanting to scrape her up and peel off what she was wearing.

Now that his mother's house was rented, he had to either visit his daughters at Jez's house or take them to his uncle's where he was staying. He'd agreed it with Dudley that if things got difficult at Jez's he'd bring the girls over, but after he'd handed out the presents he'd brought back for them, clothes and shoes that he hoped would fit, and au de cologne and toiletries, the girls went out to show off their wares and left their parents to talk.

'You look good Jez,' Lukan ventured as soon as the girls were out of earshot.

'You don't look too bad yourself,' she offered, 'it look like England agree with you.'

'It's the same thing Uncle Dudley said.'

'There's not much me and Dudley see eye to eye on, but him right.'

'Why didn't you write to me Jez?' he asked quietly in the silence that was growing between them.

'I did write' she retorted, crossing one long leg over the other and sitting up straight, as though preparing for battle.

'Just one line?' To him that was not a letter.

'It only take one line to say what I wanted to say.'

'And why didn't you send the girls to Issy.'

Jez changed legs.

'I'm surprised she didn't tell you.'

'She seh you seh there was no point sending them to somebody who wasn't their parent.'

'So if you know why you asking me again?'

'Jez, I want my children to know each other, to grow up together, I don't want you…'

'Then you should stay with them and…'

'You not going to tell me what I can and can't do with my life and when…'

'Don't shout at me Luke. You can't just come in my house and start shou...'

'Is my house too, don't forget.'

At this she stood up, flames flickering in her eyes, hands on hips and chest pushed up like a cock about to peck.

'This stop being *your* house the minute you married that woman.'

'She's not *'that woman,'* she's my wife,' he stood up too, partly to defend Issy and partly because he felt disadvantaged by her height, 'you should show some respect after all she do for you.'

'Oh, so is that what you come here to tell me? That I should bow down to that money grabbing, bible-thumping woman, who would send her husband to the other side of the world for a few sheckles.'

'Don't tell be you don't benefit from the money I earn, Issy make sure she...'

'She make sure she spend your money the way she want to...'

'Shut up Jez!' he was losing control, he'd only ever seen her like this once, so hot and fiery, he didn't know how to handle this.

'Or what Lukan?' she challenged him, pushing her face into his.

Without any warning, any forethought, any planning, any reason; he kissed her, put his hand behind her head, pulled her to him and silenced her with his lips. He pressed hard, flattening them against his, before pushing his tongue deep inside her mouth, taking charge of her tongue, pulling her to him till her neck tilted up and her body arched against his.

She felt his body hard against the thin material of her dress, felt the stiffness in his pants and reached down to stroke him. He ran his hands up her legs, under her dress and felt the tops of her stockings. That's why her legs look so smooth he thought as he carried on his search for her mound. She spread her legs to let his finger in through the side of her panties, into her warm moistness. There was an ache in him that he knew only she could satisfy, one that he'd been trying to deny since the last time they were together. He thought he'd eradicated this desire for her, but here it was again, pulsing through every strand of him, running like bushfire through his body. He allowed her to pull him to the bedroom they once shared.

'Jez, the girls,' he said weakly.

'They're not coming back for now. They gone to show off their things. They know you not leaving for now,' she assured him in hot, panting puffs.

She unbuckled his belt and he let his pants fall to his ankles, lowering herself she slid his underpants down to join it, exposing his erect and hungry shaft. She took it in both hands and began massaging, when she lowered her lips over the tip and slid it into her wet mouth, sparks ricocheted around his body, like lightening bouncing off mountains.

'Sit on the bed,' she instructed as she removed her panties. Sitting astride him she lowered herself onto his upstanding rod. She moved on him teasingly, tantalisingly till his pleasure receptors were full and he emptied them gratefully into her waiting receptacle. She looked down at him and smiled.

'Didn't I tell you you would be back? You and me are made for each other.'

'Jez,' he said feebly, already filling up with self loathing, 'this have to stop.'

'It wasn't me that started it Luke.' Her voice was soft as she wiped the sweat from his forehead.

By the time the girls came back it was nearly dark and he'd watched Jez cook, moving nimbly and happily around the small kitchen. He had time to take in the changes Issy had made, the fresh paint, the new curtains, the rugs on the floor. She was a good woman, the best. As he left them to go to Dudley for the night, full of callaloo and salt fish, fried sweet potatoes and boiled yam, he felt confused and very ashamed.

Chapter 19

Lukan and Issy's life continued in the same vein as his home coming. One or the other of the children was always sick, Ivan's skin cleared up inexplicably, but Lloyd got a sore on his big toe that became infected. The antibiotics didn't work, but a poultice Luke made, did. Lilly-Mae's ear infection got better, but Lennox got whooping cough and kept the household awake at nights for months, so they were all fatigued in the day. Lukan picked up work straight away, making furniture at first, then within a month he was back on a building job, but always seemed irritable from lack of sleep and hard work.

He went to church on Sundays, and even joined the prayer meeting group. He prayed often for forgiveness, but was never convinced that he was totally forgiven, as, although he hadn't been with Jez again, he still thought about her in that way. Issy put his distractions down to tiredness.

The girls were old enough now to travel on the bus if Jez put them on at one end and he met them at the other. There was no need for him to see her so often, but Darcie was beginning to shape up so much like her mother that he couldn't help seeing Jez when he looked at her.

The stress of the children being sick was affecting Issy. She had difficulty sleeping, was irritable, and little things that they would laugh off before, blew up in to big arguments; where he put his shoes, where she hung her hat, his insistence on putting up the bags of herbs Inez left them, that Issy had kept out of respect, but didn't want hung up around the house anymore. She couldn't understand why he was doing it.

He started to criticise her food, the amount of hours she worked, and how often she left the children with maids or with Ivan or Irene. He implied that if she stayed home more, the children wouldn't be so sick, as if she could be directly responsible for whooping cough. An uneasy undercurrent ran between them, which intensified when Darcie and Gloria came to visit.

Then Issy vomited one morning as she prepared breakfast. Oh God, not now she thought, not in the middle of all this. She called Irene to finish the breakfast and went to lie down. When Luke returned from the bathroom he seemed irritated to see her lying there.

'I thought you was making breakfast,' he said, pushing the door shut with his foot and allowing his towel to fall to the floor.

'I don't feel too good,' she said weakly.

'Not you too,' he raised his eyes to heaven, as if asking God what he'd done to deserve this.

It was too much for Issy. She looked at his naked body, toned and chiselled, and wondered what was happening to them. Time past he would have rushed to her side, put his hand on her forehead and checked if she was alright. He'd want to know where it hurt, would even joke about kissing it better. Now he was looking at her like an unwelcome cockroach. It was too much. The tension she'd been feeling for the past few weeks, the fatigue of trying to manage work and home, the distance that was growing between them, that look on his face, was more than she could take, and the dam that she'd so carefully constructed began to crack, sprung a leak which trickled silently down her face, and opened swiftly into a gushing torrent. There was not a finger big enough to plug it and it crumbled under the weight of her tears.

Luke was alarmed. He flashed back to Lennox's birth.

'Dear God,' he prayed silently, 'not this, not now,' while Issy's body racked with the conflicting mission of letting go and holding back her tears. He was on his knees in front of her, lifting her chin up to look into her face, and for a moment, in the blink between the curtain of tears, she saw her panic reflected in his eyes. She was not a crier; she faced things head on, buckled down and dealt with them. This must be something big.

'Issy, what's the matter?' Anxiety spiked his words. She was too choked to reply. He sat on the bed beside her, arm round her shoulder and waited with her till her body calmed and the flood dwindled to a stream.

'You want some water?'

She nodded and he pulled on a pair of shorts as he headed for the kitchen. She gulped it down, desperate to replenish the reservoir she'd just emptied.

'I'm pregnant Luke.' Her voice was lifeless, at odds with the new life she was declaring. She searched his face for something to encourage the life back into her, a spark of joy, the little dance he did at the news of previous declarations.

He slumped onto the bed beside her, heavy, like wet cement.

'Luke? What you thinking?' she asked, when he said nothing.

'It's bad timing.'

'I know.' She burst into tears again, partly because she agreed with him, but more because he didn't disagreed with her. She was willing, was prepared, to be persuaded otherwise.

Irene's knock on the door to tell them the breakfast was ready halted her blubbering for a second. She didn't want the children to see her cry. She didn't want them to think she was weak. She had to show them she was strong for when Luke was away and she was in charge of their discipline. They couldn't see her crying.

'Alright Irene, we're coming,' Luke answered.

'Just tell her I'm still not feeling too well,' Issy curled up on her side, pulling her knees up, protecting the seed that had just begun its incubation. Lukan flashed a glance at her as he walked to the door. He remembered that posture, and didn't want to go there again. He'd have to make sure she stayed out of that place.

In two strides he was back by her side. Dropping to his knees, he stroked her arm, and allowed his hand to trail over her hip and down her folded leg.

'Issy, it's going to be alright. This baby is a gift from God, and we should be grateful. God wouldn't give us something we can't manage.'

She stopped in mid sob, and he saw a flicker of light in her eyes, like his words had illuminated a corner of her soul. It was his first recognition that she needed him, his approval, his endorsement, his consent. He'd only ever seen her strength, now he knew her vulnerability. He saw in that moment how much he'd relied on her strength, had accepted her authority without question and had acquiesced to it. Now he was seeing her for the first time, seeing all of her. He saw the toll his absence had taken on her and felt ashamed that he hadn't seen it sooner.

'Oh, Issy, I'm sorry,' he said, trying to caress her curled up body. She straightened her knees and he lay down beside her and held her close. 'It's going to be alright Issy, I promise you.'

Irene's light tap on the door reminded them again that breakfast was ready.

'Go on,' Issy urged him, 'I'll come out soon.' She didn't feel so lonely anymore; felt she had Luke back from wherever he'd gone the last few months.

Despite the children's sickness and the work, Lukan felt light, like he'd taken off the heavy chain mail suit he'd been wearing for the last few weeks. Nothing had changed, and yet everything had changed. He caught himself looking at Issy from time to time, seeing her through new eyes. She wasn't invincible as he'd thought, and it made her more attractive.

Issy didn't want to tell anybody about the baby till she started to show, that's how she preferred it, in case anything happened. She was superstitious that way. She'd seen too many disappointed would be mothers at the hospital. She knew she was strong and carried her children easily, but she still preferred to play it safe. This one started the same as all the others. The vomiting would soon pass, her breasts were already getting tender, she was putting on weight which seemed to go on quicker with each pregnancy, but Lukey loved her when she was pregnant. It wasn't what they planned, but it was the way of the Lord.

As she and Luke walked in to church on Sunday the children filing in behind them, Pastor Morgan shook their hands and quietly asked if they could stay behind after church. He wanted a word with them. Issy found it difficult to focus on the service, partly because she was tired and still feeling a little nauseous, and partly because her mind kept wondering what Pastor might want to talk to them about. He looked so serious. Lukan too was preoccupied with thought other than that of the sermon, though he tuned in enough to hear that God hated a deceitful man.

'Just because the Bible says 'man', the women shouldn't think God don't mean them. God hates deceit whoever it is, man, woman or child. There is no place for deceit in heaven, no place at all for it at God's right hand, and if that's where you hope to be you'd better drop deceit from your life.'

Lukan shuffled in his seat, his mind drifting to Jez. Yes, he had been deceitful but he'd asked for forgiveness, and hadn't God blessed him and his wife with another child? Surely that was Gods way of showing him that he was forgiven. They came today to give God thanks, and to ask for his strength to cope with everything that was happening. The pregnancy had drawn them together, and yes, they were still struggling without enough sleep, but they were united, moving forward together again, invincible, able to overcome anything.

'Sit down Sister Levy, Brother Levy,' Pastor Morgan waved at the small table in the corner of the side room, around which were four chairs, 'Sister Pauline won't be long.'

'Sister Pauline?' Issy and Lukan both said, surprised.

'Yes, she soon come, she asked me if it was alright to talk to you.'

'Why didn't she just talk to us herself?' Issy was puzzled. She and Pauline got on quite well, true they weren't bosom pals but she didn't think they'd done anything to upset her that they couldn't sort out themselves. These kinds of meetings between Pastor and members of the congregation were only required to sort out quarrels that the members couldn't resolve themselves.

'She wanted me to hear what she's going to say. She came to me and asked for my advice about whether or not she should tell you.'

'Tell us what?' Lukan was feeling a little uneasy. What if someone had discovered about him and Jez? But, he consoled himself, nobody but him and Jez knew. He hadn't told a soul, and he hoped to God she hadn't either.

'Oh, here she is now. Over here Sister Pauline, come and take a seat.' Pastor Morgan held his hand out, guiding her into the straight back wooden chair, before sitting down.

Sister Pauline, a thin light-skinned spinster in her early forties, was one of the pillars of the church. She'd been saved for a long time and had worshipped at this church for most of her life. She knew Issy well, if fact had been one of the women who'd attended to her as she thrashed on the floor that night when she bared her soul to God, and asked him to send her a good Christian man. Church was her life. She had no children, no husband, and no social life; she dressed simply and wore her hair in a tight knot on the top of her head. She often stayed behind after church to talk to the Pastor, sometimes with other members, sometimes on her own.

Pastor Morgan cleared his throat, looked down at his hands, then up into the perplexed and anxious faces of Lukan and Issy. He had sought divine guidance on this matter, and in the end, had been persuaded to hold this meeting, because he knew what was going on in the family of this devoted couple.

'Sister Pauline said she had a dream,' he began, tentatively, as if choosing each word from a rack and putting them out one by one on the table to form the sentence. 'She came to me and asked my permission to tell you about it.'

'Why couldn't you just come and tell us yourself?' Issy couldn't help blurting out to Sister Pauline. This was feeling weird.

'Because she feels it was a vision from God, and she didn't want to frighten you. She wanted my reassurance that if it wasn't a message from God that she should not pass it on.'

'What's this dream?' Issy felt a surge of fear like a swelling wave rise up in her, she felt like she was going to vomit, and had to swallow hard. If they were hoping not to frighten her, they had failed.

'Tell them Sister Pauline.' Pastor Morgan handed over to her.

'Wednesday night I went to my bed as usual, drink a cup of hot chocolate and seh me prayers asking God to take charge while I sleep.'

Pastor Morgan cleared his throat again. 'Sister Pauline, I think you just need to tell them about the dream, I have another appointment this afternoon.'

'Yes Pastor,' she apologised, and continued. 'For some reason I see you,' looking straight at Issy, 'and Brother Levy holding a child wrapped up in a white shawl. At first it looked like it was a christening, but then I saw that the two of you was crying, and then you,' looking at Issy again, 'lay the white bundle in a little coffin and you just break down and start to scream. Nothing Brother Levy could do, could console you. Then a big hand came out from nowhere, clapped itself over your mouth and tried to suffocate you. You fall over on your back, struggling and trying to catch your breath. Brother Levy was fighting with the hand, trying to pull it off you, and he was getting more and more tired. And I was watching this and feeling helpless because, try as I might, I couldn't move to come and help you. Then I screamed out, God let me help them!'

She paused, looked at the Pastor who nodded his permission for her to continue.

'Then I hear a voice as clear as you and me talking seh, *tell them they have to leave Clarendon*. Leave Clarendon? I asked, I don't understand. *Tell them they're not safe here, they have to get away from the hand*. Then I wake up and I was sweating, my nightie drench from top to bottom, and for the whole night I was too afraid to go back to sleep.'

Issy and Lukan sat, carved pieces of rock, mouths open, gaping at Sister Pauline's reddened face as she wiped away perspiration with her already damp hanky. Neither knew what to say, and Sister Pauline continued. 'I talked to Pastor about it the next day, that's when he told me that your children them sick. He said we should pray about it and ask for God's guidance about whether I should tell you.'

'And what did God say?' Luke finally found his tongue.

'Well, Brother Lukan, I speak to the Overseer about it, because I know that some people get visions, and I know that Sister Pauline have seen things before and they have happened, but never anything like this, and it's only because I know the struggles you've been having with…'

'And the Overseer seh to tell us? The Overseer believe it, believe that we in danger in Chapeleton?' Luke's voice shook.

'He said to tell you and for you to pray about what you

should do. Only you can decide whether this is a message to flee from danger like the Israelites from Pharaoh or stay and seek the protection of God like Job.'

'Or we could just dismiss it as a dream.' Issy finally spoke, not liking either of the examples or the choices.

'Sister, Brother Levy, whatever you decide to do we will pray with you, we will support you, we will bring the power of God down to guide you and see you through whatever troubles and tribulations you may face.'

Issy looked at him wide eyed with disbelief. She didn't doubt he would support her, but she wasn't ready for any more troubles and tribulations. She had enough on her plate, and had come today to celebrate what she saw as a turning point in their lives.

Sister Pauline, having delivered the bad news, sat quietly looking down and twisting her handkerchief on her lap. She sometimes wished she didn't have what some dubiously called a 'gift.' She felt a bit like Joseph, people generally want to hear about the seven years of plenty, but never about the seven years of lean.

'When did you say you had the dream?' Issy wanted to know.

'Wednesday night.' Sister Pauline raised her head again, but her voice was quiet, as though the recounting of the dream had drained her.

Issy, oscillating between anger, resentment, and mounting panic, wanted to swear at God, wanted to shout at him, ask him what he was doing. Didn't he think they had enough already? She knew she should be grateful to Sister Pauline for telling them, but what was the use of information like this if they couldn't change anything anyway? Did she really have this 'vision' or was she just making it up to get in with Pastor Morgan? At that moment the loathing she felt for Sister Pauline, messenger of darkness, was etched into every muscle of her face. She felt the bile rising in her throat, and ran out of the room, just in time to spew the remnants of her breakfast out in the church yard.

'Let us pray with you before you go,' Pastor Morgan called as Lukan ran after his wife.

'Yes Pastor.' He knew why Issy ran out, he got there just as she was dabbing her lips with her handkerchief. She turned into his arms and shook like a leaf in a turbulent river.

'Pastor wants to pray with us before we go,' he said, when she showed no sign of stopping the trembling. She allowed him to guide her back to the room, and shook all the way through the prayer, where Pastor Morgan asked God to give them wisdom and clear sight to make the right decision, for protection in everything they do, and to know that his love goes with them always.

Issy was glad Irene had taken the other children home. It gave them some thinking time as they walked slowly back down the streets they had, only hours before, tread with such hope and optimism. She shook spasmodically, and Lukan kept his arm around her to steady her. Anyone watching would have thought them very brave to walk down the streets with such open display of affection, especially after being married for so long.

'What we going to do Lukan?'

'I don't know. I can't just make a decision like that.'

'I know. Do you believe her?'

'I suppose so. The Pastor believe her, you heard what him say, that she see things before.'

'We should've asked her what other kinds of things she see, and how many people believe her.'

'I suppose we can still do that.'

'Yes.'

It wasn't till the children were in bed that they raised the issue again.

'Where would we live if we moved from here?' It was Luke who voiced the question in Issy mind.

'I was thinking we could go to Sav-la-Mar. We could ask the tenant to leave and move into Miss Inez house till we can sort out something better.'

'I don't think that would be such a good idea.' The last thing Lukan wanted was Jez and Issy living next door to each other.

'I suppose you're right.' Issy, on reflection realised that's not something she would relish either, even if it would mean the children would get to see more of Darcie and Gloria, but what about Ivan, he would be too far away. 'There's no good schools… I mean the schools in Sav are not as good as the ones here.'

'And Irene's scholarship is for Clarendon College.'

'And my job at the hospital…'

'Yes, and there's not so much work in Sav…'

'Where else then, we could move back to Brandon Hill or even Rock River or…'

'Issy she seh Clarendon, not just Chapelton.'

'I don't even want to think about this Luke. I'm going to sleep, and when I wake up tomorrow, if I still believe her we can talk about it then.'

She was just turning over to nuzzle into his shoulder when she heard the sniffles and scratching on the door, and Lloyd's faint 'Mama.' She flew out of the bed and opened the door just in time to catch him as he collapsed into her arms, drenched in sweat and twitching like someone was passing intermittent electric shocks through his body. His eyes rolled in his head and his tongue flopped about in his mouth. She recognised straight away that he was having an epileptic fit.

'Luke… quick… we have to get him to the hospital,' she screeched, forgetting about the other sleeping children. Her heart pounded as she tried to lay him flat and hold his head so he wouldn't hurt himself.

'How?' Luke looked on in alarm.

'You'll have to use the bike.'

'I can't take him on the bike like that.'

'I'll come with you.'

'Issy, it's not safe.'

'We have to risk it. It's not stopping,' she said as Lloyd's body twitch violently, and then flopped like an exhausted rag doll.

'It stop now.'

'For the time being, but we have to get him to the hospital. I'll sit on the back with him. Hurry up Luke.'

It was a slow and painful journey transporting Lloyd on the back of the scooter, maybe only God knew why Luke had it on trial from one of his work mates who wanted to sell it. Issy didn't think they could afford it, but after tonight she might have to change her mind. Neither of them breathed, and bound by their mutual fear, they each made their decision to believe Sister Pauline.

Chapter 20

Kingston seemed the obvious place. Issy had lived there before, and Mavis was still there. At least she'd have one member of her family to call on for help, and it was Mavis who helped to find them a house to rent. They couldn't afford anything like their own home in Kingston, even with the rent they would get when they rented it out. Houses were so much more expensive in Kingston.

They did everything within a month. Issy asked for a transfer from Chapelton Hospital to Kingston Public Hospital, and as they were short of nurses, they accepted her. Lukan stayed in Chapelton till he finished the contract he was working on while Issy scouted for work for him in Kingston. He picked up a few days here and there and filled in with making furniture till they took him on full time. It made a welcome difference to their budget and their depleted savings which they'd had to dip into to buy more furniture for the house in Kingston.

It was hard to explain the move to the children, they told them it was because Lloyd needed specialist treatment in Kingston and it was too far to keep taking him backward and forward. It wasn't wholly untrue because Kingston Public did have a better epilepsy department than Chapelton. Irene suspected there was more to it than that but she never asked and they never told her about Sister Pauline. For the first few weeks while they settled in they didn't go to church. Lukan and Issy prayed together and with the children, asking for God's guidance and protection.

'Where's Darcie and Gloria going to sleep when they come?' Lennox asked one evening as he and Lloyd fought over who was going to sleep where on the bed.

Issy and Lukan looked at each other, both realising that, in the drama of the move and the incidents which made it necessary, they'd forgotten about Luke's girls. Sav-la-Mar was nearly twice the distance from Kingston as it was from Chapelton, and the fares would be almost double, and as Lennox had noticed, they didn't have as much space in this house.

'I think it would be better if you go up to see them Luke, till things settle down here, maybe till we can afford a bigger place.' Issy really didn't feel she could take on anymore. She was beginning to feel the pregnancy more now, the constant tiredness, and the extra weight. They still hadn't told the children yet, but she'd confided in Mavis, and asked her not to say anything to anybody. Mavis was the only one who knew about Sister Pauline and Issy made her promise to keep it to herself.

'I'll go on Sunday when it's quiet.' Luke interrupted her thoughts.

'Alright then, and I'll take the children to church as I'm off.'

'It would've been good if we could go together.'

'Next week. I have next Sunday off as well.'

'How comes?'

'I swapped with somebody.'

Lukan's head was so full of Kingston and Issy not feeling well, that it wasn't till he was about ten miles from Sav, that he had begun to think about Darcie and Gloria. He hadn't seen them in over three months, not since that time… he couldn't bring himself to think about that last time. So much had happened since then that he'd hardly thought about Jez. He focused on the small gifts he was bringing for the girls and on telling them that they'd all gone to the market in Kingston to choose the socks and hair grips, and that he had personally chosen the sweets. Issy hadn't had time yet to make any sweets. She told him to apologise to the girls for her, to tell them that she promised to make some next time.

'Look after your mother today, she not feeling too good,' he'd said to the children as he left.

As he walked up the lane to the house, he saw everything with new eyes. The events of the last few months had brought a new maturity to Lukan. He'd never know fear like this before, it's true he'd grown up being afraid, but that was different. That was fear of what people would think about him, fear about whether he would get a girlfriend, fear about whether he would cope in a new situation. Not fear for his life, or more precisely, fear for his children's life. It would be better if it was *his* life that was in danger; at least he would know how to look after himself, but his children... that was something else. He saw Lloyd's face superimposed on the trunk of the bird cherry tree as he passed it, the rolling eyes, the lolling tongue, and hoped Issy would be alright today.

'Daddy! Daddy!' Gloria's voice interrupted his reverie. He'd been in such a daze he hadn't seen her coming. She nearly knocked him over as she flew at him.

'Daddy!'

'How's my little girl?' Holding her at arms length, 'Look like you not so little anymore. Lord how you getting big. I soon won't be able to pick you up.'

'I miss you Daddy.'

'I know, I miss you too! Where's Darcie?' It was very unusual for Darcie not to be the one knocking him over.

'She's inside, she went to the toilet and I see you first. Here she is,' she said looking over her father's shoulder at her sister coming down the steps of the veranda.

Lukan had to look twice. His daughter was the spitting image, the dead stamp of her mother, even had her hair up like the last time he saw Jez. Her skin had always been smooth, without the blemishes of either of her parents. She was a striking girl; all this had happened in the three months he'd not seen her.

She walked to him, her long limbs graceful and swaying, in a way Jez never did, she was more like Issy in her movements, in fact if he didn't know better he would say she was copying the way Issy walked.

'Who is this young lady?' he asked Gloria in mock shock.

'It's Darcie, Daddy, it's just that her hair is different.'

'Don't I get a hold?'

She gave him a limp squeeze, like she was annoyed with him.

'Boy, if I did leave it any longer, I wouldn't recognise you two.'

'Why did you leave it so long Daddy?' Gloria reproached him.

'Baby, it's a long story. The move to Kingston took up a lot of time.'

'When are we coming to Kingston to see you and Lennox and Irene and Lloyd and Lilly-Mae?'

'And Issy, I mean, Miss Issy?' enquired Darcie.

'Soon.' He didn't know how to tell them that there wasn't enough room, or to explain the difficulties of their current situation, so he changed the subject.

'I bring a few things for you from the market in Kingston.' They'd reached the steps of the veranda. 'We all went there last week and…' his voice trailed as he looked up and saw Jez. There was something different about her, not like last time, she wasn't dressed up; just in her regular pants and t-shirt, and her hair was in plaits again, not hanging down but cane rowed up to the crown of her head. Her smile was warm and welcoming, which wasn't surprising after what happened last time, but it wasn't that. He couldn't put his finger on it.

'Hello Jez.' He greeted her, cordially, determined to keep everything out in the open. He had no intention of being alone with her and had made plans for his uncle to pick him up. He planned to stay on the veranda for the whole of this visit.

'You looking a little…tired, Luke.' She cocked her head to one side and looked him up and down.

'I feel it.' He answered, 'that's why it's a lightening visit. Uncle Dudley going to drop me to the bus later so I can get back at a reasonable time, seeing as I'm working tomorrow.' He'd arranged to take the girls to Dudley's for the afternoon, and *he* would drop them back home. He was determined to spend as little time with Jez as possible.

'I need a quick word with you before you go.'

'Alright girls, give me a few minutes with your mother.'

They wandered down the street as he climbed the stairs to the veranda.

'You want a drink?'

'No thanks Jez.'

'You want to sit down?'

'Is this going to take long, you said a quick word.'

'It *is* a quick word, but I think you should sit down.'

Hitching his pants legs up, he sat on the edge of the bench. He looked at her, trying to work out what was different about her, he knew that look from somewhere, and remembered, just as she said, 'I'm pregnant Luke.'

Once, when he was playing cricket, he was daydreaming and didn't see the ball coming till he felt the force of what would have been a six if he hadn't stopped it with the side of his head. He recalled that feeling now, and was grateful that she'd suggested he sat down. He opened his mouth but no sound came out. She folded her arms across her chest and smiled, 'one day you will be as happy about it as me.'

'Jez, are you mad!' he found his voice.

'No Luke, I'm not mad, I'm pregnant.'

Then a thought hit him, maybe it's nothing to do with me. 'Whose is it?' he asked, and knew instantly that he'd insulted her. It was a long shot, but a drowning man will clutch at anything. He'd known for years that Jez refused to go with anyone else, at one stage he'd even been flattered. Now he wished she had, at least he could have legitimate reasonable doubt. But as he sat there, he knew in the eyes of God that this woman was pregnant for him, and he had a wife at home, also pregnant, and he didn't need to ask her how far gone, because he knew, and it would be weeks away from Issy.

He wanted to drop to his knees and pray for God to wipe out the last three months, but instead he sat staring at her, not making any sound.

'You ready Daddy?' Gloria called.

'In a minute, baby.'

Jez laughed. 'You'll have somebody else to call that soon.'

'You can't be serious about keeping it, Jez.'

'What are you suggesting Luke? Tell me. What is *Brother Lukan Levy* suggesting?' the sneer was physical, he felt it hard across his face.

'I don't know,' he slumped into the bench, like someone had taken the hanger out of his shoulders. 'We need to talk.'

'That's what I said, and that's what we're doing.'

'Jez, I have a wife.'

'You shouldda think about that before you come fishing round me.'

'Jez, Issy's pregnant.'

Now it was Jez's turn to look hangerless. This was not what she was expecting, this was not in the plan, her eyes flashed the questions forming in her head, 'why not? Why wouldn't she be?' She'd allowed her heart to override her common sense, had somehow manage to fool herself that because he was with her, he wasn't going with Issy any more, thought she'd done enough to cut that link, but maybe she'd been too hasty, maybe his easy return had lulled her into a false sense of security.

'And what do you want me to do?'

'It would be easier for you to…'

'To what, Luke?' she could feel the hysteria building, and she mustn't get hysterical, she must stay calm, mustn't lose control.

'Jez, I can't afford to have two babies now, can't you see that?'

'Yes' she said slowly, very slowly, as though an idea was filtering in. 'Yes… I see that Luke…'

'So you will make sure…'

'Yes, I will make sure you don't have two babies. I will do this for you Luke, if you don't want two babies.'

Breathing out slowly, trying to hide his relief, he said, 'I will help you with it, let me know how much and I will help you.'

'I don't need your help Luke, I'm going to take care of this one myself. I just want you to remember *it was your choice.*'

'Thanks Jez,' he was almost running down the steps, 'I'll get Uncle Dudley to drop the girls off.'

It was nearly ten o'clock when he got home. After the disastrous start it had turned into a good visit. He hadn't seen his Uncle for a while, and it was good to spend time with him and the girls. He felt he had to tell his uncle why they'd suddenly moved to Kingston.

After a long silence his uncle cleared his throat, 'I would be surprised if it's not Inez that come to that woman in her dream.'

'What would Mama have to do with Sister Pauline?' His mother had never met her, in fact his mother was never very keen on churches, always said they were full of hypocrites and backsliders.

'She was always talking about you and your family needing protection. I used to tell her you look like you were doing just fine without her protection, but she insisted on making those bags of things and that blasted stuff in the bottles. She always said people could put their faith in prayer if they wanted, there was nothing wrong with that, but sometimes prayer needed a helping hand.'

Luke's mind flashed back to the night of Issy's prayer meeting. 'I didn't know she talk to you about those things.'

'There's a lot you don't know about your mother Luke. She was deep, she knew a lot, but she kept it to herself.'

'You don't believe in it, do you Uncle?'

'I keep an open mind Luke. You have your church, and she had that. Your Sister Pauline, you say she have visions. Well your mother could see things too, only they wouldn't call it visions. That's why she keep herself to herself.'

'Anyway, I need to be on my way now.'

'There's just something I need to tell you, because I promised Inez that if you was ever in a situation like this that I would.' He hesitated, trying to find the right words.

'What?' Luke urged.

'She say to try and keep away from Jez.'

'Jez? Why should I keep away from Jez? She's my children's mother, I've known her almost all my life.'

'I'm just telling you what I promised Inez, and this don't have anything to do with what I think of her personally, I'm just passing on a message. And one last thing,' he added, as Luke stared at him bewildered, 'she said if you ever feel unsafe to sprinkle salt all round the house, and around any body that you want to protect. Almost all of those bottles she used to give you had in salt water, plus some other things I help her to write down to give you, if you ever ask for it.

Lukan's head couldn't handle anymore. His daughters came with him as far as the bus stop and he promised to come and see them again soon. Maybe next time he'd get his uncle to pick them up and he would meet them at his house.

They must all be tired and gone to bed early, Lukan thought, as he pushed the door open. He didn't put on any lights, went to the toilet in the dark, brushed his teeth by the full moonlight that flooded in through the bathroom window. There was an unusual quiet in the house, no gentle snores, no grunts or snorts. He crept into his bedroom and reached across the bed for Issy. She wasn't there. He flicked on the light, the bed hadn't been slept in, he went to the children's rooms, nothing, no-one was home. Then he saw the note on the dining table.

I have the children, Issy in hospital Ward 2. Mavis. He wished Mavis had a phone. What had happened to Issy, why was she in hospital? He ran out and flagged down a taxi.

'Kingston Public Hospital.' he ordered.

'You sound like you in a hurry.'

'Just get there as quick as you can.'

'Is a good ting it late,' the driver tried to make conversation but gave up when he got no response.

Why was she in hospital? Did she fall over, did she break something, was she in an accident? With every yard his stomach tightened a little more.

'I'm looking for Isabell Levy.' He told the receptionist, who checked her papers before answering.

'Ward two. Down there on the right hand side.'

'What's wrong with her?' he asked.

'They will tell you that on the ward.' She answered.

He ran to the ward where the ward sister beckoned him over. 'It's not visiting time,' she said in hushed tones, 'who you looking for?'

'Issy, I mean Isabell Levy.'

'Who are you?'

'Lukan Levy, her husband.'

'Alright Mr Levy, as it's you, you can see her.'

'What's wrong with her sister?'

She seemed surprised. 'Nobody tell you?'

'I just got back from Sav-la-Mar, there was only a note on the table that she was here.'

'She had a miscarriage, sir, she loose the baby.'

Lukan didn't hear whatever else she said as she took him to the bed at the end of the ward where Issy lay, crumpled and creased with a thin sheet over her.

'Ten minutes sir,' the ward sister said, 'patients are trying to sleep.'

'Issy, I'm sorry, I'm very, very sorry,' he said, holding and squeezing her hand.

'You don't have to say sorry, it wasn't your fault.'

'You don't understand...' he began, and stopped. He didn't know how to explain that he now understood the look on Jez's face when she said, 'I will make sure you don't have two babies.'

Chapter 21

'We're going to have to use savings to pay Irene's school fees again this month,' Issy said as she sliced the roast breadfruit and arranged the wedges in a circle on the plate. Lukan broke off the tip of a slice and dipped it into the cooked down mackerel sauce still sizzling on the stove.

'I suppose we don't have any choice.' He licked his fingers.

'I wish she could get a scholarship for Excelsior. Maybe if somebody leave…'

'Come on Issy, who going to give up a place at Excelsior, especially if they not paying for it. It's hard enough to get in there even *if* you're paying.'

He dipped another piece of breadfruit into the sauce, breaking off a bit of mackerel with it.

'You should feel lucky that she so bright.'

'She's not the only one though Luke. I want Lennox to sit the exam for Woolmer's Boys when he's old enough. That's going to mean fees too. The competition really fierce down here for places, people send their children to live with relatives so they can go to these schools.'

'You think Lloyd and Lilly will be bright enough to go to Excelsior or Woolmer's?'

'If they keep going like they going now we might have to find school fees for all of them. I don't know how we would manage that, and I really don't want to send them to any riff-raff school.' She sighed, weighed down by her lack of vision.

This was the difference between Issy and Jez. Issy was all for education, she even paid for extra lessons for Irene before she sat the exam for Clarendon College, just to make sure she passed. Jez would prefer to buy clothes and shoes. Darcie and Gloria always look good, but he'd never seen Jez sit down and read a book to them. They just went to the local school, there was never any suggestion that they would go anywhere else, or sit an exam to get into a better school. And yet they were bright too, but they didn't do half the things their children did, like read in church, mostly because they hardly went to church, even though he begged Jez to send them, even if she didn't want to go. They didn't learn to play the piano, or any other musical instrument, didn't go on trips with the school or with church. That's where a lot of their money went, educating the children. It wouldn't be such a worry if they could get good education for free, but it was almost impossible to get that for all of them.

'You know, you don't have to pay for schools in England,' the thought leaked out before he was ready to release it.

'The food ready, go and call the children for me.'

'All right.'

'Wait! What you mean you don't have to pay in England? What you suggesting? That we move to England? Because if that's the case you can get that idea right out of your head Lukan Levy, don't even let it lodge there. It was bad enough moving them here, much less to…'

'Issy, stop! I wasn't suggesting anything, and if I was I would scrub that one out right away. You don't have to…'

'Good, go and call the children, and check the salt round by the back, there was some chickens scratching around there this morning, sprinkle some more if they scratch it away.

'Yes maam.' He saluted bringing both his heels sharply together, 'anything else want me to do maam?'

Laughing, she threw a kitchen cloth at him, and laughed

even more as he ducked to avoid it, tripped over, and fell on his back. She loved Sunday mornings like this, when the children were outside and they just chatted while she cooked breakfast.

'Where's the salt maam?' he brushed himself down, looking wounded and in search of sympathy, which was not forthcoming.

'In the cabinet over the sink.'

Lukan poured some salt into a brown paper bag and took it outside, hoping that no one would see him sprinkling it around the house. People might not understand. He was prepared to say he was doing it to stop ants if anybody did ask, though he had no idea if salt would stop ants. He wasn't sure if it was working, but after what his uncle said, and what happened to Issy, he wasn't taking any chances. He'd started sprinkling it the same night he came home from the hospital after Issy's miscarriage, and had carried on secretly till she caught him one morning when he thought she was sleeping.

'What you doing, Luke?' she'd asked, leaning over the veranda balcony, watching him as he bent low to stop the salt from blowing away in the brisk breeze. Jumping, he'd dropped the bag and spilt the salt, like a sprinkling of dandruff on an old man's bare skull. He'd told her then, fully expecting a backlash, and was wondering how he was going to defend himself against her accusations of heathenism, of believing in obeah and of going against God and all the church stood for. But after listening to him recounting all his uncle had told him, she sat back on the bench, sighed that worn out 'aah' that came from a place where the fight was being lost.

'I suppose it's only salt, it might be good to keep some of the insects out of the house. It's not like those bags of things your moth... Miss Inez used to bring. I wouldn't want anybody seeing you sprinkling herbs and things round the house.'

'You don't mind then?'

'I suppose not, just as long as you don't expect me to go out there and do it.'

It was the first step in her acceptance of the wisdom and ways of Miss Inez, in a belief that was not totally rooted in God's protection. The other step she took some months later, when Lukan was back in England and she had to face things by herself.

It hadn't been an easy decision for Lukan to return to England, but the pressures of finance, and the need for Irene's fees, finally drove them to see another stint in England as a short term fix. It was a different kind of parting, the kind you get when you know the territory and know that you will return. The airport was not as daunting, the goodbyes, although sad, were not as distressing. There was no need for Dudley to come and take him to the airport. One of Lukan's workmates who had a jeep did, and only charged them a few dollars toward the gas.

When Issy stepped back through the door of their house she felt alone in a way she hadn't felt before. With Luke gone, she had the full responsibility of the children again, they were a little older now and there was help from Irene, but she'd had to ask to be transferred to days so she didn't have to pay someone to be at home with them at night, and days didn't pay as much. She had to help with homework and to make sure they were in bed on time. She was being mother and father again, it felt like the night Easton left and she knew she was on her own, at least till he got better, but he never did. He didn't even see Irene anymore, not since she started at Clarendon College. She was always so busy with homework, and it was always up to the children to visit him. Sometimes, when things got really bad for him he would go and stay with him mother, that way Ivan got to see him, but she wasn't entirely happy that he was setting an example for Ivan she hoped he would never follow. Luke was more of a father to

Ivan and Irene. It wasn't really his responsibility to have to find the fees for Irene, but if it was left to Easton, they wouldn't eat, let alone pay school fees.

They hadn't settled into church too well, hadn't had time yet to build up the strong relationships they had at home. They'd asked Pastor Morgan not to say anything to their new pastor, as they wanted to make a new start. People in Kingston seemed preoccupied with their own lives. They were too busy to join any of the bands, so for many weeks were little more than visitors. She couldn't rely on the members support, Mavis had finally been promoted to manageress and seemed to spend even more time at work, she helped out when she could, but it wasn't that often any more. Issy felt alone. She sighed again, not least because they'd agreed that Luke would stay for a year. They'd begin saving as soon as Luke paid off her Uncle William for the emergency plane ticket he used to come out. Issy sighed again. This wasn't what she wanted now; she was feeling exposed, vulnerable, a little less sure of herself.

The miscarriage had shaken her badly. She'd always carried a belief that only weak women lost babies, had always prided herself on the fact that she carried her children well, and delivered them easily. Even Lennox, she had no problem delivering him, it was only the memory of Isaac that had thrown her into that strange place for a while. But she had come out of it, had gone on to have other children easily. Although she didn't believe Luke one hundred percent about what Miss Inez said, and still put her faith in God, without him here she felt like the only one on the beach after everyone had gone home, easy to see, an easy target.

She sat at the dining table, hands in her head, and allowed herself to cry, warm salty streams bursting out from under her eyelids and snaking their way over her cheekbones, before sliding off the end of her chin onto the unwelcoming plastic table cloth, where each drop found a companion and huddled together to form a lake of wretchedness. She tried to count her blessings, but self pity had taken hold, she tried to thank God for all he'd done for her, but her loss got in the way, and she could only see the difficulties ahead. Maybe tomorrow she would be able to appreciate her good fortune in having a man who was faithful to her, who believed in the sanctity of their marriage, who looked after his children, and hers. She would be grateful that her children were all well, that Lloyd's epilepsy had virtually disappeared with the treatment from the hospital. She should be grateful he had such a wonderful consultant, who took so much interest in him. She knew she should be grateful that they were able to leave Chapelton at such short notice and find somewhere from which to rebuild their lives. But all that seemed to be filling her head was the reason they had to leave, and the fact that she was now alone.

The lake had become a reservoir before she was able to move. She needed to lie down, just for a couple of hours. It had been an early flight and she hadn't slept the night before.

Chapter 22

'It's up to you.' William looked at him over a glass of Guinness stout.

It was another one of those differences between the church at home, and the church here. At home alcohol was strictly forbidden, but here, if it was mixed with milk and drunk as part of a meal it was OK. William always had a bottle of Guinness, mixed with condensed milk with his Sunday dinner.

'Would you go?' Lukan wasn't sure. Wales was a long way from Birmingham, from the safety and support of his family.

'If I didn't have Hazel and the church trip to plan, I'd say yes the minute they offered it. Luke, the money's good. Much better than anything they're paying round here,' he coaxed, 'and it's just a couple hours down the road,' William added, sensing Luke's hesitation. 'I mean man, look how far you come already. Remind me again exactly what you come for?'

'To make some money to send home.'

'Then take the job Luke, come back here at the weekend. I won't charge you any rent for the days when your not here, pay that to the bed and breakfast people in Newport.'

He was on the move again, in a strange place, in a strange bed, with new work mates. He didn't know if it was the speed of the move from Jamaica to Birmingham to Newport, or the fact that he didn't know anybody in Newport, or the harshness of the winter, or the friendliness of his landlady that made him follow her to her bed one night, and stay there till the end of his contract. When he returned to Birmingham at the end of the six months, he was in a much better situation financially, but with a lot more worries.

It was a Friday night that would run like a silent underground river in his subconscious for the rest of his life. Opening the door to William's house, weary from the long journey from Newport, chilled to the bones from the lack of heating on the coach, and rattled by Cindy's demands for him to spend more time with her at weekends, he was looking to getting his head down early and getting a good night's sleep. He hoped William and Hazel would understand if he didn't want to sit and chat with them tonight.

The living room door on his left opened as he headed down the long narrow corridor toward his bedroom.

'Lukan!' William greeted him, a little more jovially than usual. He seems to have had a better week than me, Luke thought.

'Good to see you. How was your journey?'

'Alright, I suppose. Cold though, and the coach was crowded. I couldn't even stretch out my legs. Then the bus take ages to come, but at least it wasn't as packed as the coach.'

William was looking at him like he wanted to say something but didn't know how. Lukan knew the look; it's the same one Issy had when she was building up to tell him something she thought he wouldn't want to hear. Must be something in her side of the family.

'Come in here,' William beckoned him into the living room.

'Let me drop my bag in my room.' He felt his stomach tighten. Had William found out about Cindy? Is that why he was waiting for him? He started to search his mind for how he would deny it. It would be Cindy's word against his, the other lodger had move out before he and Cindy started to…and she couldn't find another one. He suspected that she hadn't tried too hard; she wanted the place to the two of them. A few times he'd asked her how she was managing without the extra money.

'Don't worry about me. I can manage,' she'd replied the last time, ladling out the soup in to the bowl before sitting down with him at the table in the small dining area of the kitchen. Then she'd asked him about his day, what he did, how it was with his work mates. He liked the way she listened to him, showed real interest, even though he pretty much told her the same thing every night.

Such evenings would go one of two ways. Either he would go to his room because he was so tired, sort out his things for the next day, write a letter, read his Bible or prepare his Sunday school lesson for the next week, or they would go into the small living room where she would sit next to him as they watched a bit of TV, then go to her bedroom.

The first time it had happened her heating had broken down. The gas people couldn't come out till the following day and the house was freezing. She'd put a paraffin heater in the living room but the bedrooms were like ice boxes. She'd been very apologetic, and had joked about how lovely it would be to cuddle up to someone for warmth.

'I bet you wish you had your wife with you tonight,' she'd laughed.

'I don't think Issy could deal with this cold,' he'd answered, rubbing his hands together while trying to picture Issy huddled over a paraffin heater.

'She's a lucky woman, your wife.'

He pulled himself back from the open invitation in her eyes. He'd never thought of Issy as the lucky one. It was he who was lucky to have her. Nobody had ever suggested to him before that it could be the other way round. Cindy was only saying it because she'd never met Issy.

He hadn't wanted to admit that he missed having

somebody in his bed at night. Mostly he was too tired to think about it, or if he did, he made himself think of something else, but when Cindy tried his lock, found it open and crept into his warm bed that night, he didn't protest for long.

'Cindy, what you doing in here?' he'd whispered, even though there was only the two of them in the house.

'I can't get warm in my bed. Can I stay in here with you?'

'Why don't you put the heater in your room?'

'The paraffin's almost finished,' her voice rose and fell in her soft Welsh lilt. 'I have to save a little for the morning otherwise we will freeze.'

He could have said no, could have told her to go back to her own room and use extra blankets, but he too, wanted some extra warmth. He could just hold her, feel a woman in his arms even if all she wanted was a heater. He knew, as he pulled back the blanket for her to get in, that she wanted more than his body heat. He saw again the look in her eyes when she told him his wife was lucky, and tried to still his rising erection, tried to push it down into his underpants. But it would not be submerged, and she felt it poking against her as she slid in between his sheets.

Nothing was said as she wriggled into his arms, found his mouth and kissed him. The weeks of isolation, of aloneness, of holding his wanting in check found expression as he crushed her lips with his, hard and hungry. She wore a long nightie with a scooped neckline. A warm breast popped into his hand as he reached inside the top of her nightie. The nipple was as hard as a pimento grain, as he massaged it between his fingers. Her breath came out in little pants, like she couldn't cope with his kissing and stroking at the same time. The smell of her dark perfume filled his nostrils as he buried his head in her bosom, looking for the other nipple. She oozed a deep moan as he found it, ran his tongue around it and nibbled as though chewing the flesh from a sweetsop. She wriggled her nightie up to her waist while pushing his head deeper into her large gourd-like breasts. She had wide hips and thick, solid legs, she would hold his weight well, keep him firmly anchored as he paddled in her lake. As he sunk his oar into her deep waters, and she arched her back to receive him, he asked God to forgive him his weakness. She panted, and gasped, and sighed, and groaned, all in muffled tones, as though trying not to disturb the household. He made his moves in her silently, swift, smooth, sure strokes, back and forth with an urgency to reach the other side as quickly as possible. He had little thought for her needs, for prolonging the moment. She seemed as eager as he, moving with him all the way, staying with him stroke for stroke. She was wet and slippery, he was hard and fervent, together they brought the boat to the other side, riding the whirlpool that threatened to pull them into oblivion. With one final thrust he hit her wall, splashed his whitewash all over her, and rolled off her still panting from his efforts.

Laying on his back, looking up at the ceiling which was barely visible through the thick curtains and streetlight, he wondered what to say. He could think of nothing to excuse his behaviour, so remained silent until, pulling her nightie back into place, she said, 'Lukan, you're good you know, has anyone ever told you?'

Despite his resolve of just a few seconds earlier to just ask her to leave, go back to her own bed, and to just behave in the morning as if this had never happened, he found himself tingle with a flush of pride.

'Hmmmhum.' He muttered.

'No?' she sounded surprised, 'then either you're just a tiger with me, or you been missing out on some praise.'

He didn't have the heart to ask her to leave as she seemed content to stay, and after all, it was the warmth she came for. He waited till she was asleep, turned his back to her, and slept with his face to the wall, his heart heavy with all kinds of regrets.

But the precedence had been set, and despite the repaired heating, she still found her way into his bed from time to time. They had an un-discussed code. If his door was locked he didn't want to be disturbed, but if it was open she was welcomed. He heard her trying his door some nights as he lay praying for strength to resist the temptations of the flesh, and felt redeemed and blessed by God who saw his attempts to walk a good and righteous path.

Over the last few weeks she'd been hinting that she'd like to share more of his life, would like to go out with him, maybe for a drink or to a restaurant for something to eat. She's sneered at his insistence that as a Christian he couldn't go into pubs, and had offered to pay for the meal when he confessed he couldn't afford to take her out because of his financial commitments. She'd suggested staying over some weekends and at least going to the park, or swimming, or something else other than going to church. He'd declined all her offers, conscious of how it would look to Hazel and William, and everyone else. He didn't for one minute forget that William was Issy's uncle, and he really didn't want to do anything to threaten his marriage.

Had she contacted William after all, told him about their liaisons? He would just have to look surprised and deny everything, and find somewhere else to lodge next week, even if he had to pay the extra for a hotel, while he looked for a new place.

'These come for you today,' William handed him two letters and a telegram.

He recognised Issy's handwriting on both the letters, but didn't have time to think about why she'd written two, because he was apprehensive about the telegram.

'When did this come?' His voice was shaking.

'About four o'clock this afternoon, I was just coming in the door because we finish early today. I was praying you would come home straight and not work overtime tonight.'

'There wasn't any on offer tonight,' he said as he dropped the letters on the table and, with visibly trembling fingers ripped open the telegram. William scanned his face anxiously, trying to get a clue as to the contents.

'It's Lloydy, he's in hospital. A truck hit him.'

'A truck? That sound serious.'

'Him still unconscious. At least he was when she send this.' He stared at William blankly. 'What do I have to do?' he asked, having no experience of this kind to draw on.

'Sit down,' suggested William, rapidly searching his own memory bank for an answer.

Lukan began pacing the small empty spaces between the furniture.

'I have to go home. I'm going to go home. I have to go home,' he muttered to himself, almost oblivious of William's presence.

'Why don't you sit down and read Issy's letters, there might be something in them that will help you make your mind up what to do.'

'Yes.' He walked from the living room along the freshly polished Minton tiled hallway into the kitchen for a knife to slit the thin flimsy airmail letters.

They both had the same date; one ran on from the other. Issy's writing was smaller than usual, like she was trying to cram as much in as she could.

'Why don't you phone Pastor and ask him what to do? He's bound to have come across this before, and if nothing else, he has a phone. If the worse happen maybe you could phone the hospital in Jamaica.' William had read the telegram when Luke went to get the knife. 'Lloyd in Kingston General Hospital. Stop. Hit by truck. Stop. It's serious. Stop. Still unconscious. Stop. Issy.

'I'll read this, then I'll go to the phone box.'

He began scanning the letter for clues, but realised the lunacy of that, as the letters were written weeks before the telegram.

Dear Luke,

I hope when this letter reaches you it finds you in good health and on your knees asking God's forgiveness for the sins that you have committed. I have already asked His forgiveness for my sins, and I'm sure I'm forgiven because he could see that I was severely provoked.

I had a message from your Uncle Dudley the other day that the heavy storms that they had up there caused some leaks in the roof of Miss Inez's house and some of tenant's things got damaged. He wanted me to see how much I thought they were worth, because in his view, the tenants was asking too much. I managed to persuade Mavis to sleep in the house with the children for me while I went up because I didn't want to have to make the journey in one day, you know how busy she is these days and how hard it is to get help now, and even though Irene stay with them most nights while I'm at work I didn't want her in the house by herself overnight, especially with Lloydy's epilepsy.

When I got up there, the house was in a bad way. We're going to have to paint the living room and bedroom again because so much water came in. Dudley says it's our fault because there was a leak in the roof and he will sort our fixing it, but it was the clothes that he wanted me to give him an idea of price for. I could see that we're going to have to spend some money, but not as much as they were asking for, I can even get some of the things in the market in Kingston the same as theirs for half the price they want to charge us. But really Luke that's not the main reason I'm writing to you.

While I was up there, I wanted to see the girls because it's been such a long time since I see them. Dudley said he forgot to tell them I was coming up and was trying everything to stop me going into the house to see them, but I insisted. When I called out, Gloria came to the veranda. She was happy to see me and wanted to know if I'd come to see the baby.

I asked what baby she was talking about, thinking Jez was looking after somebody's baby. 'Mama's baby,' she said. She seemed surprised that I didn't know, 'My baby brother.'

I didn't know what she was talking about, so I asked her where her mother was. 'She inside sleeping,' she told me, then asked me if she should wake her up. I couldn't understand why Jez would be sleeping at two o'clock in the afternoon. 'Yes, wake her up' I tell her, because Luke, I was getting a very uneasy feeling about something, but I couldn't put my finger on it. I started to think maybe Darcie had got into trouble and they were trying to hide it. It's a long time since I see them.

I waited at the bottom of the steps till Jez came to the veranda rubbing her eyes. She suddenly woke up when she saw it was me. 'Oh, him send you?' she said, like she was expecting me. Continued in other letter.

He quickly opened up the other one and read on, the writing was even smaller.

'Nobody sent me,' I told her, 'I had to come up, and as I haven't seen the girls I wanted to come and see them. I told Dudley to let you know I was coming, but he forgot.' She laughed a funny kind of laugh and said 'you sure him forget?' Then Gloria asked Jez if I could see her baby brother. 'I didn't know you were expecting.' I said to her. I felt pleased that she finally found somebody, and realised that's probably why she just cut off contact with us, not that she ever kept in touch when you're not here, but not even Dudley was mentioning her, I figured that was why.

'You might as well,' she said, 'but you'll have to come up as him sleeping, and I don't want to wake him up.' I was relieved that it wasn't Darcie, but the funny feeling wouldn't go away, and when I saw the baby, sleeping in the basket in her room I knew why. She was watching my face all the time, and I wanted to slap the conceited look off her's as she folded her arms over her swollen breasts and looked at the miniature version of you, chest rising and falling, eyes flickering under his lids, lost in his own dreams. I could only stammer, 'what's his name,' and she knew it was like a whip across my face when she said, 'Luke. I call him Luke, after his daddy.' Luke, he looked just like Lloydy when he was a baby.

I don't know what made me do it Luke, but I slapped that self-satisfied look off her face, my hand just fly up of its own free will and land a clout bang across it. I saw the surprise as her face twisted round and I slapped the other side. She tried to grab my throat, but I caught her hand and she went off balance and fell over. I don't know what got into me, but I was kicking and kicking her and calling her a bitch and a whore and a thief and a liar, and then I was crying and kicking and calling her more names that I'm too ashamed to write. And all the time she's laughing a weird laugh, like she's not feeling any of the blows, just laughing and laughing. Then she just stood up, grabbed my shoulders, pushed me hard against the wall, with the strength of a man twice her size, and screamed at me, 'Get out of my house, and if you ever come in here again, I'll kill you! It's not me you should be mad at, it's that dog of a husband of yours!' 'If he's such dog, why don't you leave him alone,' I shouted back at her. 'Because he was my dog first, did you really think you could take him from me? Now get out my house, and mind you take *good* care of them pickneys you have for him, because that's the only thing holding him to you. Get out! Get out!'

I ran like I was being chased by the devil, but she wasn't following me, just standing on the veranda laughing. I can still hear her voice in my head Luke. I don't know what you going

204

to do about this, but you have to do something. After everything that's happened to us, now this! You had to go and do this! And you know what was funny, your son slept through all that was going on. Luke, you have to do something, because I can't take any more of this.

Issy.

He sat looking at the letter, a million and one images running through his head vying for his attention. Issy, Jez, fight, the baby which he could only picture because Issy said he looked like Lloyd. Gloria, did *she* witness it? Lloydy in hospital, Issy crying, leaking roof, Dudley. The only thing that was no longer in his head was Cindy.

'You alright?' Hazel asked, touching him lightly on his shoulder.

Her voice and touch brought him back to his present situation. The letters were obviously sent before the telegram. He should have told Issy about Jez and Luke; he knew it was only a matter of time before the girls told her anyway, or Dudley, or somebody else. He knew Jez wouldn't tell Issy, she said she was leaving that to him, and he had never found the right time. She had so much on her mind, dealing with everything for the children and her job, that he didn't want to add anymore to her basket. Several times he'd picked up a pen to write to her, but found something else to do.

'You don't look too good,' Hazel continued before he could formulate an answer. 'I'll make you a cup of tea,' and she busied herself with the kettle and cups, as he continued to stare into space.

Hazel was a quiet woman, she always seemed to be just on the edge of her husband's shadow when he was in a room. When he wasn't there she allowed herself a little bit of space for herself, but always retreated, make herself smaller, when William entered. He often observed how different their marriage was to his. Issy was the flamboyant one, and while he was never in her shadow, she always shone more brightly, was always more engaging. At first he thought it was because she knew the people in Clarendon, but she was the same in Sav. People he'd known since he was a boy were prepared to tell her their life story within a few minutes of meeting her. She had an ease with people that he envied. He saw in Hazel a female version of himself, and wondered if she had a secret life that William knew nothing about.

He suddenly felt crushed by his secrets. Like Damocles he'd been waiting for the sword to fall, and now it had, piercing straight through his family, threatening to rip apart everything he held dear. He couldn't find a way out of this on his own; he'd have to seek help.

'Is William still here?' he looked up at Hazel with watery eyes.

'Yes, of course, he's waiting for you in the front room. I'll bring the tea in there if you want.'

'Thanks.' Already trying to formulate what to say to William.

'Sit down son,' William invited, but Luke began talking before he got to the sofa, and remained on his feet pacing backward and forward as he told his story, pausing only long enough to receive the tea from Hazel. He told William about the baby first, then worked backwards to how it had all come about. He knew it was a mess, he knew he had sinned, but other people shouldn't have to suffer because of him, if anything it should be him that got run over by a truck.

'But Lloyd getting hit by a truck don't have anything to do with the baby.' William tried to calm his distress.

'That's just the point though William, it does. Issy said after the fight, Jez told her to look after my children because it's the only thing keeping me and her together. And then two weeks later Lloydy get run over by a truck.'

'That's just a coincidence. A lot of people say a lot of things that they don't mean.'

'Not Jez, you don't know Jez,' he said fiercely, and went on to explain why they moved to Kingston, Lennox's birth, Inez's warnings, Sister Pauline's dream, Lloyd's epilepsy. William had a rational explanation for all of them, they were all coincidences, but when he saw that Luke was firmly fixed on his own explanation, he knew they'd have to find a solution to put his mind at ease.

'First things first,' he said briskly. We need to see if Pastor's at home and can make the call to the hospital. I'm sure he'll say yes.'

They both grabbed their coats, and headed for the phone box at the end of the road. The pastor was in, and saw it as part of his pastoral obligation to help in situations like this. He considered it important enough to come and get them in his car, leaving his wife to get the number of the hospital from directory enquiries.

Lukan was a coiled spring as he waited for the hospital to pick up the phone. They'd had several false attempts and he was praying that this time the connection would be made.

'Hello,' the voice on the other end sounded like it was coming from down the road.

'It's Lukan Levy, is he alright?'

'Is who alright sir?'

'My son, Lloyd.'

'Lloyd who, sir?'

'I told you, my son Lloyd Levy.'

'When was he admitted?' Why was she asking so many questions, there couldn't be that many Lloyd Levys in the hospital?

'Today. I'm his father, and I'm calling from England and I don't have much time, because I got a telegram today that he's in the hospital and that he was run over by a truck and I just want to know how he is.'

'Alright sir, I have to put you through to the ward.' Then she disappeared. Lukan looked at the phone puzzled.

'She was supposed to put me through to the ward but she's just gone.'

Pastor McCullough took the phone from him and listened. 'Hello. Hello. Hello.' He repeated, as though trying to contact the dead. 'Hello, oh hello, I'll hand you back to Mr Levy.'

'How is he?'

'He's alright sir, he's stable now, his mother just leave his bedside to get something to eat, I will tell her you telephoned, she's been asking all day.'

'What's wrong with him?'

'He's concussed. I'll tell your wife that you phoned.' She sounded impatient.

'Thank you,' he said and was about to add, 'is she alright?' But the phone was already dead.

The two men looked at him expectantly. 'She said he's concussed. I was going to ask her about Issy but she hang up.'

'Is Issy injured too?' Pastor McCullough asked perplexed.

'No but she's at the hospital with Lloydy.'

'Sit down Brother Levy, you look like you could use a drink. Do you want a Guinness or a Mackeson?'

'What Pastor?'

'Guinness or Mackeson?'

Even in his befuddled state he knew that both of those drinks were alcoholic, why was the pastor offering him alcohol?

'But pastor, they have alcohol in them, don't they?'

'At a time like this the body needs a tonic. There's not enough alcohol in them to outweigh the tonic. If you prefer though, I'll get Sister McCullough to make you a hot drink. What about you brother?' he asked William.

'I'll have the Guinness.' He answered without hesitation.

'I'll have one too,' Lukan ventured. It had been a long time since he drank alcohol. That was one part of his baptismal vows that he'd taken seriously, that he'd been able to stick to. But if Pastor thought it was alright...

Maybe it was the heightening of his senses by the alcohol, or the anxiety of the telegram, or the worry about the letters or the unfamiliar surroundings of the pastor's house, but Lukan found himself telling the pastor about Issy's letters, and the whole matter with Sister Pauline and the vision.

'Brother Lukan,' the pastor cautioned, sipping on his Guinness, 'you have to be careful not to put too much reliance on what these pastors in the district churches say about these matters. Some of them still haven't lost their superstitious natures.'

'Are you saying Pastor Morgan was just superstitious? That we should never have moved to Kingston?' Maybe if they hadn't move Lloyd wouldn't be in hospital now. Maybe they'd taken Sister Pauline's vision too much to heart, after all, Lloydy epilepsy had just been a coincidence, and now it was him again that had the accident. Maybe Lloydy was just unlucky. But Lennox had got pneumonia, and had to stop going to school for a few weeks, and Lilly-Mae had the same sore on her foot as Ivan. The only one that didn't seem to get anything was Irene.

He voiced his concerns to William and the Pastor, a little agitated by the alcohol, which seemed to run through his blood like tiny red ants making him itch from the inside. He couldn't sit still, kept getting up and walking about. Pastor McCullough, sensing his anguish, offered to pray with him, but whatever Pastor said could not penetrate the severe anxiety Lukan felt for the safety of his wife and children. He was convinced Jez had something to do with Lloydy's accident. He couldn't prove it, but his mother had tried to warn him in her own way, with the water, and the bags, and the salt. Sister Pauline had seen it, it didn't matter what Pastor said, he hadn't see Sister Pauline's face, or Lloyd's twitching body or his rolling eyes, and it wasn't his son in hospital right now, concussed. He had to get them out of there.

'I have to get them out of there,' he said out loud, just as Pastor was coming to his 'in the name of the Father, the Son and the Holy Spirit. Amen.'

'I have to get them out of there,' he said again, fearing that they hadn't heard him the first time.

'Who, out of where?' Pastor rejoined Lukan on his wave length.

'I have to get Issy and the children out of Kingston.'

'Where else you going to move them to?' William asked. 'You only just move them, and they just getting settled. Lukan, you just need to sleep on it, tomorrow it will look different, you're tired and you've had a big shock. You've done what you can already tonight. Let's go home, you can get a good night sleep and we'll talk about it in the morning.'

'That sounds like a good idea,' Pastor agreed.

The short journey in the pastor's car was done virtually in silence. It wasn't till they got into the house and William locked and bolted the door that Lukan broke down and wept. William held him, a little awkwardly at first, then with a tenderness he didn't know he had. 'Let it out,' he said, patting his back. 'Let it out.'

'I have to get them out before she kill all of them,' he said between his laboured breaths.

'She's going to kill them otherwise.'

Chapter 23

My Dear Issy,

I don't know how to begin this letter. I don't know what to say to you. I've been praying for forgiveness like you said in your letter, and I'm really hoping God sees it in his heart to forgive me. I hope you can find it in yours to forgive me too Issy. I know I should have told you about Jez and the baby, but I just didn't know how to. Every time I tried, I just felt weak and cowardly. I know you deserve better than me Issy, and I was afraid you would leave me. I don't want to lose you or the children Issy. I've tried to be a good husband, but I think Jez have something on me. Uncle Dudley warned me about her, or at least Mama told him to warm me against her. It was when I told him why we had to move from Chapelton. I didn't want to believe it because of Darcie and Gloria, and I believed she wouldn't do anything, because she know that our children is brother and sister to hers.

I know I should have told you this before, but the day she told me she was pregnant was the same day you lose the baby. I'll never forget the look on her face when I told her you was pregnant too. Issy I didn't want to leave you to come to England, and that's why every time I keep reminding you to put the salt round the house. I don't know if you're still doing it, but if you stop you need to start doing it again.

I've been praying and praying for an answer to this whole problem, and the only one I can see is that I have to move my family right away, put water between her and them. I keep having a dream that we're all in a big waterfall, and everybody is frightened, especially as none of us can swim. We're right at the edge, about to fall when we all hold hands and go over in one long line, then somehow we can't hold on and we fall one by one separately, but at the bottom we all find each other and hold hands again. Issy, I think it's a sign that we should all be together.

I talked to William and Hazel and to Pastor about it. I was going to come home but they agree with me that the best thing is to send for you and children to come here, right away from that woman. It's going to be tough, but if I have to work every hour that God send I'm going to do it. I don't want anything to come between you and me again Issy.

I phoned the hospital again last week, they say Lloydy is a little better, but not wonderful, that he's not out of the danger period yet. I don't know how you're managing. I suppose you're not going to work. I've put in for extra overtime to try and send you more money.

Issy, as God is my witness, I love you, and I want you to come over here. Think about it and let me know.

Your loving husband,

Luke.

Chapter 24

'Mrs Levy... Isabell, I think you should go home and get some rest. There's nothing else you can do here, and he's sleeping now. I think you should go and do the same.'

'But what if he wakes up when I'm not here. He won't know where he is, it might frighten him and send him back in the coma.'

'He's not in a coma Issy, he just drifting in and out of consciousness. Can't you get somebody else to come and sit with him?'

'There's only my sister and my daughter down here and they're helping me to take care of the other children.'

'You don't have a friend who could...'

'Maybe Sister Mullet from church could come...she's the one that does the hospital visits.'

'Why don't you ask her? Anyway, I'm here, if he wakes up I'll tell him where he is.'

As Issy waited at the bus stop she wondered what was going on in the lives of her fellow passengers. Did any of them have a child that might be dying? Did that woman wiping her face with a limp and already damp handkerchief have somebody who had just died? Is that why she didn't smile or answer the people who walked past and wished her a good evening? And the young woman, who couldn't be more than seventeen or eighteen, with the baby on her hip, did she have somebody she was worried about? The baby had hooked its finger through the straps of her dress and was resting its head on her chest, content. The man pulling hard on his cigarette and pacing up and down, like he was late for something that mattered to him.

Everybody in Kingston was going through something, or so it seemed to Issy. A few years ago the only thing she was going through was how to go out without Mavis's permission. Then, she walked with a spring in her step, held her head high. Now she found it hard to lift her feet or her head.

She got on the bus and found a seat by the window. It wasn't too crowded this time of the night, and she was glad she didn't have to sit next to anybody. She could gaze out at the brightly lit shop windows decked in the Jamaican Independence colours, at the people lining the streets, some in huddles outside their houses taking in the cool night air, enjoying a beer, throwing their heads back and laughing, temporarily forgetting their troubles. She wished she could forget hers, even for a moment, but she seemed to wear them like a second skin. The day in Savanna-la-Mar was etched indelibly in her mind. She couldn't rub out Luke's miniature face, or Gloria's horrified stare as she watch her mother being kicked by her father's wife. But the image that was brightest, boldest, biggest, that was the filter through which she saw everything else, was Jez's face as she said 'look after your pickney them.'

She couldn't understand how Luke could put her in this situation. She felt let down by him, but most of all she felt let down by God. How could he have brought her another Easton? Yet, somewhere in her heart she knew he wasn't Easton, that he had more strength than Easton, but he had let her down. She had never felt so alone. It wasn't the fact he was in England, or the physical distance that was weighing her down, it was that she didn't know him anymore. All the time she was trying to build a family that wouldn't exclude his children, he was busy extending his family with Jez. She didn't feel she had any more say to him. How was she to explain that her husband had a younger child with his older children's mother? She felt shame as a heavy weight, pulling her down into a dark night sea, and she didn't have any energy left to pull herself up. Anyone watching her would have thought her twice her age.

That's what Irene thought as he mother opened the door and dropped her bag in the chair, then dropped herself in the one next to it.

'How's Lloydy?' she asked anxiously.

'A little better,'

'That's good.'

'I suppose so.'

'You want some dinner?' Irene was concerned about her mother, she'd lost a lot of weight in the last few weeks, and since Lloyd's accident had virtually stopped eating.

'No, just make me a cup of chocolate tea.'

'You eat anything today Mama?' It felt like the roles had been reversed.

'Yes, I got something from one of the nurses at the hospital.'

That probably meant half a sandwich, or a little bit of somebody's lunch, but Irene decided to drop it and go and make her the tea.

'How's Lennox and Lilly-Mae?'

'They're alright,' she said from the kitchen, waiting for the water to boil. 'There's a letter on the dresser from Daddy. It came this morning.'

Daddy, how easily Luke had accepted her children as his own, and although Ivan's grandmother would never allow him to call Luke Daddy, she knew Luke was more of a father to him than Easton. She'd trusted him with her children, trusted him with her money, with her love, she'd trusted him with her life. Now, she didn't know what she could trust him with. Because of him, Lloyd was in hospital. Because of him, she lost the baby, because of him they had to flee to Kingston. She didn't know if she could trust him anymore. Yet life without him seemed inconceivable.

Issy's eyes travelled to the airmail letter propped up on the vase on the dresser. She wasn't expecting to hear from him so soon; he's not a letter writer, he must have written the same day he got hers. She'd told to him to do something, and had assumed that he would try to repair things between them, to beg her forgiveness and God's. She assumed that he would beg her to stay with him because he was the one that had sinned in the eyes of God and the church. But for the first time she saw a different possibility. What if that letter was an intact hand grenade, waiting for her to pull the pin, waiting to explode into her face the fact that he wanted to go back to Jez, to forsake his marriage vows, to risk his soul, and go back to her? He had proved that she was not enough for him, had gone back to her, lain with her and created another life, a permanent reminder of his betrayal.

'Do you want me to pass it to you?' Irene had returned with the tea.

'Yes, and pass me a knife.' Issy turned the letter over and over as she waited.

Having convinced herself that the letter contained explosive matter, she opened it very slowly. Nothing in her own musings and misgivings had prepared her for Luke's solution to their problem.

'What!' she exclaimed a little louder than she'd intended, which brought Irene running back into the living room.

'What's the matter Mama?' These days her mother was always on edge.

'Your daddy want all of us to move to England!' she said, the incredulity raw in her voice.

Irene sat down.

'To England?' Things were getting weirder and weirder.

216

'Are we going to go?' Irene couldn't hide her excitement, even though she knew her mother's views about England. It was alright for her mother to stay near her family, but…

'I don't think that the solution.'

'To what Mama?

'To what your daddy did.'

'I don't know what he…'

'Anyway, it's not anything to do with you children, it's between him and me.' She wished she'd kept her mouth shut. Irene was a bright girl, it wouldn't be long anyway till everybody would know about Luke Junior. Maybe it would be better to leave all of it behind, but she was too tired think clearly.

'Is it true we're going to England?' Lilly-Mae bounced onto Issy's bed, her excitement fizzing like freshly stirred Cool Aid.

'What nonsense you talking about?' Issy muttered, rolling onto her back and rubbing the sleep from her eyes.

'Irene says we going to England. Are we going tomorrow?'

'Irene don't know what she talking about.'

'But Mama, she say Daddy want us to go to England.' She was now snuggled up to Issy, and if she wasn't firm, would worm her way under the sheet. She and Lilly-Mae were very close, maybe because she was the last one, but since the move to Kingston she'd become clingy, always wanting to sit beside Issy, to get into her bed. She was finding it tough, Issy spending so much time at the hospital, and no Daddy to plug the gap.

'It's not everything your daddy wants he's going to get.'

'You mean we're not going?'

'I mean, get out of my bed and stop asking me questions.'

'But Irene said…'

'It don't matter what Irene said, if we're going to England you will be the first to know, alright. Now get out of my bed and let me sleep.'

'But it's time to get up Mama,'

'Not for the time I went to bed, now scoot.' She gave her a gentle nudge. 'And you can tell Irene that sending you in here didn't work.'

But she didn't need to, Irene had heard every word, and was already plotting how she could persuade her mother to change her mind. England! She would be the envy of her friends. She'd overheard her parents discussing how much easier it would be in England because the schools were free, no school fees, maybe they wouldn't need to work so hard.

It wouldn't go away though. It not only joined the stream of things constantly running through Issy's head, but it became the central thing. Like a pyramid towering over sand dunes, it could be seen from whichever angle she look. She had a lot of time to contemplate the benefits of moving to England while sitting at Lloyd's bedside. She knew them all, she and Luke had discussed them plenty of times, but she couldn't see any reason for uprooting her children and planting them in, from what she heard, a hostile place. England in her books, was somewhere to work and make enough money to come home, and it had been working well for them. In another year they would have been able to build their second house. For as long as Luke could do it, he could come and go and they would build their lives. It wouldn't take him more than ten years, then they could sit back pretty. She was convinced it was still possible; if they could ride this storm.

Then the bandaged Mummy that had been sleeping in the pyramid sat up and stretched, and Issy could ignore it no longer. What if Jez wasn't the only one? What if Luke had other children that he hadn't told her about. After all, he never told her about Luke Junior, what if she ran into other mothers with babies that look like Luke? And what was he doing in England, if he could do this right under her nose, what was he up to all those miles away. Maybe she was too confident to think he would never do anything like this, or maybe she trusted God too much to send her a faithful man.

The more she thought about it the angrier she got, because of him she had to be putting salt round her house, creeping out at night like a robber because she didn't want anybody to see her, and she couldn't give that job to any of the children without having to explain why. Yes, she had lapsed with the salt; it was a lot to remember everything. Now his letter was making her wonder if things would have been different if she'd remembered every day, would Lloydy be in hospital now but for a handful of salt? She didn't know who to trust any more. Not Luke, not the doctors who she was sure wasn't telling her the whole truth about Lloyd, not God.

What kind of life could she have with him if she didn't trust him?

'What kind of life would you have without him Issy?' Mavis curled her leg up under her as she sat on the sofa and sipped on her lemonade. 'I mean, you say him sorry, him begging your forgiveness. How many men you think out there would do that? Some of them would just expect you to put up with it. There's many a wife out there who never get a single apology, not the first, second, third…'

'Alright, alright.' She wasn't expecting Mavis to be making a case for Luke, 'is whose side you on Mavis?'

'I'm not on anybody's side. You asked me what I think and I'm telling you, if you just wanted somebody to agree with you, you shouldda asked somebody else.'

'Yes but…'

'I'm not making a case for him, or for you. I know what him do is wrong, but him still your husband, and him still have a lot of good points.'

'But he could be doing the same thing over there Mavis.

What if I pick up myself and go, only to find some other little Lukes running around.'

'Issy, talk sense. Why would he be sending for you if him have somebody out there? Don't you think he would want you to stay here?'

'But what if…'

'And another thing. If there *is* somebody over there, don't you think you should go and get your husband back? You put a lot of work in to this marriage Issy, and a lot of work into Lukan.' Issy raised her eyebrows. 'You don't need to look at me like that; everybody can see the difference in him since him married you. You going to throw all that away, just let some other woman step in and walk off with your hard labour?'

'But all my family's here Mavis. I don't have any…'

'That's rubbish, and you know it. Who's Lukan living with?'

'Uncle William.'

'*Our* uncle Issy, not Lukan's. And you think he's going to be doing anything under our uncle's nose? And don't forget, him say Uncle William agree with him.'

'What about you Mavis? Would you go?'

Without hesitation, as though she'd already given it prior thought, she answered. 'If I loved him. If I loved him I could forgive him and start again. Some people do it for the children, but I would have to do it for the love. Don't you think that's what Jez did? If you give up on him, she wins. Don't let her beat you Issy, she might have his child but she don't have him, you still have him, go to him, but only if you still love him.'

'I can't just get up and go, what about the children, and Lloydy still in hospital, and there would be so much to sort out here.'

'I wasn't suggesting you leave tomorrow, and I'm sure he wasn't either. At least think about it Issy.'

'You think I haven't been thinking? I'm going to talk to the pastor.'

'Why? To see if him agree with Lukan's pastor? It look to me that everybody can see sense, except you.'

'But his pastor don't know me, not like Pastor Morgan.'

'Oh him! You going back to Chapelton. Wasn't him the same one that tell you to leave Chapelton?'

Mavis seemed to have every angle covered.

Any thoughts of moving to England disappeared from her head when she arrived the next at the hospital to a group of doctors and nurses around Lloyd's bed, administering oxygen and looking anxious.

'This is his mother' one of the nurses said.

Trying hard to push down the huge ball of bile that was rising up and threatening to engulf all her organs on its way out of her mouth, Issy asked, 'What's happened to him?' Her voice was small and thin, like she was pushing each word through a tube of vermicelli.

'He stopped breathing, we're giving him oxygen.'

'Why?'

'To make sure he's got enough in his...'

'I mean why did he stop breathing?'

'We don't know.'

Just then, as if sensing his mother's presence, Lloyd gulped, drank deeply from the mask, and started breathing again normally.

Everyone relaxed, relieved that the crisis was over.

'Why did he stop breathing?' Issy asked again to no-one in particular.

'We don't know Mrs Levy, but I'd like to run a few test to try and find out.'

'When? What tests?'

'We'll do them now, in case it happens again.' The doctor who was in charge said to Issy, then turning to the nurse, 'we'll have to x-ray his chest. Tell them it's urgent.'

She waited with Lloyd till they came to take him for the x-ray.

She knew she couldn't go in with him and headed for the hospital's prayer room, overcome with fear and anxiety. She begged God to make sure there was nothing seriously wrong with her son. She prayed there'd be no complications due to lack of oxygen. She told God that she would do whatever he wanted her to do, would dedicate her life completely to him if he made Lloyd well. She argued with God. Didn't he think she'd suffered enough? Wasn't loosing one, no, two children enough? How much more did he expect her to bear?

She alternated between pleading and telling, between fear and anger, between hope and despondency. Why was she going through this when Luke was so far away? Why wasn't Jez going through this? At the thought of Jez, she remembered that she forgot to put the salt out this morning, so preoccupied was she with Mavis's advice from the night before. 'God, show me what I have to do, tell me what I have to say. I know that only you can save him God, but tell me what I can do to help. Then the idea popped into her head. *Sprinkle salt around his hospital bed.*

She ran outside the hospital down the road to the little shop on the corner where she usually bought sweets to take home for the children after work.

'Little bag of salt.' She panted to the keeper who was just about to serve someone else.

'This lady's before you…Nurse Levy, I didn't recognise without your uniform. I was just…'

'I need to save a life,' she panted, still trying to catch her breath.

Sensing the urgency in her voice he raised an apologetic eyebrow to the customer, and reached behind the counter to get the salt. Throwing a note at him, she ran from the shop, not waiting for her change. As she reached reception she slowed and put the salt into her bag, no point alerting anyone to her unorthodox approach to healing.

Pretending that she wanted to wait by her son's bed because it would make her feel better, she sat quietly until the nurse got busy with another patient. Slowly she walked around the bed, leaking salt from the hole she'd punctured in the plastic bag all the way around the bed. Satisfied that the white salt on the white floor was invisible she sat down again, waiting in the safety of the salt ring, and repeated *Psalm 23* over, and over again.

Chapter 25

Dear Luke,

I'm sorry it's taken so long to write back to you, but you know what I've been going through with Lloydy and everything else. Thank God he pulled through as I told you in the telegram. He should be coming out next week if he continues to improve. The doctors couldn't find anything physical why he should stop breathing, and think it was a massive panic attack, maybe from remembering the truck hitting him. Anyway, since then it hasn't happened again. They think he will be all right to come out soon. God is indeed to be praised. The other children are fine, happy now that they know Lloyd's going to be all right. I think the whole thing put a strain on everybody, especially Irene, who had to take on a lot of the responsibility for the children when I was at the hospital.

Luke, I've been thinking about what you said about coming over there. You know it's never something that I ever saw for myself or for the children. Mavis sit down and show me all the advantages, but it's still a big step to take. Look how hard it was to move the children to Kingston. What if they don't like it there? I don't think I would like that cold you're always talking about, and who's going to help with the children if I get a job. And what about Ivan? When will I get to see Ivan? They're just the practical things though Luke. I'm more worried about you and me. I don't know if I can trust you any more.

What if I come there and you start the same thing again, who am I going to turn to?

Anyway, just suppose I say I want us to come, how you plan to do it? I wouldn't want to leave the children here, I'd want all of us to come together. That would cost a lot of money, and where're you going to put us? I don't think there's enough space at Uncle William's for all of us.

I talked to Mavis and to Pastor Morgan, and I prayed about it. I'm not saying no, but you have to tell me how. And Luke, you have to tell me if there's anything going on with you and anybody else over there. I don't want any more revelations like the one with Jez. Talking about Jez, how do you plan to keep in touch with her children, or are you planning to bring them over too?

The children all send their love.

Your wife,

Issy.

She read it through several times, making sure she hadn't left anything out. It was such a hard letter to write. Usually she looked forward to writing to Luke, to telling him about what was going on with everybody, and to try and make him see their life through her letters, but today she had to pick and choose her words, like picking rice, or weevil from corn meal. She was still feeling raw, exposed, like someone had sliced her in half and turned her inside out so all her organs were available to the wind and the rain and the hot sun. She felt like there was no place to hide, that she walked down the street naked, her hurt and fear heavy in her breasts. Every time Jez or anything connected with her was mentioned it was like a razor through one of her vital organs. Issy walked an emotional tightrope from which she could topple with the slightest push, and that push was not long in coming.

Lukan got to the end of Issy's letter and felt more hope

then he'd done for a long time. There are things you take no notice of until it directly affects you, like wasps, or nettles or mortgages. Luke had heard them discussed, understood them well, but didn't see them as something for him, because, like so many others, he was simply working to build a life back home. William, on the other hand, in his twenty years had bought several houses. After finding the deposit, he filled them with tenants to help pay the mortgage and the bills, which left most of his own money available to save for more deposits. As well as the house he lived in, he had two others and was soon to complete the transactions on a third.

Luke had listened well to his strategy, and had seen it as the way forward for him and Issy, but at home, not in England. They already owned two houses, three if you count Jez's because they had never done anything to sign the house over to her, so it was still his. When all the mess was over, they were going to start looking for another piece of land to start the process over again. Luke had worked out how he could put up a house even quicker than the last time. After ten years he and Issy wouldn't have to work. As he wasn't ready for that yet, he didn't take much notice of who to apply to for loans to buy houses. But now that Issy was asking where he would put them if they came, he suddenly had a burning desire to find out.

A week after Lloyd's oxygen episode she was thinking of going back to work, because she needed as much money as she could to pay for someone to stay at home when he was discharged. She couldn't keep stopping Irene from school, even though she was bright and could catch up; she had exams coming up and needed to give them her full attention.

Work was happy to have her back, and to allow her to change some of her shifts to fit around her domestic situation, her colleagues were also very understanding, being mostly women with children themselves, and recognised that there but for the grace of God went their lives.

Issy and the children settled to a routine which involved tightening their belts a little to pay for the help. Issy had to make sure her pardner money was paid every week and as funds were getting tight she began making sweets and cakes again to supply to shops and stalls. She was so tired most days she didn't know if she was coming or going, and had little time to think about Jez, Darcie, Gloria or Luke Junior.

Some may say that she deliberately tried to shut them out, and that she'd successfully managed it until the Saturday afternoon she came back from work to find them all in her living room, being entertained by Irene and the other children. They filled the room like an overcrowded bee hive, and for no reason that she could fathom, Issy pictured wasps and bees trying to live together, although they looked the same, their way of life was different.

Hush fell on the room as she walked in, everyone looked to her expectantly. She could find no suitable words for the situation, and it was Jez who broke the expanding silence.

'Good day Issy.'

Issy nodded, still unable to speak.

'Good day Miss Issy,' Darcie and Gloria chorused, mimicking their mother.

Issy nodded at them also, but her gaze went to Irene who was holding Luke Junior and cooing over him.

'Mama, don't you think he's the dead stamp of Lloyd?'

Lilly-Mae, sensing the building tension, ran to Issy, held on to her skirt and stuck her two fingers into her mouth.

'What you doing here?' she asked looking straight at Jez, who was sitting on the edge of the seat, as though she was about to get up when Issy walked in and changed her mind. She sat back a little, trying to compose herself, before answering, with a slightly wavering voice which belied the stiffness of her back, and the rigidity of her neck.

'We came to look for Lloyd.'

No one moved, everyone was barely breathing, it was the first time they'd all been in the same room, and while the younger children could sense the tension but not understand the reasons, Irene, and her comment about Luke Junior, certainly grasped the significance of this meeting.

'Why didn't you tell me you were coming?' the words were shards of ice sharpening themselves against Issy's teeth as they forced themselves out, carrying their chill into the room.

'I did tell Dudley to tell you. Him never tell you?' Jez leapt to her own defence. She was conscious that she was on Issy's territory, and didn't feel so safe. They'd always met on her turf, but as Issy had refused to come to her, had stopped inviting the girls to stay, and had stopped sending little gifts for them via Dudley; she had to make the journey herself. She needed to know what was going on, and Dudley had clammed up too, only telling her that Lloyd was in hospital with something to do with his lungs. She'd had to prize the name of the hospital out of him. Issy seem to do everything through him, the money for the children, there had even been a slight increase for Luke Junior, so it wasn't like they weren't acknowledging him as Lukan's child. But instead of bringing more contact with Lukan, it had brought her less. With so little news she felt she was losing her grip, and no wonder, the woman had the house surrounded with salt.

Lukan had stopped writing to her, even though she'd written him three letters he hadn't replied to even one. It was as though they were cutting her and her children out. She had to let them know that they couldn't just brush her away like a troublesome fly.

'No, he didn't tell me.' It was clear she didn't believe Jez, but Lilly-Mae's tug on her dress made her realise that they couldn't continue the stand off, with weapons drawn, in full view of the children.

'Irene, did you offer them a drink?' Issy re-directed her gaze at Irene.

'Yes Mama, they have a drink already.'

'Then why don't you children go and play outside while I talk to Jez?' She didn't want an audience for what she was about to say, but seeing the look of disappointment on Darcie's and Gloria's face at her lack of acknowledgment of them, she relented.

'Come here girls, come and give me a hug, it's a long time since I see you. Boy, look at you, look how you've grown, and Darcie, you looking like a proper young woman.' Standing her at arms length she took in Darcie's brown mini skirt, orange scooped neck top which showed the tops of her still developing breasts and her golden thin strapped sandals sitting snugly at the end of her long legs. Both girls were going to have Jez's height but Darcie was the curvy one, more like Issy but taller. Gloria was going to take her mother's boyish frame.

'Thanks, Miss Issy.' Darcie glowed. It was clear, seeing them together, that Darcie was trying to emulate Issy. Jez saw it, but choose to ignore it for now.

'You see how you are, Mama. You won't let me wear a mini skirt but you think it look good on Darcie.'

'Darcie's older than you Irene.' Issy tried to defend herself

'Only by a few months, so can I get a mini skirt?'

'Not now Irene, we can talk about this later.'

'You promise?'

'Yes.'

Gloria, who'd patiently waited her turn for Issy's attention, hugged her in silence, letting her body transmit to Issy how much she missed her. It didn't show in Gloria's face, not in a smile, or a twinkling eye, or a furrowed brow. No, it was all in her touch. But despite this, Jez knew, and they knew that she knew.

'Now, all of you, go outside.' Issy instructed as Gloria

peeled herself away, and Lilly-Mae promptly took her place at Issy's side.

'D'you want me to take the baby outside too?' Irene asked.

'Yes… I mean no…I mean… ask Jez.' It suddenly occurred to her that someone outside might recognise the likeness between Luke and the baby and start asking questions.

'She can take him out if she want.' Jez gave her consent.

'What do you want from me Jez?' Issy asked as soon as the children were out of earshot. She didn't, for one moment believe Jez had just come all the way from Savanna-la-Mar to see Lloyd, when she could get updates on his progress from Dudley, who had visited the hospital and also got regular reports from Issy.

'I don't want anything from you,' she said standing up, feeling at a disadvantage from her perched position on the chair, 'I just want Luke's children to get to know each other.'

'Since when's that worried you? For the last how many years it's me that's been pushing for the children to keep in touch. You forget that you wouldn't even send them to me when we lived in Chapelton, and now that we all the way in Kingston, you suddenly want them to get to know each other?' Issy was trying to control her rising anger. The audacity of the woman, to come into her house to lecture her about family cohesion. She hadn't seen Jez since that day when she'd lost control, but she could still see the self-satisfied look on her face as if it was yesterday.

'I know, I'm not arguing that it was you who show me how important it is. But since Luke born him not even meet him other brothers and sisters.'

'You should have thought about that before you…'

'Issy, I didn't come here to fight. I don't want another beating from you. I come because the girls wanted to see Lloyd and I think Luke should know his…'

'Yes, so you seh.' Issy didn't want to hear her say it again, because, as much as she didn't like Jez, and didn't want her in her house, she agreed that the children should stay in touch. It was something her father had drilled into her, that the children didn't ask to be born, and shouldn't be punished for the indiscretions of their parents.

Jez waited, arms folded, for Issy to continue.

'OK, but you can't just turn up – we have to plan it.'

'It's not me you're talking about, it the girls…'

'But I thought you just said you wanted them to get to know L…L…Luke?' she struggled to get the name out.

'I can send him with the girls. Darcie can manage him now.'

That put a different complexion on things for Issy. It wasn't a good time for them to come and visit now, but in a few months when things were back to normal, they'd be able to squeeze up and they could visit.

'Alright, but it won't be for a few months. I have to get Lloydy out of hospital first and let things settle down.'

'That's alright for me. I'm easy.'

Issy was far from easy about it, but felt she had to do the right thing. At least Lukan wasn't here for her to get near him.

'Are you going to send them down on the bus?'

'Dudley say he will bring them down if you want, that way he can see your children too.'

Issy didn't bother to enlighten Jez on the fact that Dudley came down to see her children regularly. He liked coming to Kingston, and they gave him a good reason. He was a great source of comfort and condolence, and had even sat with Lloyd for her once when she was too tired to do it. Clearly, he had not told Jez this, and there was no reason why Issy should.

The rest of the visit, which didn't last long, was cordial. The children came back in which removed any further need for direct conversation between Issy and Jez. Luke Junior was passed around, all the children wanted to hold him, play with him, treat him as a new toy. Issy busied herself in the kitchen and tried to quell the rising resentment that it should be her baby her children should be cooing over. She could not hide her relief when they left in a taxi for the bus station.

She was kneading flower and cornmeal for fried dumplings when Irene came into the kitchen, scanned her mother from head to toe before asking, 'Did you know about Luke Mama?'

It was the question Issy was dreading. Irene knew Luke was her step-father's child. No one had actually said it, and the emphasis for future visits had been around maintaining contact with Darcie and Gloria, bit Irene knew, and she looked at her mother with a mixture of love and pity. She realised, as Lukan had done some time earlier that her mother wasn't invincible, that she could be attacked, and that her wounds could run so deep that she dared not speak about them.

'Is it because of Luke why we moved to Kingston?' she asked, while Issy was still trying to formulate her answer to her first question.

'Yes.' Issy said, rolling the dough in her hands before flattening it into an ellipse, and dropping it into the hot oil in the frying pan.

'Does Daddy know?'

'Of course your Daddy knows!' What does she think they were all doing here if her Daddy didn't know? But Irene was giving her a look that was way beyond her years, the one that said, '*the Daddy doesn't always know.*'

'If you're going to stand there and ask me questions you might as well help me pick the calaloo.'

'Is that why Daddy went back to England?' She asked, picking the seeds from the top and the tired looking withered leaves from the sides of the calaloo stalks.

'That was part of it.' She was glad to have her hands occupied with turning the dumplings, have her mind focused on something practical. She didn't want to admit to her daughter that her husband had been too cowardly to tell her himself, that she had to find out the same way Irene had, by seeing Lukan's face staring back at her from Jez's baby's body.

'What was the other part?'

'There was a lot of things going…' Issy caught herself. This wasn't the right time or person to be unburdening herself to. She needed to let go of so much, needed to uncurl her spring a little, but not to her daughter. She would have to face the treacheries of the world soon enough, the fickleness of men and the heartache of deceit, deception and abandonment, no point introducing her to them now.

'Yes Mama?' she reminded her mother that she hadn't answered her question.

'We needed more money for the school fees once we moved here and you lost your scholarship from Clarendon College, and we'll need money for Lennox's fees for Woolmer's Boys.'

She was quiet for a while, seemingly giving her attention to the calaloo, plunging them into water to allow any small insects still taking refuge to float off. But Issy knew that silence, knew Irene was digesting this and thinking of her next question, which predictably came.

'Daddy hasn't seen Luke, has he?'

That's what the silence was, she was doing the sums.

'No, he was already in England.'

'Doesn't he want to see him?'

'I suppose he'll want to see his so…, to see him.' She couldn't bring herself to call Luke Junior, Lukan's son. It was one thing adopting a child that was there before you came on the scene, but it's hard to accept one afterwards, even though she was a Christian and knew that God loves all children equally, she couldn't bring herself, not at the moment anyway, to love Luke's son.

'Then why does he want us to go to England?'

'I haven't said we'll go yet.'

'So he might come back and we'll all be together like before, like when we lived in Chapelton?'

'I don't know Irene, I really don't know. There's so much happening I don't have time to think about what Luke want or why him want it. Right now, I have to work out how to look after Lloydy when him come out of hospital. I can't keep taking you out of school otherwise we are just wasting good money paying for days that you not getting any teaching.'

'I don't mind Mama, I can always use one of my friends books to catch up, they don't mind, we do it for each other when somebody miss a class.'

'Yes, but your friends not missing as many classes as you,'

'Some of them miss even more…'

'and they didn't just have a big move and they don't have so many thing going on at home.' She didn't really know any of Irene's friends, so she was just speculating that nobody else's life could be as complicated or as disruptive as hers. She was still looking for reasons for not going to England, but the thought of having to share her Sundays with Jez's son, was one good reason to pack her bag and go right now.

'You want me chop these?'

'No, it's all right, I can finish it up.' She would have been grateful for the help, but Irene was asking too many questions.

'But you look so tired Mama.' Irene protested.

'If you want to help, you can iron the boys' shirts for church tomorrow.'

Realising that she wasn't going to get any more out of her mother, Irene went to find the ironing board and set it up in the bedroom.

Issy knew it was going to be hard to keep fending Irene off, especially when she was tired, and that was everyday. She almost let it slip that Luke Junior had already rocked their marriage, that it was one of the reasons she didn't want to go to England, because she didn't know if she could trust Luke anymore. She was praying for a break from all of this, for a quiet space by one of the lagoons, soaking up the salt from the turquoise water like she and Luke did on Saturday or Sunday afternoons during the children's school holidays. Life just seemed such a grind these days, just one thing after another. But the rest Issy craved was not about to happen, not till she'd climbed another mountain, faced another challenge, and they both happened on the same day.

Chapter 26

Lukan was grappling with a few challenges of his own. His wife's letter, whilst encouraging was not definite. She wanted to know how he was going to bring them over. He'd been thinking about it because he knew she would ask, and he had to have a plan in place.

Willam came up with the perfect solution. Lukan should buy a house in England.

'Instead of sending money over to buy land over there, use it to put down a deposit on a little house over here. You can get a nice three bedroom terrace one in Handsworth for a decent price. You can get a mortgage on your wages, and if need be, I'll stand as a guarantor for you.'

The house was found, the applications made, and the mortgage approved in principle. All this he wrote to Issy about, stressing in every letter that she could trust him, that there were no more surprises for her, especially as he was now back working in Birmingham, away from the temptation of Cindy. It might take a while to get everything sorted, but there're grammar schools in Birmingham that were probably better than Excelsior College or Woolmer's Boys, and they were free. The children would still have to sit an entrance exam, but they wouldn't have to pay anything once they were in. If she said yes, he would try to put even more money aside to start paying for the tickets, he would work round the clock if he had to, so they could all be together.

He still didn't know what to say to Jez, so he didn't answer her letters. He sat looking at the four of them, all waiting for a reply. He knew she wanted reassurances from him that he couldn't give. He was making sure she got money for Luke Junior as well as the girls, but that was all he was willing to do. There was another reason he wasn't writing back. One day some of the men on the site were joking about the ways women can trap you. One of them said they can use your handwriting to perform some kind of ritual that will tie you to them, after a while it wears off and they have to do it with new handwriting, a bit like the way the smell of perfume fades and you have to top it up with a new squirt.

He was a Christian, and he prayed every night for protection for him and his family, so maybe that conversation was a message from God that he should stop writing to Jez. In her last letter she said she and the girls went to look for Lloyd and went by the house. She said Issy agreed with her that the children should all know each other, and that she'd be sending Luke down to Kingston with the girls once every three months.

He wasn't sure whether it was a good idea, and Issy hadn't written to tell him, so he didn't know if it was even true. Maybe Jez was saying it to irritate him, or to show that he couldn't keep her away if she wanted to be in touch with them. It might be her way of saying she will find them wherever they are. Issy was a more reliable source of information, she would tell him if it was true. He didn't have to wait long.

When he saw the two letters on the table in the hall, his heart did a double beat, like an excited drummer. His mind skipped immediately to the last time he got two letters at the same time.

'Evening Luke.' Hazel greeted him from the open door of the kitchen, wiping her hands on her half apron as she came out into the hall way. 'you have a couple… I see you find them

237

already,' her voice trailed as she saw the two airmail letters in Luke's large hands. 'You want a cup of tea?'

'Coffee, if you're making one' he said absentmindedly. He couldn't get used to the amount of tea people drank. Every half hour somebody at work would be stopping for a brew up or a drink from their flask. It's no wonder they worked so slow. They should have Maas Vincent to work for, that would put a bit more speed into them. Not that Luke minded too much, especially when they were on piece work. He knew he would always make his bonuses, by just taking half as many tea breaks.

'I'll bring it in to you.'

'Thank you.' He was already opening his door.

He opened the second letter first, and couldn't help scanning to the end to see how Issy had signed it. He could always tell what was coming if he checked the signature. Just 'your wife, Issy.' She was either tired or annoyed with him, which was pretty much the state of play for the last few months. Ripping open the other letter he began reading.

Dear Luke,

I hope when this letter reaches you it finds you in good health and under the protective wings of the Holy Spirit. Luke I don't know where to start. I want to talk about your plans for the houses first in case I run out of space. I think it's good to have a back up plan, and it would certainly be good to be together as a family again. But I need to tell you about some of the things that's been happening here.

Jez turned up with the girls and the baby a couple of Saturdays ago. I wasn't expecting them. She said she told Dudley to tell me she was coming, but when I check with Dudley he said he don't remember her telling him that. I don't believe her either, but anyway, she went to see Lloydy. I don't trust her Luke, especially after what she said about looking after your children, but I suppose it was good for Lloydy to see his sisters. Even so, I ended up agreeing with her that the children can visit once every three months. I don't know how I'm going to manage it, but Darcie and Irene are sensible enough to look after all of them even if I have to work. That was causing me a lot of stress till the other day I got hit by two things at once.

Lilly-Mae's school contacted me at work to say she was playing in the yard and got a rusty nail jammed in her toes. What she was doing running around without her shoes I don't know, but they wanted me to come and get her. I asked them to put her in a taxi and send her down to me but they said they couldn't do that, I would have to come and get her. I had to ask for the time off work, and although they said yes, I think they're getting sick and tired of it now. The thing is, just the day before I found somebody to stay with Lloydy when he comes out of hospital tomorrow. She's a nice girl, down from Manchester, staying with her auntie and looking for work. Somebody at work put me on to her, and I think the children will like her.

Anyway, I had to take Lilly-Mae for a tetanus injection at the hospital, and they let me through quickly because she was crying so much. They dress it and send her home, but of course it's still the middle of the day. I had nobody to leave her with so I took her home. As I open the door I hear a lot of moaning and groaning coming from Irene's room, Oh Lord I'm thinking, don't tell me they send her home from school sick as well, (you know how she suffers with her monthlys sometimes). Then I hear another voice groaning as well, a deep male voice, and I don't want to believe what I think I'm hearing. I couldn't help myself, I walk straight over to her door, push it open and there she was, she and some boy from somewhere, naked in the bed, legs wide apart and moaning like a grown woman. As soon as they hear the door, he flew off her and stand up by the side of the bed, his hands over his privates, like I wanted to look at them.

'What are you doing here?' I screamed at them. Irene started reaching for her clothes while the two of them continue to look at me like a couple of frightened rabbits. No answer. 'Why aren't you at school?' I scream at her again. I don't even want to look at him, shivering like a wet dog by the side of the bed.

'It was half day today.' She said, pulling the sheet to cover herself.

'So why didn't you tell me?'

'I didn't remember.'

'And this is how you use your free time. Get him out of here Irene, get him out! And then I want a serious word with you!'

All this time I forgot that Lilly-Mae was standing in the living room. I picked her up and carried her into my room. I didn't want her to see him leaving, at least she didn't see what they were doing.

When I talked to her after he'd scuttled away, she said it was the first time, that he was a boy from Kingston College and that he had been asking her for a long time but she had always said no.

'What made you say yes today?'

'I don't know. I was just fed up. We never do anything anymore.'

'What do you mean we don't do anything?'

'I'm either at school doing work, or at home doing work, or looking after the children, or sitting with Lloyd at the hospital. We don't do anything interesting or fun since Daddy went to England.'

Luke, she might as well have slapped me round the face with a dead fish. She was saying it was all my fault, as if she couldn't see the struggle I've had trying to keep things together. The worse thing is Luke, he wasn't wearing a rubber.

240

And you know what she had the nerve to say to me, that it didn't get that far seeing as how I interrupted them.

Well, I told her she had to go to church and pray for forgiveness, that she should never, never, never bring anybody else into my house, that she needed to show more respect for her body and not be giving it to every Tom, Dick or Harry. I told her I was ashamed of her, and asked her if that was the kind of example she wanted to set to her brothers and sisters. She ran off crying to her room, muttering about how Jez didn't treat Darcie like I was treating her for doing the same thing. She wouldn't repeat what she said, but if this is the kind of influence Darcie is going to have on Irene I don't want her around them. I'm going to tell her straight when they come down in a few weeks time. Maybe you should write to them Luke, tell them they should put more value on their bodies.

So things are a little tense still. The new girl started the next day. She gets on well with Lloydy and Lilly-Mae, (though she still hook on to me like a leech as soon as I come in the door.) Lilly-Mae's toes gone septic and I have to be changing the dressing every two days. It's a good thing that now is when Lloydy's at home and I have somebody here for him, other wise it would be more problems with work to take time off for her too. Any more of this and you might get your wish after all. I might just pack them up and send them to you.

All of us miss you. Not a day goes by when one of them don't ask about you or talk about you.

Your wife,

Issy.

Lukan looked at the letters as though he was expecting them to talk to him, to tell him what to do. It seemed the harder he worked here, the worse it was getting there. He was tired, and *he* didn't have to come home to a houseful of children. He knew Issy worked hard, knew too that there was probably more that she wasn't telling him. He knew he was responsible for the situation they were in, and he knew he didn't know what to do anymore. He wished he could undo that night with Jez, wished he'd listened to his mother, listened to his Uncle. He'd tied Jez and Issy in a knot together and it seemed like Issy was coming off worse.

'Sorry, the kettle take a long time to boil.' Hazel entered with his coffee, 'you want me to put it down here?' She indicated the chest of drawers at the side of the door.

'You alright Luke?' she asked as he stared at her blankly.

'Yes.' He dragged himself back from the house in Kingston to focus on her concerned face. 'Yes, it's just that Lilly-Mae stood on a rusty nail and she's not been going to school for over a week now. But the good news is that Lloydy's on the mend.' He heard himself and marvelled at how easily he was slipping into the English way of speaking *on the mend.*'

'God be praised!' she said, 'God be praised. Send them my love when you write to them.'

'Yes, I will.' But before that, he needed to talk to the pastor, wanted to ask his advice about writing to his daughters.

They discussed it over a Guinness punch. It had become quite normal for them to discuss even church business over a Guinness punch. Sister McCullough made a fine punch and Pastor liked to show it off. Lukan, on account of William being an elder and joint treasurer in the church, had quite a lot of access to the pastor who passed around sometimes. As he did on the night Luke received the letters.

'Come over to my house, relax a little and let's pray together.'

Luke was happy to accept, release the pressure building in him before it blew a hole in his head.

'Is there anyone you can send it care off?' He wasn't just a holy man, he was a very practical one.

'Uncle Dudley!' It came to him immediately. Why hadn't

he thought of that before? He would write to Darcie and Gloria via Dudley. He would ask him to get them to read the letters and leave them with him, so there would be no chance of Jez getting hold of them. The pastor didn't actually believe in what he called Lukan's 'old wives' tale' but he could see it had an impact on his brother, and he felt it was his duty to bring people from where they were to the Lord one step at a time. He preferred it if they came to his church because they trusted him, not because they were fearful of him. He was good at earning people's trust.

'Why don't you come on the church outing to Rhyl on Saturday, I think there're a few more places left. It would do you good to relax, have a little fun. I suggest you tell your wife that too. Your daughter is screaming it out to her, she should listen.'

Chapter 27

Issy was already listening. Even though she was always tired and sometimes had to force herself to go, she began going out with the children again. Not to places that cost money like the cinema, but to the markets, shopping for trinkets and cheap toys. She bought them ice cream, fudge and candy floss. Things she didn't make but she knew they liked. When Dudley came down to visit they went to the beach, spent the whole day there with food. Irene was eager to help with the preparations, and was keen to help her siblings build sand castles, hunt for shells, race on the sand, and play games. Issy found it hard to relocate the picture of her in the bed with whoever his name was. Here she was still a child, not a forced-ripened woman. She was gradually rebuilding her trust in Irene.

She took them up to visit her family in Brandon Hill. Mavis came with them. They stayed overnight with her sister, all squeezed in like sardines in Beatrice's small two bed roomed house. They picked and ate mangoes straight from the trees, picked gungo peas and dug up a couple of heads of yam to take home. Things they couldn't do in Kingston.

When the children went to bed Issy, Mavis and Beatrice sat out on the veranda, the cool breeze tickling their skin and brushing their hair. Her sisters drank rum and coconut water, Issy drank lemonade and longed for some rum, but was staying true to her church vows of abstinence. They reminisced about growing up, about the rivalry between them, about Issy's waywardness, her skills as a seamstress and her gift with anything that included sugar.

'Do you remember the dresses she used to make?' Mavis asked.

'Yes. Papa would almost always make her let out the seams, or let down the hem, or take up the neck line. The girl was hell bent on showing off her body.' Beatrice laughed.

'And it was worse when she came to Kingston. You couldn't even keep her in at night.' Mavis added.

'It's only because you two didn't have the figure for it.' Issy retaliated.

'We didn't have the nerve.'

'What happen to that figure Issy?'

'It's still in there somewhere,' she joked, 'just waiting for an easier life and a bit more exercise. What do you expect after seven pickney?'

'At least you have the excuse of seven pickney. I don't even have one to show, and I'm bigger than you.' Mavis confessed.

'Yes, but you born bigger. You nearly killed Mama when you born.'

'Is how you know, you was there?' Mavis leaned forward touching Beatrice's knee, 'is how much older you think you are than us?'

'I'm just telling you what Papa used to say.'

'Him must be only say it to you, because I never hear him say that, and I was around him a lot.' Mavis joked.

'Yes, but it was me him trusted with the family secrets.' Beatrice winked at Issy.

'You just make up things all the time.' Issy interrupted.

And so they went on, remembering a time when they were carefree, when fashion and boys and homework were their only concern, when there was always a room in Papa's house for them, and always a word of wisdom from him. So much had changed, yet so much stayed the same, the smell of roasting corn from somewhere in the distance; the high pitched arguments of the crickets, the fleeting flashes of light of the peenie wallies, the heavy beats from a distant party, the howl of a frightened dog, the moon, like a giant torch, changing the shapes of trees and houses, picking out splashes of colour, red hibiscus, yellow crotons, purple bougainvillea.

One of the children was snoring so loudly it made them all laugh.

'That will be Lloydy,' Issy volunteered, 'he never seem to be able to get enough air.'

As they reminisced, laughed, drank, or just sat, Issy knew that she couldn't go to England, that she couldn't give up this. It was bad enough being in Kingston. The noise and the hussle and bustle she'd found so attractive as a young girl had lost its appeal. She couldn't sit on her veranda in Maxfield Avenue and listen to the mating calls of frogs. No frogs, no family. Even Mavis was always busy. She would have to write to Luke and tell him. Whatever they have to face they have to face it here, not run away from it. The two of them with God *must* be stronger that Jez. Maybe they were giving her credit for things that had nothing to do with her.

'I hear you had Luke's boy down the other week' Beatrice said, as if she read her thoughts.

'I see you been talking to Mavis.'

'Well, you didn't tell me it was top secret.' Mavis reached for the bottle to pour another shot into her glass.

'How that worked out for you?' Beatrice was concerned.

'It was alright, better than I was expecting.'

She hadn't confronted Darcie as she had planned, deciding at the last minute that it was her father's job to do that, she merely warned Irene before they arrived that she was not to be influenced by what Darcie said she was doing. It was still early days and it was still painful, and there were times when she felt the anger rising that Luke had left her this to cope with, but she managed to suppress it. They sat round the big dining table and ate and talked and laughed. There was a lot of discussion about the various ailments and accidents of Issy's children. Not wishing to be left out Gloria told them about the day a big dog chased her and Jez. It was coming after them and barking and snarling and baring its teeth. They couldn't run fast enough, it was catching up with them. Then her mother suddenly turned round, said something to it in a language she didn't understand. The dog stopped, screeched to a halt, hung its head, then slinked off, tail between its legs, looking over its shoulder occasionally as it headed in the direction from whence it had come.

'Gloria said when she asked her mother what language she spoke to the dog in, Jez said 'dog language'.'

'Your mother can speak dog language?' Poor old Lilly-Mae was intrigued.

'Nothing about that woman would surprise me.' Mavis said sourly.

'Well we laughed and laughed, and you could see Gloria felt good because she's usually so quiet, and don't normally have much to say.'

'So when you going to England then?' Beatrice, who was always very direct, asked.

'Who say me going?' Issy retorted.

'Is not you same one tell me about the big plans your husband have for you all? You losing you memory as well as your figure?' Beatrice mocked. 'Girl, you better make your mind up before him find another Jez over there.'

'Is the same thing me telling her, but she keep talking about how she don't want to leave Jamaica.' Mavis joined in.

'You know how many women would love to go to England? Would sell them pickney to go, and there's your husband begging you to come and you keeping him waiting.' Beatrice took a sip from her glass.

Issy knew both her sisters were getting drunk. They were likely to say anything without a thought for how she may receive it; they were losing the capacity to think before speaking. She didn't want to hear any more. They could say what they liked, she wasn't picking up herself and travelling all that way, leaving all this behind. Anyway, things had settled down now. Lloydy was back at school, Lilly-Mae's foot was the last catastrophe that had happened, and that was a good six months ago. She still kept the girl on to help with the cleaning and the cooking three days a week, and she was keeping a closer eye on all the children, especially Irene.

From what the girls said, they received a letter from their father, through their Uncle Dudley. They couldn't understand why they had to leave it there, but then they didn't always understand their father or his Uncle. They accepted a lot, questioned little. It was something Issy wished she could change about them, make them a little more like Irene, who would keep digging till she got an answer.

No, she wasn't going to England, there wasn't any point discussing it with two drunken women. When she failed to divert the conversation from herself and her reluctance to travel, she excused herself and went to bed. She slept soundly that night, in the safety of her family, in the village of her birth. There would be many occasions when she would remember this night and long for it. If she'd known what was to come she'd have stayed talking with her sisters for longer, savoured the intimacy of the strong web they formed with their words and their reminiscences, snuggled into the security of their lifelong knowledge and acceptance of her foibles.

Chapter 28

Lukan took Pastor's advice and went on the trip to Rhyl. A handful of members were already waiting outside the church doors, even though it would be at least an hour before the coach was due to leave. He'd arrived early with William who was responsible for booking the coach and needed to be around to ensure everything ran smoothly. Lukan enjoyed the nods of deference paid to him by the other members, a recognition of his close association with the pastor and Brother William. He noted the bags of food, Hessian baskets with brightly coloured tea towels as lids, Thermos flasks poking through the tops. Umbrellas firmly wedged under armpits and coats and jackets draped over bent arms. This was a million miles away from the sea side trips he'd been on in Jamaica. If there were towels for the beach they were not evident, and he assumed, given the temperature today, that any swimwear worn by members under their clothes would remain safely hidden. On William's advice he hadn't bothered to go to the expense of purchasing trunks.

'You won't need them, Rhyl's too cold. Save your money,' he'd laughed.

Within half an hour the coach, and most of the members had arrived, excited anticipation filled the air. For some, like Lukan, it was their first trip with the church. Other more seasoned tripsters offered to take them under their wings. William had asked Lukan to help count members on and off the coach, so of necessity they were the last ones to get on. William had reserved a seat at the front of the coach, but the only seat left for Lukan, as they had manage to fill the coach, was next to Sister Sadie who was taking the trip on her own because her husband had been called into work at short notice. Fortunately she'd managed to sell his seat, but it did leave her feeling spare.

'You mind if I sit beside you?' Lukan asked out of politeness as there was nowhere else for him to sit.

'No, not at all.' She sounded like she'd been in England a while, had developed, not just the accent but the sentence structure. 'It's Brother Lukan isn't it?'

'Yes. I'm sorry but I can't remember your name.'

'Sister Sadie, Sadie Price.'

'Oh, you're Brother Price's wife?'

'Yes.' He heard the pride in her voice. Brother Price was a member of the choir with a rich dark baritone voice, the one often chosen to deliver powerful solos that moved the congregation. Lukan had seen the persuasiveness of his voice at alter calls. It wasn't always clear if people were moving to be closer to God or closer to Brother Price. Maybe it was his beautiful voice that had attracted his beautiful wife. Lukan had noticed her in church, always modestly but well dressed. Her figure was never on show, but was always outlined with the use of a well placed belt, or a well cut skirt.

'We don't see you too often on these trips.' She said.

'This is my first one.' He confessed. 'Maybe you can show me what to do.'

'Happy to. But there's really nothing to it. We go, we have some fun on the rides, eat a little, drink a little, walk on the beach a little, then we come home.'

'I think I can manage that.' Lukan laughed.

'It's just about a change of scene and a bit of sea air, and a chance for the members to get to know each other outside of church.'

William summonsed everyone to attention to join him in prayer for God's protection on the journey and for a happy and enjoyable day. Luke settled down to hearing about Sister Price's journey to God, His hand in her career as a nurse, and His guidance to the church and her husband. She was easy to talk to, had a soft, light voice that reminded him of Jamaican evening breeze. He found himself reciprocating with information about himself, ending with why this was his first outing, and why because of work she didn't see him in church so often. They were so engrossed in conversation they hardly noticed the three hours it took to get them to Rhyl.

As the coach pulled into a big car park on the edge of the town people began gathering their things. Excitement was mounting as William announced the arrangements for leaving bags and coats on the coach and the time for returning. He got everyone with watches to synchronise them, before issuing a plea to look out for each other as Brothers and Sisters in Christ. There had apparently been trips where people had got lost, had not realised the time and had turned up over an hour late. It was church policy not to leave anyone behind, and everyone had to contribute to the extra costs of paying the coach driver's overtime. From what Luke heard, there'd been some very un-Christianly comments made about the late-comers. William had explained in his briefing to Lukan before they set off, that it's better to apply peer pressure than to have the embarrassment of leaving one of the flock behind. It wouldn't look good.

It was his job to make sure everyone left the coach, and that nothing was left on show. He invited Sister Sadie to leave if she wanted, but she said she'd wait, especially as he was sitting on the aisle seat and she'd have to squeeze past him. So it was that they were the last two off the coach. Little groups had formed and were already drifting away. William had waited for them, wanting to make sure Luke was OK. He didn't want to spend the whole day with Luke, as the objective was for Luke to get to know other members better.

'Are you joining anyone Sister Sadie?' William asked looking around at the disappearing groups wrapped in hats and coats, and wearing sensible shoes. Not a pair of sandals in sight. Some of his church members were dressed more for a mountain expedition than a day on the beach.

'No, I was just going to join up with whoever was free.'

'Well it looks like the only free people are me and Brother Luke here.'

'Then I am happy to join you.'

'We..ee..ll, it's just that I promised Brother Marshall that I would spend some time with him today sorting through church business before we relax and start to enjoy ourselves.'

'So it looks like it's you and me, Brother Lukan.' She smiled up at him.

'You don't mind do you?' William asked, gratitude oozing like tooth paste out of a tube.

'Not at all.'

'Thank you.' He clasped her hand with both of his, 'thank you. I'll catch up with you later. It's not such a big place that I won't be able to find you.'

'So it look like I'm the child and you're the teacher.' Lukan looked down at her small oval face in which twinkled two equally oval and mischievous eyes.

'I will teach you everything I know, but you are far from being a child.' The twinkle was in her voice too.

'Thank you. Can you remind Willi... I mean Brother William about that some time?' he was only half joking. He felt a novice in the church compared to William, and the issues going on at home made him think William saw him as incompetent. 'Do you want me to carry that bag for you? It looks a little heavy?'

'No. Thank you anyway. Shall we walk?'

She headed left from the coach park to the toilets, and no sooner arrived than asked him to hold the bag as she didn't want to take her food in with her.

'That's why it's good to travel with someone.'

'All this food is for you?' he was incredulous. He only had a few sandwiches, a couple of ripe bananas, and a piece of sweet potato pudding. William said there would be a lot of places to eat and get hot drinks so not to weigh himself down. But here she was with a basket heavy enough to feed, if not five thousands, then pretty close.

'I always pack extras to share with others, sometimes people don't bring enough, they don't realise how the sea air's going to make them hungry, then they're too embarrassed to ask. It all goes in the end, especially on the way back. Did you bring any food?'

He pointed to his small canvas bag, the one he took to work each day. She laughed that tinklely laugh again.

'Looks like I might have to feed you,' she said over her shoulder as she disappeared into the toilet.

Lukan couldn't remember the last time he'd had so much fun. Sadie was a great companion. She knew Rhyl, having been there several times, knew the best rides to go on and laughed all the way through the dodgems and the waltzers. He tried roller skating and they laughed and laughed as they fell over time and time again. He drew the line at the donkey rides, protesting that he could ride a donkey at home for free and didn't see why he should pay for it here.

They sat on a bandstand and ate a well earned lunch before venturing to the beach. The sun, which had woken with such energy that morning, soon lost its potency to the bracing north winds that made walking on the beach a push against an invisible wall.

'Boy, what I wouldn't give to be on Hellshire Beach right now.' Lukan said, thinking of the long stretches of white sand, the glistening water, but most of all the blistering sun. He could almost smell the fried fish and dumplings and feel the sand between his toes. 'I will never complain about the heat again.'

Lukan watch in amazement as people ran into the sea, dressed only in trunks or swimsuits.

'These people must me mad,' he shivered. She'd recommended a sea front café from which they could watch the beach and its population, warmed by the radiators and the hot chocolate they both sipped on.

'They don't know any different, this is the only sea they know, so they don't think anything of it.'

'Do you ever go in there?'

'I did once... in the summer.'

'Was it any warmer?'

'The water was freezing but the sun was hot, so I dried out quite quickly.'

A picture of Sister Sadie in a bathing costume flashed involuntarily across his mind. It unsteadied him.

'Are you OK?' she quickly spotted his discomfort.

'Yes. Just the thought of it makes my blood run cold.'

'You look like you could stand a bit of cold, big strapping man like you,' she laughed.

'I can stand cold alright,' flattered by her description of him, 'I have to work in it a lot of the time. I just don't see the point of putting myself in it when I don't have to. That don't look at all like fun to me.'

For some reason they both got the giggles, and from then everything they said reduced them to tear jerking hysterics.

'We should be going now.'

'Or Willi... Brother William will be sending out a search party.'

'He will chastise me for leading you astray.'

'He would have to get past me first.'

'Are you offering to protect me from Brother William's wrath?'

'I'll protect you from him and anybody else. No point being a big strapping man for nothing.'

He laughed and she giggled as they gathered their things and started making their way back to the coach.

The bracing air outside did little to dampen their spirits and they were still laughing, bumping into each other, holding theirs sides and wiping their eyes when they arrived.

'Well you two seem to be enjoying yourselves,' one of the brothers who looked like he'd just had an argument with his wife grumbled.

'The Lord knew I needed a laugh and sent Sister Sadie to help me.' Luke answered boldly.

'Is how much you pay for that big teddy bear?' his wife asked Sister Sadie.

'I didn't buy it,' she giggled, 'Brother Lukan shot down some ducks and won it. The man wouldn't let him play again because he was so good. He gave it to me.'

The woman gave her husband a 'why have you never won anything for me?' look as she stepped onto the coach.

Maybe it was the chill, or maybe the thought of paying extras, but there were no late comers. Lukan checked them all back on and found his seat beside Sister Sadie. That's when she offered her basket containing sandwiches, patties, fruit, biscuits and cake to be passed around the coach and for people to help themselves to what they wanted. Within minutes the basket was returned empty. She winked at him, 'Told you.' He smiled his acceptance of her wisdom.

Sea air, and especially Welsh sea air have a way of tiring you out, even if you didn't do much, and within minutes of the homeward prayer, and a few excited sharing of wins and losses on the fairground attractions, of people making themselves almost sick on the rides, and of the rip off cost of drinks, the coach settled into the gentle hum of snoozing passengers. Lukan was running the day through his head and smiling at every frame when he felt a tap on his shoulder. He turned to find Sadie's head resting there, her breaths deep and even, her eyes lightly closed. 'Sadie.' He whispered, but she was asleep. He was grateful for the cover of dark. This may be frowned on by many in the church, despite its innocence.

She looked uncomfortable with her head at that angle, but he resisted the impulse to slide his hand behind her back to cushion it more securely. He was far from sleep. He hadn't experienced this side of England, going out and just relaxing for the day. This was probably what Cindy wanted him to do with her. He hadn't thought about her in a while, maybe it was because he was in Wales why she came to mind. This kind of life would certainly make it more bearable, even enjoyable being in England. He'd have to write and tell Issy. Her last letter hadn't left him with much hope that she wanted to come. He was confused; making plans for her to come and her saying she's not sure. If she was here they could be doing this together, they could bring their children like some of the members did, and it would be like it was in Jamaica, just with a little less heat.

Maybe it was the sea air, or maybe the woman asleep on his shoulder, but he was feeling aroused in a way he'd managed to suppress for many months, since moving back to Birmingham. He really wished Issy was here. He started to compose the letter in his head that would convince her to come.

Chapter 29

'Mama, I got top marks in the Biology test today.' Irene met Issy as she dropped the shopping bags she was carrying.

'Good. It's time you were back on top. You see what you can do when you settle down?'

'Mama, you bring anything for me?' Lilly-Mae was by her side, fingers in mouth, eyes looking up expectantly.

'Even if I did you wouldn't get it with those fingers in you mouth. How many times I must tell you to stop sucking your fingers? I'm going to put some chicken dodo on them, and see if you want to suck them then!'

'Mama, Mama, a dog bite me today when I was coming home from school.' Lloyd chipped in.

'Where?'

'On my arm.'

'Let me see it.' Lloyd showed her the mark on the inside of his right arm. 'Oh, it's only a scratch, I'll bathe it later and put some iodine on it.'

'Mama, there's a letter from Daddy on the dresser.' Lennox said.

'Good, I'll read it later.'

'Are we going to England?' Lilly-Mae asks, in the same tone she uses to ask if they're going to the beach, like the two are similar.

'Anything happen to you Lennox?' Issy asked.

'No.'

'Why can't you two be more like Irene and Lennox. Either bring me good news or no news, which for Lennox is good news.'

'Did you cook the rice Irene?'

'Yes Mama'

'Did you put on the mutton to heat up?'

'Yes, it should be ready now.'

'Good, then if you and Lennox can pack out these things out I'll share it up. Lloyd, get the plates out and set the table.'

'But Mama, what about my arm?'

'Lloydy, it's only a scratch. Let's eat first, I'm hungry, and if I don't feed Lilly-Mae soon she going to chew off her fingers for dinner.'

It was like this most evenings. She'd managed to get some cross over shifts so she could be at home most nights with the children. For the few shifts when she had to work nights the help stayed till she came home. It was working out OK. They were settled into a routine now, she was a good worker and the hospital did their best to accommodate her, figuring it was better to have her there consistently between eight and six than to not have her there at all. Even if one of her children was sick, it was easier to get help during the day than at night. Irene was settled in school again. Lennox was same old Lennox. Nothing ever troubled him. He had a few friends that he walked home with after school, and sometimes went to their houses. He seemed to have adapted easiest to the move, he demanded little of her at a time when she had little to give.

By the time they'd eaten, washed up, did their homework and their Bible scripture – it was time to start the round of showers. When they were all in bed Issy sat with a mug of fever grass tea and opened Luke's letter.

Dear Issy,

It's good to hear that things are a lot more settled there,

and that all the children are well. I know it wasn't easy, and I wish I was there to help, but things are moving here with the house. I find a nice three bedroom house that would be big enough for all of us. It needs a bit of work, but we knocked quite a bit off what they were asking for it. The work is nothing too big for me, and the money I'll save will help with the cost of fixing it up. Don't get me wrong, it's liveable, just not to the standard yet that I would like you to come over to. I put in an offer, and they accept it. William going to help me with the paperwork and as the mortgage approved already it could be mine in just a few of months. I'm learning a lot from him and Pastor McCullough, as both of them buy and rent out houses.

I went on a trip to the seaside to a place called Rhyl a few weeks ago. You and the children would like it. There was a fairground with all kinds of rides. I can just see Irene and Lennox on some of them. You would love them too, especially the one called the Watlzers. They had all kinds of sweets, candy floss, toffee apples and a kind a candy called rock that when you bite it have 'Rhyl' running all through it. I would love to take you there Issy.

I heard from the girls. I think they like getting their own letters. I don't know why I didn't think about it before. Darcie say she doesn't have a boyfriend, that she was only trying to show off to Irene. Gloria says she nearly got bitten by a dog, now she's frightened of dogs. That child would be frightened of her own shadow if it said boo to her. They're going to see Uncle Dudley once a week, and he's giving them some extra pocket money out of his own money.

Seems like you all managing out there without me. Issy, I miss you and the children. Although William and Pastor keep telling me that buying a house here is a good investment, and I know you think so too, it doesn't make any sense if my family still in Jamaica. It's either you come over here Issy, or I come back home. I can leave the house for William to manage.

Kiss the children for me and tell them I love them. I love you.

Your loving husband,

Luke.

Issy stared at the letter for a long time, fatigued, desperate for sleep, and painfully aware that in a few hours she would have to start it all over again. Conscious too, that she was going to climb into an empty bed, while her husband was doing the same thousands of miles away. But she couldn't think about it tonight, she couldn't think of disrupting the children again, not now when they had just settled. It's a shame he was buying the house over there already, but even that could work out for them, especially if Uncle William managed it like Dudley was managing the one in Sav-la-Mar. England rent could mean big money over here. They wouldn't lose anything if Lukey bought the house then came back home. He could come and go like they'd planned. It was only the thing with Jez that had them flying about all over the place, and everything seemed fine now. Maybe coming to their house and seeing that Issy was prepared to accept Luke Junior was what did it. Maybe she realised that she couldn't win, that she and Luke were too solid for her to come between them. She'd write back to him on her next day off.

That weekend Dudley came down and they went to the beach. Issy told him about the house Luke was buying and confided in him that she didn't want to go to England.

'Well, you can't really lose with houses, here or in England. I personally think it's a wise move for him to buy there if him have the opportunity. Luke is a very lucky man.'

'It's not just luck Dudley, he's a hard worker.'

'I know, but he could be working just as hard and have some woman spend it on foolishness. Him lucky to have you.

Look where him reach, three houses in Jamaica and one in England. How many men from Sav you think do that? Come to think about it, how many men from Jamaica do that? And with seven pickne...children?'

'So you think I should write and tell him we're not coming, to buy the place and rent it?'

'I can't tell you want to do, but I know you have a good business head, and you're a hard worker, and you two are good for each other.'

'Thanks Dudley. I'll write to him tomorrow after church.'

Issy didn't make it to church, she sent Lennox and Lilly-Mae with Irene so she could stay home with Lloyd who seemed to have caught a chill from the beach and had a bit of fever. She decided, seeing as he was so sickly, to leave him in bed, sponge him down with some Bay Rum, and feed him fever grass tea. When he wasn't better by the night she asked the help to come in the next day. She was used to being at home with Lloyd and was glad for the work. What Irene took in school fees, Lloyd was competing for in nursemaid money.

Two days later he was no better, didn't want to eat anything, and when she made him sit up to drink some chicken soup, he brought it right back up, all over the sheets, giving her extra work to strip his bed and put on clean sheets, which he soaked with sweat within a few hours. If he wasn't better by tomorrow she was going to have to take him to the doctor.

Over the evening meal Lennox complained that Lloyd was talking rubbish in his sleep and thrashing about so much he could hardly sleep himself, could he sleep in Issy's room or in the living room? As if on cue Lloyd emerged from his room, looking drunk and lost as he tried to find the toilet. Lilly-Mae pointed and laughed at the dribble running down his face.

'Lloydy, wipe your face, you look like a baby,' she screeched.

Lloyd didn't appear to hear her, but continued to stumble around, not knowing where to turn.

'He don't look like a baby, he look like a drunken man.' Lennox laughed.

'Mama, what's wrong with him?' Irene, noticing his rolling eyes was as alarmed as Issy, who rushed over to him and tried to guide him to the toilet.

'The toilet is this way Llo…' she began as Lloyd lashed out at her, his arm catching her across the face.

'Lloyd!' she shouted, shocked, and grabbed his arms. He tried, but couldn't focus on Issy's face.

'The toilet is this way. Do you want the toilet?' He nodded and she guided him firmly toward the bathroom door, her hands sliding off his hot, sticky skin.

'Did you wash your hands?' Issy asked as he left the toilet. 'What's the matter Lloyd, what's the matter?' She held him as he trembled like young bamboo in a hurricane.

'What's the matter with him Mama?' Irene was beside her, silently offering help as the others sat rigid, not knowing what to do or think.

'Help me get him back into bed.' Lloyd was shaking so much he couldn't move. He was big for his age, following in his father's footsteps. Irene and Issy took one arm each and half pulled half guided him into his room, struggling to get him to sit down.

'What's the matter with him Mama?' Irene's voice shook in time with Lloyd's body, as he began to gasp for breath.

'It must be the fever, he's delirious. Or maybe it's his lungs. Or maybe he's having another panic attack' Issy didn't want to admit that she didn't know what was happening, not when the children were relying on her for answers. She couldn't let them down. 'Maybe he's going to need oxygen like last time. I'm going to have to get him back to the hospital.'

'How?'

'Call a taxi. If it's his lungs I have to get him there quickly.' She was trying, unsuccessfully, to keep the panic out of her voice.

There are many disadvantages to living on a main road, but one big advantage is readily available taxis.

Irene ran outside and two minutes later returned with a taxi. Issy with no time to change Lloyd's clothes wrapped him in a sheet, and she and Irene guided him into the taxi.

'You have to stay here with the others,' she told a relieved Irene, who'd somehow sensed the depth of her mother's concern. Something was very wrong, although Lloyd was breathing a little better, he still didn't look good.

'Not again, Lord,' she prayed silently as the taxi drove off toward the hospital. He was making whimpering, whining noises, a far cry from the lashing out of a few minutes ago, and his breathing was a little easier. She just hoped the waiting room wasn't too full.

The two middle-aged male patients, a little worse for drink, gawked as Issy guided her son, wrapped in a white sheet, to the reception desk, and had a brief conversation with the receptionist before guiding him to a seat as far as she could away from them.

'I'll get him in next, and if they complain I'll tell them his case was more serious. Don't worry, Doctor Pike's on tonight, he's good with children.' Issy breathed a sigh of relief, Lloyd had seen Dr Pike before, he knew his case, she felt a boost of optimism, like having the final straw lifted off again.

She stood anxiously as the doctor examined Lloyd, listened to his chest, took his temperature, checked his reflexes, asked Issy how long it had been going on, whether there were any other symptoms that he wasn't showing now. She told him everything, the words tumbling out like marbles down a steep hill, in her eagerness to help him make a speedy diagnosis,

'Is it his lungs doctor?'

'I'm not quite sure yet Mrs Lukan, there's something not quite adding up.'

'What do you mea...'

'What's this for?' he interrupted her pointing to the plaster on Lloyd's arm.

'Oh, I put that on, a few days ago. He said a dog bite him, but it was only a scratch.' Issy was more concerned about what was going on with his breathing, there was something the doctor wasn't telling her, she knew the look, she saw it often enough in her work.

'When did the dog bite him?' why was he so concerned about that little thing when Lloyd had much bigger thing wrong with him?

'It was last week on Wednesday,' she said slowly, doing the calculations in her head, 'yes, last week Wednesday.'

'Mrs Levy, I just need to go and check something, I'll soon come back.'

He hadn't done a good enough job hiding his unease, and by the time he returned Issy had convinced herself that Lloyd was going to need an operation or at least more oxygen.

'Mrs Levy,' he was very brisk now, like he had the answer, 'I want to run some test on you son. I'm going to keep him in tonight, but I think for his sake and the other patient's sake it would be better for him to go in the barrier room, especially as you say he gets disoriented.'

'Is a panic attack like last time doctor?'

'I can't say for sure what it is till I get the test results back. I'll need to take some blood.'

'Can I stay with him tonight doctor?'

'I don't think there's any need to Mrs Levy. I'm going to give him a sedative so he can get a good night sleep, you would only be watching him sleep. Come back in the morning.'

'Can I stay till he falls asleep?'

She helped to prepare him for bed, all the time wondering

why it was always Lloyd. She was putting her faith in God that it wasn't anything too serious, just a bad fever. Maybe it was something to do with his concussion, she imagined brain tumour or...but it couldn't be that or they wouldn't be giving him a sedative and being so calm about it.

She carried the image of his peaceful slumbering face to bed, having assured Irene that the doctors didn't seem too worried, and thanked her for putting the others to bed. She'd already alerted her work that she wouldn't be in, more days loss of pay, but at least they were letting her keep the job. She just hoped it wasn't going to be a long time off with Lloyd again.

By late afternoon the results were back. It had been a pretty distressing morning with Lloyd alternating between complete lethargy and talking to people no one else could see, even cowering on the bed like someone was going to hit him, some person he was terrified of. Issy had shaken him a couple of times to bring him back to the reality of the room. She was convincing that he was having another panic attack. He'd just been given another sedative and was drifting into a fitful sleep when she took the opportunity to get something to eat.

There were three of them around his bed when she pushed the door open. A momentary hush fell among them, as though they'd been caught gossiping.

'Oh, you're back Mrs Levy. We have the test result.'

'What is it doctor?' She sensed with a mother's instinct that it was not good news.

'Where's your husband Mrs Levy, where's Lloyd's father?'

'He's in England. Why you asking?'

'Is there anyone you can call to come and be with you for a few minutes, somebody responsible?'

'Why doctor? Why?'

'We're just waiting for one more result within the next hour, I don't want to say anything till then, but it would be good to have somebody with you, you look tired, you might need some support.'

'Doctor I'm a nurse, I've been looking after my children by myself since…'

'Mrs Levy, take my advice, ask someone to come.'

She heard the firmness in his voice and knew there was no point arguing. The only person she could think of was Mavis, but she was at work. Maybe they'd let her come if the hospital called her.

'What's the matter Issy?'

'I don't know but it must be something bad otherwise they would tell me.' She'd gone over all the possibilities, if it wasn't to do with his concussion, and he didn't need an operation, then it was probably nothing physical. Her biggest fear was that they were going to tell her Lloyd was going mad. He'd certainly been doing some weird things: lashing out, being frightened of invisible people, talking to himself.

'Well, it looks like they're going to tell you now.' Her sister observed the two doctors walking towards them.

'Mrs Levy, we have the final test result and it is what we thought it was. I think you should sit down.'

'Is it psychiatric doctor? Is he going mad? He's only a ba…'

'Who's this?' the doctor turned his gaze to Mavis.

'This is my sister doctor, she came from work.'

'I'll get to the point then. I'm afraid it isn't good news. Mrs Levy your son has rabies.'

'Rabies!' the two women exclaimed in unison. It was the last thing either of them expected to hear.

'Yes, all the tests confirm it.'

'But how him get rabies?' Mavis asked the question that was in Issy mind.

'Mrs Levy you said Lloyd was bitten by a dog last week, about eight days ago, you said that's why he had the plaster on his arm.'

'Yes, but it was just a little scratch, it didn't give him any trouble, it didn't bleed for any time. I only put the plaster on it because he's such a cry baby, that little scratch couldn't give him...'

'What does that mean doctor?' Mavis asked the question Issy didn't want to hear the answer to. She knew what it meant, but maybe they were mistaken, maybe it didn't have to mean what she knew it must. She understood now why the doctor insisted she had someone with her.

'It means we can't save him. It's set in too far. There's nothing we can do for him but keep him comfortable.'

'You mean he's going to die?'

'By the time it gets to this stage there's nothing we can do. If we'd caught it earlier, if you'd brought him in as soon as he got the bite, we could have given him a vaccine, but it's too late now.'

'But how did it happen so quick?' her understanding was that it took weeks, months even, for rabies to develop, 'how did it happen so quick?'

Was it her fault, should she have acted sooner?

'When did the dog bite him?' Mavis asked.

'Last week...' it was such a trivial thing she didn't thing to mention it to anybody.

'But Lloydy usually get on so well with dogs, them always seem to like him, even that one up in Brandon Hill that everybody scared of come to Llo...'

'Oh my God,' Issy's eyes open wide as she recalled the conversation with Gloria about being chased by the dog, 'Jez.'

'Who?' asked he doctor.

'What's she got to do with it?' asked Mavis.

'She's trying to kill him.' Her answer made sense to neither the doctor or her sister.

'Mrs Levy, do you know the dog that bit your son, because it should be found before it bites anybody else.'

'I don't know. He was coming home from school.'

There were a lot more questions, and instructions that she couldn't take in because all she could focus on was that the doctor just told her her son was going to die, that there was nothing they could do.

'How long him have doctor?' she asked cutting across some instruction he was giving to Mavis.

'A few day, maybe a week, it's quite aggressive.'

'She might be able to stop it.' Issy muttered to herself, as the doctor continued his explanation of what was going to happen to Lloyd, how they were going to treat him. She'd stopped listening and was formulating her own plan to save her son's life. If it was Jez doing this she was going to have to ask her to stop it. Plead with her, agree to whatever she wanted. She could have Luke if she wanted, but she couldn't let Lloyd die.

'I have to go and see Jez.' She said emphatically to Mavis after the doctors had gone.

'Girl, you mad?' Mavis was incredulous. 'Even if it was her, you hear what the doctor said, it's too late.'

'If it's she doing it, she can stop it.' Issy insisted. 'She *have* to stop it.'

'And if it isn't her, what kind of fool you going to look like, going up there crawling to her. You know how she would laugh at you?'

'You think I care about how much she laugh? I'll do whatever I have to do to save Lloydy.'

Mavis realised it was pointless arguing with Issy in this state, she'd been her sister for too long, the only thing she could do was help her pick up the pieces afterwards.

'Anyway, you can't go anywhere today, it's too late, but you have to let Lukan know.'

She hadn't thought of him, but now she did, anger bubbled up in her, red and raw, a volcano popping its glowing bubbles, threatening to spill over and engulf her, burn her to cinders, singe her flesh and leave her bones exposed, clanging and rattling.

She had Pastor McCullough's telephone number which Luke had sent to her in case of any emergency. She'd have to go home to get it but she didn't want to leave Lloyd. She felt she had to stay with him, even though he was sleeping and wouldn't miss her. She didn't know what to do, stay with Lloyd, go and see Jez, or phone Lukan.

'But there would be no guarantee he'll be at Pastor's house.' She said eventually to a waiting Mavis.

'Just leave a message with him.'

'You could go and send him a telegram for me.' Issy suggested, not wanting to leave Lloyd's bedside.

'No Issy,' she had to be firm, seeing her sister's confusion, 'you have to do it, in case he wants to ask you any questions.'

After much persuasion, Issy agreed to go and get the number, but only on the promise from Mavis that she'd stay with Lloyd. Although Mavis thought Issy needed someone with her more than Lloyd did, she allowed her the peace of mind of knowing there was someone with Lloyd. Running in to find the number she'd written down for an emergency she never thought would happen, she almost tripped over Lilly-Mae.

'Mama Veronica stood on my foot at school today and the teacher didn't…' the rest of the complaint was squeezed out of her as Issy scraped her up and hugged her tight. Shocked but pleased Lilly-Mae looked as though she was making a mental note of what to do on future to elicit this response from her mother. Scanning the room for her other children she asked Irene, 'Where's Lennox?'

'He staying over at his friend's house for a while. How come you're home so early Mama?'

'I have to go to the post office,' she suddenly remembered

her mission. 'I have to get there before they close.'

Putting a very happy Lilly-May down she headed to her room, took the number off the bedside table, and headed straight out of the door.

'I'll be back soon.' She left the two girls gaping. Their mother was running, whatever it was, must be serious, she never ran.

It seemed to take an age to get through to the number, and for the pastor to come on the line, but in reality it was only a minute. Conscious of the cost she passed her message on in telegraphic speak.

'Please tell Brother Lukan, Lloyd have rabies. Doctors give him one week to live. Tell him *not* to come. I'm trying to sort it out. Thank you Pastor.' She hung up, not giving him time to ask questions. She didn't know till she said it that she didn't want Luke to come over. She didn't want him here complicating things with Jez, because she was certain *she* could stop Lloyd dying.

Her next stop was to the police station. She wanted them to phone the station in Sav-la-Mar and get a message to Dudley.

'Please tell him Lloyd's dying, I'm coming to see him tomorrow. I'll be on the early bus; please tell him to meet me at the bus stop.'

'Who's Lloyd?' the police officer, a young man in his late twenties in a crisp, fresh uniform asked her from behind the desk.

'My son.' Her breath caught in her throat, but she told herself she couldn't cry, wouldn't cry, not in front of this young man, this stranger. Besides, she knew that if she started crying she wouldn't stop, and there was still too much she had to do.

Issy was thankful that it was Carley's day to work tomorrow. She'd ask her to stay on longer. She had to go back to the hospital, but first she had to make sure her three other children were alright. She wouldn't say anything to them tonight. No point upsetting them for something that wasn't going to happen. She was just a few yards from her house when she remembered to pray. 'Dear God, you can't let him die, you have to save his life,' she instructed God. 'I *can't* go through this again,' she added for emphasis.

Now that Lennox was back she told them all that they were still waiting for the results of the tests, that she had to go up to Sav tomorrow to sort out some things with the house, and that Carley would be staying over later. She warned them to come straight home. She tried to ask as casually as she could if any of them knew which dog bit Lloyd, but it was too long ago and none of them were there.

By the time she got back to the hospital Issy was as tight as a guitar string. One more twist and she would snap. Lloyd had just received another sedative to make him sleep through the night and Mavis suggested Issy went home and tried to get a good night herself, but it was just words, because she knew that Issy couldn't sleep, no more than she could.

Chapter 30

'What does she mean him have one week to live and she don't want me to come?' Lukan was pacing the living room floor, unable to heed pastor suggestion to sit. He didn't know what he was feeling, the fear was like freezing fog, the kind that descends suddenly and engulfs you so you can't see where you're going and have to walk from memory. Only, as he'd never been down this road before he didn't know where to walk, was putting his hands out to find a wall, a building to hold onto, but there was only fog, and with each step, and each second that passed he was felt increasing lost.

'What does she mean him have one week to live?' He looked at Pastor McCullough through the fog.

'Ring the hospital, Brother Lukan, find out for yourself. Come round to the house and use the phone.'

All they told him was that Lloyd was comfortable, and was asleep. It probably didn't help that his first question was, 'is it true my son is dying and only have one week to live?' Despite taking his details all she would say was that they're not allowed to give out that kind of information on the phone.

Pastor persuaded him to trust his wife's judgment, that if she felt he should come she would tell him, to wait for her next call or telegram, or even send her one if he was feeling helpless. So he sent Issy a telegram the next day, which she didn't get till she returned from Savanna-la-Mar.

Chapter 31

Dudley was at the bus stop scanning the alighting passengers for Issy. She looked tired, creased, like a faded version of herself. He was not a tactile man, but his embrace was gratefully received.

'What's going on Issy? What's happening to Lloyd? What do you mean he's dying?'

'They say he's got rabies, that it's gone too far, and that he might have just a week before it spreads through his system and kills him.' It sounded so stark, so matter of fact. It didn't describe the boy in the hospital bed, gasping for air and fighting off imaginary assailants.

'So what you doing up here? It would've been easier for me to come down there to you.' Dudley was puzzled.

'I've come to see Jez.'

'I could've told her about Lloyd for you, you didn't have to come all this…' Then it dawned on him. 'You think she have something to do with this?'

Issy told Dudley as quickly as she could the basis for her suspicions and her proposal to confront Jez, and appeal to her compassion as a mother. Dudley looked uncertain. He wasn't sure Issy should be going anywhere near Jez, anyway, even if it was her, things had gone too far, not even Jez could bring people back from the dead.

'He's not dead yet Dudley. God will save him.'

'If that's what you believe, why are you up here talking to Jez?'

'God help those who help themselves. I couldn't just sit at home and do nothing, and wait for my son to die.'

Still unconvinced, Dudley took her to Jez's house and, to comply with Issy's wishes, sat in the car while she went up the stairs to Jez's veranda.

'Jez!' she called, just once before her husband's other baby mother poked her head out from the door.

'What you doing here Issy?' she seemed genuinely surprised. I guess if she was expecting visitors she would have put on some descent clothes and combed her hair. The triangle of cloth, a small Jamaican flag, failed to encased the unruly plaits that poked out from the sides of her head. She wore a loose pair of pants that was once orange but now looked like St Elisabeth mud, and a grey vest that clearly showed she wasn't wearing a brassiere.

'I want you to stop it!' Issy said emphatically.

'Stop what?'

'Take whatever you put on Lloyd, off him!'

'I don't know what you talking about Issy'

'Lloyd and the dog. Gloria told me about the way you turn on the dog when it was chasing her. You know how to talk to dogs. That's what you did with Lloyd wasn't it Jez, you set the dog on him? Now he's going to die.'

'Sit down Issy, you not making any sense.'

'Don't 'sit down Issy' me, and don't tell me you don't know what I'm talking about. You know you can't get away with this, not while there's a God in heaven.'

'Issy, is who you think you is, coming to my house without any invitation, accusing of killing your son and…' she paused, as if remembering something, but quickly moved on, but not quickly enough for Issy to miss her hesitation.

'So you *do* know something about it!' Issy was triumphant.

'Why don't you tell me what's happening to Lloyd?'

'As if you don't know.'

'You just going round in circles. If that's what you want to do let me go and look after my pickney.'

'He's in the hospital, he's got rabies from the dog that bite him, they say he's only got a week to live.'

Jez sat down heavily on the bench, a series of emotions flashed like a speeded up film across her face, before it stopped on horror.

'Jez, you've got to stop it.' She was pleading now, but she didn't care; her son's life was more important than her pride, she'd get down on her knees and beg if she had to, but something about the way Jez was shaking her head stopped her.

'It wasn't supposed to be for him.'

'What do you mean Jez? Who was it for?'

Looking her directly in her eyes, a thing she rarely did to Issy, she answered, 'it was for Luke.'

'You wanted to kill Luke? You wanted to ki..'

'No, not kill him, just frighten him. Him stop writing to me, won't answer any of my letters. The girls seh him write and tell them that a dog chase him and how frightened him was. I just wanted to frighten him a little more.'

'Stop it Jez!' Issy screamed at her. 'You can't let a little boy die!'

'It's too late, you shudda tell me before. It's too late now.' There was no triumph in Jez's words, no victory on her face, no air of success in the gait. She was pinned to the bench with what Issy was later to acknowledge was remorse. But in that moment, in direct disobedience of Jesus, she hated Jez. She could not love her enemy, not this one, with evil running through her like the rock from Rhyl that Luke wrote to her about.

'One day God will pay you back Jez, and I hope for your sake he don't do it through your children.'

She ran off the veranda, out to Dudley waiting by the car.

'Can you drive me back to Kingston now?' she asked, shaking with fear and anger. 'I need to go and see the pastor. I need the help of the church.'

By the time they reached Pastor McMillian's house Issy was bathed in sweat and almost incoherent. After her initial explanation of what Jez had said, the journey had been virtually silent. The pastor listened, trying to make sense of it whilst trying to instil some element of calm into Sister Isabell. He was aware of the circumstances of their move to Kingston, but since they'd become members of his congregation he'd seen no evidence of it, nor had any been brought to his attention. He knew of the sickly boy, but lots of people have sickly children and they don't automatically put the blame on evil spirits. He prayed with Issy while her uncle sat with his head bowed more out of respect rather than belief.

'I'll get the prayer group together as soon as I can, and we'll arrange a prayer meeting for you.'

'Thank you Pastor.' She felt a little calmer, knowing others were praying with her. But their prayers, in the end, was for the safe passage of his soul to heaven. By the time they got to the hospital, Lloyd was dead.

Chapter 32

One of the benefits of being a member of a church is the support you get when a member dies. An army of help arrives on your doorstep, to ensure a good send off, and it was doubly so for Issy in her vulnerable state. It would not have been possible without their help, because, although her family were willing to assist they were not familiar with Kingston, didn't have the contacts or the influence of the many church members. The funeral was organised within a week. She was adamant that Luke should stay in England, believing it was the distance that saved him.

As the pall bearers, Dudley, her brother Norman, Ivan, and Sarah's husband carried in the small coffin, Issy walked behind it, dignified and numb, with Irene, Lennox and Lilly-Mae, who gripped her hand and fixed her eyes on the ground. She had nothing left to give to her children in the way of comfort, so wracked was she with guilt, and her own grief. Mavis held the children together, taking time off work to make sure their emotional and clothing needs were taken care of, while Issy focused on the practicalities of the funeral.

They all sat quietly, respectfully, through the service while Pastor McMillan spoke about their brother in the past tense. They showed little emotion, and everyone said how strong they were, but as Lloyd was lowered into the deep hole, and they all realised that they would never see him again, it was Irene who first broke the rank of composure, and howled like a wolf, the sound that had been caged for months and had finally been set free. Issy reached out to comfort her and Ivan, Lennox and Lilly-Mae, who were already by her side, joined them. Huddled together their bodies heaved and swayed from the breaking of their hearts as the graveside congregation sang;

Yes we will gather at the river, the beautiful, the beautiful river, gather with the saints at the river, that flows by the throne of God

Mavis, Norman and Beatrice tried to comfort them, but they too were facing their own anguish, as the choir reached up to God on the family's behalf with the final verse of the song;

Soon we'll reach the silver river, soon our pilgrimage will cease; soon our happy hearts will quiver, with the melody of peace.

They found it hard to watch the hole being filled in; the separation of Lloyd from his family made permanent. They could no longer go to visit him in the mortuary, or in the funeral home. And when they said goodbye in the church, he looked so peaceful, as though he had indeed found that melody of peace that was to evade the rest of them for so many years.

Lukan, on the other side of the world, felt the loss more acutely, because life went on as normal around him, with no one aware of his misery, his anguish, his utter despondency. The news had come via Pastor McCullough. He'd known from the look on pastor's face that it was not good. He felt cheated, not even being allowed time to get used to the idea of Lloyd's impending death before it happened. No time to try to intervene, to make sustained representation to God. No time to try to imagine life without his son. And then there was Issy's insistence that it wasn't safe for him to come home, and he didn't want to oppose her as he felt responsible for the tragedy.

The only good that had come out of this was Issy's agreement to leave Jamaica, to join him in England. Her only insistence was that they all come together, and that they come as soon as possible. She would not leave any of the children behind. It was a complete turn around from her previous stance, but he couldn't see how he was going to find all that money at once. The only thing he could do was withdraw from the house purchase and use the money to bring them up, but then where would he put them?

William, Pastor and Brother Powell presented him with a solution that made it possible. Between the three of them and the church, they would lend him the money. As his house was only weeks from completion they would hold some stake in it which would be withdrawn when the money was paid back.

And so it was, that on Lennox's 9th birthday they left Jamaica for England, the children were excited, despite the circumstances that necessitated the move. Issy's need to remove them from Jez's influences overrode her concern for Irene's education and not knowing when she'd see her family again. Her biggest regret though was leaving Ivan behind. Although he'd not lived with her for years, he'd been a constant in her life, her first son. She didn't, however, fear for him in the same way as he was not Luke's child.

It seemed odd that they were leaving just as others were arriving to join in the Independence Day celebrations. They were not taking much. Luke said the children were going to need new clothes for the weather in England, so they only needed to bring what they would need for the next couple of months, so they were traveling light, despite bringing tea bush, chocolate, coconut sweets and pastries, and escovish fish with plenty of pimentos, peppers and onions.

Dudley, Ivan and Mavis came to see them off, helped them with the cases, and reassured them that leaving was best for everyone. They'd had a going away send off at her father's house and every one had come to say goodbye. The church had given them another send off and sent God's guidance with them. It felt a little hollow given God choice not to save Lloyd, but Issy was fighting to keep her faith strong.

She sat close to Ivan who didn't know the full story, but accepted that his mother couldn't continue without her husband, that raising the children on her own was too much. She'd try and send for him for a holiday some day, when she was working. Issy tried not to imagine what he was going through, losing all of them at once. She'd been forced to make the choice she'd tried so hard to avoid, take some and leave one. She hoped he could feel as she held his hand, that her heart was breaking too.

Then it was time for them to go through the departure gates and leave behind all that they had ever known. It wasn't Jamaica Issy wanted to leave, she'd never wanted to do that, but it wasn't safe for her anymore.

As the plane took off Lilly-Mae clung to her, as if the devil himself was trying to prize her off, and didn't open her eyes till they were cruising and her ears had stopped feeling blocked. After the first hour or so the children slept, worn out by the events of the months before, the early morning, and the adventures of travel. Intermittent waking for food and the toilet was swiftly followed by more sleep. Issy dosed but couldn't sleep, rewinding the film of what she'd left behind and fast forwarding to an England she'd conjured in her mind from Luke's letters, the news and other peoples' reports. She wondered if she'd fit, make new friends, find a job, cope with the cold, like the house. Luke said it needed work doing to it which he'd hoped to do before they came but now he would have to do it with them in it. She wondered about all these things, but most of all she wondered how she would be with Luke.

Things had changed between them, Luke had gained a child that he'd not even seen yet and lost one that he loved.

She knew it affected him badly. William wrote to her, told her that after Lloyd's death, Luke just wander the streets, couldn't go to work for a week, couldn't sleep, couldn't eat, would sit staring into space for hours. It was a lot of prayer that stopped him going over the edge. It was the final thing that made her decide to come, but she was still apprehensive about what lay between them.

She was coming to her husband in England and should be full of anticipation, but a weight like an undercooked dumpling lay in her stomach and stayed there all the way through the announcements about landing, about fastening seatbelts, and about what to do once they were inside the airport. It didn't shift as they touched down and she said a silent prayer to God for their safe arrival. She was willing it to go as they waited for their cases and as they walked through customs. Then she saw him, a split second before the children did.

'There's Daddy,' Irene was already waving and the others quickly followed. He smiled and waved back restlessly moving from one foot to the other, willing them to walk faster. Irene and Lennox, feeling his energy broke rank and spontaneously ran to him. Lilly-Mae waited with Issy till she reached them before joining in the embracing.

He stood them all at arms length and beamed. He hugged her briefly with a mixture of admiration, apology, excitement, desire and love. He looked paler, there were a few grey hairs at his temple, and he'd lost weight. Issy was the opposite, dark newly dyed hair and gained a few pounds.

'You look good,' he mouthed to her as he held her by the shoulders and scanned her from head to toe.

'You not looking bad yourself,' she answered quietly.

Luke introduced William to everyone.

'Do you like it Mama?' Irene asked, in awe of the size of the airport, the bright lights and the lack of black faces.

'I'm going to love it if the rest of England look like this.'

But it didn't, and Issy's first impression, once they'd loaded up the minibus, which William had borrowed from the church to pick them up, was of a place liberally endowed with factories, all belching smoke from their chimneys. She was disappointed when she realised that she'd be living in one of these factories, and that each morning they would light a fire to add to the smoking chimneys.

The inside of the house did not meet her expectations either, but then, she had been warned it needed work. Uncle William, as Issy and the children all called him, stayed with them until Luke had given them a guided tour of the house and all the cases and bags were in the right rooms. When he was satisfied that there wasn't anything else they needed he left them alone, promising to bring his wife to meet them in the morning. Luke had taken the day off but would be going to work the following day and Hazel had offered to take Issy under her wings and show her the ropes. She'd cooked a dinner of curry mutton and rice for them so they'd have a decent meal after their travel.

They ate, talked, and celebrated Lennox's birthday. He asked a hundred and one questions, about making fires in the grate, the neighbours, school, people to play with. He'd absorbed far more about the technicalities of the flight than the girls and wanted to check facts and figures with his father. Issy recognised for the first time, how much Lennox had missed his father.

Although it was still early, everyone was very tired. They had to take it in turns to have a bath, as there was no shower, and had to be careful with the amount of water they used, as it had to be heated up in a tank and could run out if people used too much. There was still so much to discover, about the house, the street, Birmingham, this place called England. But that would have to wait. What Issy and Luke most wanted to discover was what was left between them.

Without the children to focus on Issy and Luke became shy of each other, with all the things that were too big to be said in letters and telegrams expanding between them, like cavity foam, filling the spaces and threatening to insulate them from each other.

'Issy,' he said finally, finding the courage to do what he knew he must to make his way back to her. 'Issy, I'm sorry, I was wrong, but God knows I love you. I've always loved you, and I'm so glad you decided to come. I'm sorry it took what it did, but I'm happy that we're back together. I know I did wrong and I'm begging your forgiveness.'

Holding his breath he tried not to think of Jez and all that was left unfinished with her, his daughters and the son he'd never seen. That was for another day. She couldn't come between them now.

Issy looked up at him, tears welling in her eyes. One blink, and they bounced off her cheek, splashed onto her chest and disappeared into the fabric of her blouse.

'Luke, I have to know,' she sputtered through the tears, 'Have you been with anybody over here?'

His answer was instant and insistent. She looked deeply into his eyes and wondered if she could believe him. She wanted to trust him, wanted to lose herself in his pleading eyes, but he had lied to her before. He always had a way of making it right though, of winning her round. She found it hard to resist his raised eyebrows, his wide-eyed innocence and the small gap in his front teeth when he smiled at her.

He wasn't touching her yet, but she knew he would. She knew he would move towards her, slide his arms down her back, pull her in close, and hold her hard against his beating chest. He would say, 'Issy, you know I wouldn't lie to you. You know I love you too much.' And when he did she would allow herself to believe him, because the alternative was too frightening.

He stepped to her, wrapping his arms around her shoulders.

'Come here my Pint Size Beauty,' he said silencing her sobs with his mouth, soft gentle kisses to soothe and reassure her that he was still her husband and that he was glad to have her in his arms again. She felt the strength of his body, and the desire rising in him. That night, as he entered her, hesitantly, she opened her legs wide, pulled him in close and whispered in his ear.

'Come in Luke. We need to start again.'